SAVING JASON

E.J. HANAGAN

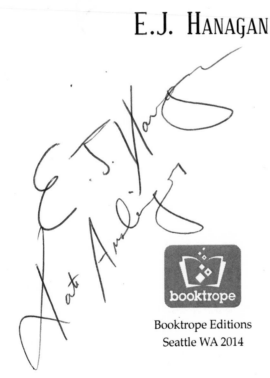

booktrope

Booktrope Editions
Seattle WA 2014

Cover Design by Shari Ryan
Edited by Erica Fitzgerald

This is a work of fiction. Names, characters, places, brands, media, and incidents
are either the product of the author's imagination or are used fictitiously. Any
resemblance to similarly named places or to persons living or deceased is
unintentional.

Print ISBN 978-1-62015-512-7
EPUB ISBN 978-1-62015-528-8

Discounts or customized editions may be available for
educational and other groups based on bulk purchase.

For further information please contact info@booktrope.com

Library of Congress Control Number: 2014915371

*This book is dedicated to our service members
who suffer silently every day.*

Their sacrifices are undeniable.

PROLOGUE

JASON PINNED HIS BODY as tightly as he could against the rigid edge of the climbing rock at Heartbreak Park. Fingers clenching the pointed edge, he raised his right leg, feeling for a protrusion to rest his foot. He looked down at the ground twenty-five feet below, where the mix of leaves coated in a fiery red and orange served as a bed for his rock climbing gear. It was the first time he'd attempted a free climb without the safety of a harness attaching him to the side of the boulder. A rush of fear passed through him when he took his next step. Putting all of his body weight into that step, he was no longer supported by the ledge; instead he was falling to the ground, face scraping against the serrated boulders along the way. Time stood still for the thirty seconds that his body descended to the ground. Silence softened his busy mind and the world was calm until he landed in a pile of leaves on top of his gear. The last thing he saw was a set of piercing silvery blue eyes flashing across his vision like lightning in the midst of a storm.

"Thirty-two-year-old male. Appeared to be rock climbing on a cliff at Heartbreak Park." Dr. Wallis went through the motions of doing vitals on Jason's limp body while announcing the stats to his young, eager residents.

"Apparently he's a daredevil too; none of his gear was attached to him. It was on the ground, covered in a pile of leaves. Good place for it. Dr. Melanson, can you diagnose the patient for me please?" Dr. Wallis's steely green eyes peered over to survey the young doctor, almost as if to extract the thoughts from her mind. Her sweaty palms gripping the clipboard, Dr. Melanson approached the side of the bed. Breathing deeply like her yoga instructor taught her, she recited what she learned in her eight years of medical school, spewing a barrage of medical terms to her mentor. "Male has been placed in an induced coma to reduce the swelling in the right cerebral hemisphere. There are several abrasions on the left side of the face that will result in minor bruises. The neurosurgery team will operate to assess the trauma to the right side of the brain. Further steps will be taken at the discretion of the surgery team's assessment."

"Dr. Melanson, you failed to notice the eighteen stitches that have been threaded through the patient's left forearm." Looking down at the arm, she turned a deep shade of red as she saw the tiny black stitches, woven in his thick tan skin, just above a black USMC tattoo. Dr. Wallis slowly moved his eyes from the top of her head down to her feet, his face a mask of disgust. She bit her bottom lip while attempting more deep breaths, her ego having been knocked down once again by the legendary Dr. Wallis. "Sorry, sir. It was an oversight."

"You're in a hospital, Dr. Melanson, not on a battlefield. Don't call me 'sir.' Why don't you assist Pediatrics with their rounds?" Dr. Wallis smoothed out his bushy white eyebrows while shaking his head and looking away.

CHAPTER ONE

Samantha

THE VIBRATION OF MY PHONE startles me out of a deep sleep. The buzzing intermingles with my dream of running across a Southern California freeway toward the shimmering sun-drenched ocean. I slowly fade out of the dream and roll over into the reality of my pulsating phone. I quietly reach for the phone on the nightstand, with a goal of not waking Alex, knowing his inability to fall into a deep sleep, as if he is always partly awake, just waiting for the new day to start.

"What's going on?" Alex sleepily asks as he reaches for my hand under the covers.

"Nothing, it's just a text. No clue who would be texting me at 2 a.m." I look down at my blinking cell phone screen: *do you have Jason's social security number, he's been in an accident, don't know if he's going to make it-Abby.*

Jason. My ex-husband. My first real love that started as an innocent, sweet flame and ended in a rapidly progressing fire. We were combustible together. We loved to hate each other and hated to love each other. It was as if we sat in the cart of a creaky, old roller coaster together from ages twenty to twenty-five—a roller coaster that dipped and twisted at such sharp angles that we had to grasp on to one another just to make it through the painful, gut-wrenching ride. It started with the stress of a long-distance relationship in the military and ended in PTSD caused by the turmoil of combat. It started with hope and a love so strong that no one could keep us apart, and ended in hate and destruction caused by the world.

The words sit on the phone like a nightmare. They instantly make my stomach twist and my throat go dry. I stumble out of bed with the phone in my hand, padding down the stairs and into the kitchen, each step on the hardwood floor launching me closer to reality. Chauncey, our Irish setter, lies curled up on the cold kitchen floor, sleeping peacefully while occasionally jerking a paw as if in a deep dream. I wonder what it would be like to be a dog, where the only responsibilities you have are to eat, sleep and play.

Nearly seven years after the divorce and his Social Security number tumbles out of my mind like it's one I see every day. My sweaty fingers type the digits into the phone and shoot it back to Abby, Jason's current girlfriend. Like all of Jason's other girlfriends, Abby has somehow managed to extract my number from his phone. There have been several occasions when Jason's flavor of the month has contacted me—sometimes out of jealousy and anger about our friendship, other times simply with questions about why he does the things he does. Like a vacuum, I'm always sucked back into his life; I will always be the ex-wife who is still somehow in the picture.

Just to ease my worrying mind, I pick up the phone and begin to dial Abby's number, baffled by what I plan on saying.

"Yeah," Abby picks up the phone in a hurry.

"Abby, what's going on? Is he okay?"

In a tone that holds bitterness and fear combined in one, "No, he's not okay. He's been in a rock climbing accident. They don't know if he's going to make it. I'll try to keep you updated."

Before I can ask her my catalog of medical questions, Abby hangs up.

Attempting to brush this off as just another one of Jason's crazy adventures ending in a few bumps and bruises, I make my way back to bed to snuggle up in the safe arms of Alex.

"Is everything okay? Who's texting you?"

"That was Abby, Jason's girlfriend. Jason's been in an accident. They don't know if he's going to make it." As the words trickle out of my mouth, reality hits and makes my heart do a back handspring inside my chest. Alex rolls toward me in silence and stares into my eyes with a comforting loyalty. He has an ability to know when silence is necessary and when comfort is needed. His love and support always make me stronger, which is why I fight back tears and pretend to fall asleep, brushing off any sign of worry so I don't appear weak and affected by Jason's pain.

Four hours and no sleep later, I open my eyes to Alex's daily goodbye kiss.

"Have a good day, honey. Let me know if you hear anything about the accident."

Though he's open-minded about my friendship with Jason, Alex still struggles with actually saying his name. Jason, an ex-Marine with severe PTSD, was raised in a rough Southern home and couldn't be more different from Alex, a conservative college-driven architect from a wealthy town in New Hampshire. Since Alex is open-minded and accepting, their differences alone wouldn't have been much of an issue. It was the dark secrets I accidentally spilled to Alex one night after a few too many glasses of Cabernet. I had told him about the time I found Jason folded up in the corner of our walk-in closet, gripping the upright rifle close to his chest and staring coldly at the wall directly in front of him. At the time, I was naive. I thought he was cleaning a hunting rifle, until I saw the remnants of tears on his face, the stillness in his eyes, the finished bottle of Jack Daniels tipped on its side next to him.

"Jason! What are you doing?" I had shouted.

"It should've been me. It should've been me."

"What do you mean? What are you talking about?" I had stayed in the entryway of the closet, afraid to get any closer.

"I should've died in Iraq. I should've died. All those other people had kids, families."

Eyes frozen on the wall in front of him, he began tapping his forehead with the metal rifle; the tapping grew faster as more tears rolled down his face. His olive skin turned scarlet as if he were about to explode.

"Jason. This isn't your fault. And it shouldn't have been you. You do have a family. I'm your family. Now put the gun down." I inched closer, certain he wouldn't turn the gun on me and he was only in danger of hurting himself.

"Come on, baby. You have a long life ahead of you. I need you. The world needs you." I slowly crouched down, folding my knees so they were crossed and angled outward, my right knee gently rubbing against his thigh. I remember how tightly his fingers were wrapped around the cylinder of the gun. The veins protruded from his forearms as he readjusted his grip.

"I can't do this anymore." His gentle tears turned into sobs as he let go of the gun; it fell to its side against the closet wall like a dead soldier. He fell over onto his side and crashed into me as he released his head into my lap and let out breath-catching sobs blending with unintelligible sentences. I rubbed his fuzzy head like he was a crying toddler, his tears leaving a coat of dampness on my pants. I sat there cradling him for what seemed like forever, and then I called the VA and asked to be transferred to Mental Health.

* * *

My alarm clock buzzes, invading my memories. I roll out of bed, my eyes dry and bloodshot from the lack of sleep. I force myself to run my daily five miles through Colby Park, trying to push the stress of Jason out with each step that hits the trail. After two severely strong cups of Godiva coffee, I'm as ready as I can be for the day that lies ahead. I go through the motions of my job at the Philadelphia VA hospital, worrying incessantly about Jason the entire time. Hoping none of my patients and co-workers in the X-ray department notices the pain growing underneath the surface, I plaster a false smile on my face throughout the day. Patients come in for scheduled X-rays as I make small talk to clear up any threat of tears invading my eyes. Eating suddenly becomes a chore, and focus is so far out of reach that Courtney begins to show concern.

"Sammy, what's going on? Did Prince Charming forget to make the bed this morning?" Courtney teases as we both catch up on paperwork between patients. I met Courtney our first day on the job in the radiology department, during orientation. Outgoing and perky, Courtney took no time before she obtrusively commented on the size of my princess cut diamond. Always single and dating, Courtney's effervescent persona meshed quite nicely with my modest, quiet approach to life. The two of us were inseparable from the start, consistently taking our 9 a.m. break together while sharing our love for gourmet coffee and running.

"No, but he did leave the toilet seat up," I attempt a joke.

"Funny. Now tell me what's going on. You were staring through this morning like I was invisible. At one point I told you that I just got finished doing an X-ray for Lance Armstrong, and you just nodded and stared ahead. Spit it out."

Before I can stop myself, I launch into the story about Jason, tears welling up in my eyes. Releasing the emotions feels great, but part of me feels ridiculous for shedding tears over my ex-husband.

"I feel so stupid; I just have never had anyone close to me die before, and I don't know if he's going to die. I don't want to always regret never saying goodbye."

"Listen, Sammy, you know I am going to tell you like it is. You spent five years of your life married to this guy, and you've been close friends for seven years. Why *wouldn't* you be upset right now? Even though I am ridiculously envious of you for already having been married twice when I can't find a guy to take me out for a burger, I think your tears and your concern are justified. If it makes you feel better, maybe you should fly to New Hampshire and see him. I'm sure Alex would understand. Seriously, when is Alex *not* understanding?" Courtney raises a perfectly plucked eyebrow questioningly as she continues gathering files.

It was around 11 a.m. when I caved in and started surfing online for flights from Philadelphia to New Hampshire. For once in my life, I wasn't going to let price become an issue. It's amazing how losing someone can change your entire perspective on such trivial matters such as the cost of a plane ticket or the need to eat. I hadn't been able to eat more than a few crackers all morning. Never in my wildest dreams would I have imagined booking a flight so last-minute, so disorganized, so off the path of my plan. Like puzzle pieces that fit together perfectly, every minute of my day is planned out, and if things move even slightly in a different direction I feel out of sorts.

I fully admit to my obsessive compulsive planning, completely inherited from my father. My mother couldn't have been more opposite. Growing up in my mom's house, the two of us seemed to just move from day to day, like children swinging on a playground, aimlessly and without a destination in mind. We had no schedule and no meals planned. We certainly weren't one of those households with a giant calendar nailed to the wall listing all of our daily chores, activities and meals. I take pride in my ability to plan, probably because it's something I can cling on to, something so different from my upbringing.

A debate ensues in my head about how to explain this to Alex, afraid he won't like the idea of my flying home to see my ex-husband, who is quite possibly on his deathbed. With a few deep breaths, I step outside into the hospital courtyard and dial Alex's work number. As soon as his voice makes contact with the connection, I become a prisoner of my emotions and burst into tears.

"I don't know what to do." I begin to sob as all of the pent-up fear and sadness erupt.

"Would you mind if I flew home to New Hampshire tonight? I'm so sorry, I—I just have never had a friend die before."

Almost as if he was expecting this call, Alex responds quickly. "I understand. You should be there." There's a pause as I swipe the back of my sleeve across my eyes, wiping away my tears. "I'll book your ticket."

There are a million and one things I admire about Alex, and this just adds to that list. His friendships last forever without any breaks in time; he has a way of catching life and throwing it back twofold like a simple game of catch. It's almost as if he was given a handbook on life and women and friendships and followed it word for word. Maybe it was his respect for his mother, a well-known English professor and author at Dartmouth College. Or maybe it was the way he looked up to his father, an architect who doted on his wife and led his children by example.

I, on the other hand, lived life differently—I soared my way through, dipping and accelerating when things got scary or too intimate or someone posed a threat to my ego. From the moment I met Alex, I knew I could learn from him, and that's exactly what I did. My less-than-perfect childhood led me to seek someone who could teach me proper life skills, and Alex had been that person since age eight. From the moment we met, Alex had been my savior.

It had been a stormy April day in 1987, and I was locked out of my house. My mother had passed out on the couch after too many of her daily dirty martinis, forgetting I was outside playing alone in the yard. Without the shelter of a roof, I sat on my front steps hugging my tiny shaking body. I remember my wet, blond hair being plastered to my face and neck as I shook with cold and the fear that this time might be the time my mother would die. After continuously banging on the front door, I surrendered to my mother's drunken state and sat, crying and drenched in the wind and rain.

That's when Alex first came to my rescue. He was letting his chocolate lab, Darcy, out for an evening bathroom break when he saw me, hopeless and frightened on the steps of the tiny ranch across the street. Alex ran over, sheltering his head with a bright red saucer sled, approaching me with concern and the directness of an eight-year-old.

"Hi, I'm Alex. I live across the street. Why are you outside in the rain?"

"I'm Samantha. Um, my mom is taking a nap and she accidentally locked the door," I said, too embarrassed to tell the truth.

"Well, you can come over to my house. My mom will make us hot chocolate with Fluff."

"What's Fluff?" I had asked, pushing the wet overgrown bangs out of my eyes.

"You don't know what Fluff is? It's the best stuff ever! I'll show you."

And from that moment on, even though I didn't know it then, I had found my soul mate. We grew apart for several years, my life dipping and bending in different directions while Alex's world maintained a steadiness that is the product of a stable upbringing.

I left work at 3:30 and was in the air by 5 p.m. for a 7 p.m. arrival into Manchester airport. While waiting in the security line, I called my dad, who had always been a father to Jason. After being absent for most of my childhood, my dad made a comeback into my life after my mother's fatal car accident when I was seventeen. Since then, Dad and I have been inseparable, putting the trauma of the past behind us.

With a stern, slightly shaky tone, the words escaped me: "I'm coming home to see Jason at the hospital."

In most circumstances, my dad would have done anything to prevent a useless trip and would have counseled me on the need to save money. Not this time though. He responded, simply and quietly. "What time do you land?"

Before Abby had called me looking for Jason's Social Security number, she had called my dad. His number had been listed somewhere in their apartment. I guessed my dad was listed somewhere

recent in Jason's phone—while my dad tried to keep his continued
close relationship with Jason a secret, I knew the two of them got
together once a week to hit balls at the batting cage. Dad always
feared his relationship with Jason would interfere with my marriage to Alex, but Jason and I both knew we were in no danger of
making the same mistake twice, of getting tangled up with one
another again romantically. Like two combustible materials, some
things just don't mix well.

My dad didn't instantly fill me in on all the details of Jason's
accident. He's a man of few words, and it was hard for him to repeat
the story. He and Jason had a bond that was hard to explain if you
couldn't see it with your own eyes. But watching them interact was
like seeing magic unfold. Jason brought words and animation out
of my father, and my father brought out a serious side of Jason, a
side that kept him somewhat grounded in between his daredevil
hobbies and his inability to sit still and think about a plan for his life.

"I'll be there at 9 p.m. I'll take a cab to the hospital and meet you
in Brookside. What room is he in?"

"He's in the ICU; just meet us in the waiting room." Right away
I notice that my dad uses the word *us* instead of a singular *me*. I
wonder whom else from Jason's life he has collided with in the
waiting room.

"Okay, see you soon." Wiping my eyes, I pick up my carry-on
and head to my next gate.

The blank white hospital walls close in on me as I make my
way to the waiting room. The tension of coming face to face with
Jason's younger girlfriend was lost somewhere in the chaos that
surrounded my fear of seeing him helpless in a hospital bed. For
the past seven years I have been a witness to Jason's relationships.
He's hopped from one girlfriend to the next, unable to make any
of them work out quite right. Even the ones who approved of our
friendship managed to get away, somehow giving up when they
discovered who Jason really was: ridiculously free-spirited, moody,
and tainted by the war. Always younger and somewhat naive,
Jason's girlfriends never had enough patience to work through the
rough times. They still had their looks and energy to lock down a
man with less baggage and more money.

Chapter Two

Abby

I STARE AT THE MOONLIT CEILING, stuck in a losing battle with insomnia once again.

"Ugh! I give up!" Untwisting myself from the crisp blue top sheet, I toss the comforter to the ground. Now I know why Jason hates sleeping with a top sheet—it's like having a snake coiled around your limbs. This tiny studio apartment seems to be closing in on me. Looking around the messy room, I see several of Jason's and my things muddled together. A pair of his swimming trunks dangles over the drying rack, still damp from this morning's trip to the beach. A snowboard leans against the white walls, awaiting the winter months, as one of my bras hangs over it, blending our lives together like intertwining branches. I turn on the tiny television set, a homemade antenna taped to the top. Jason convinced me we didn't need to waste money on a cable plan, that he could just as easily create a way for us to watch the basics for free by angling the antennae in just the right direction. I instantly argued that the ugliness of the contraption wasn't worth the free TV, even though I was the first one to tune into my reality shows when I got home from the restaurant for the night. He preferred to read books about anything from wildlife to positive thinking.

He was reading a book titled *Power of the Mind* right before our argument. Once again I had to defend my disapproval of his relationship with his ex-wife, Samantha. It's the same argument every week, different things triggering the fight. Once it was his need to visit her and her dad when she was home for Christmas. Another time it was his ridiculous need to call her when he heard from one of their old mutual friends. This time was the worst of the fights. He apparently didn't know I was in the apartment when I caught him on the phone with her discussing *our* relationship. *I just don't know if she completely gets me, Sammie. What if she's just like the others?* I had gotten off work early and came home to surprise him with his favorite nachos from the restaurant, extra spicy with fewer chips and more cheese. My quiet attempt to eavesdrop failed when a creak in the floor gave me away. Silently cursing old New England homes, I dropped the Styrofoam container of nachos on his lap, grease oozing from the sides, and locked myself in the bathroom.

"Abby. What's the matter? Don't you want to eat these delicious nachos with me?" Jason's soft voice had serenaded me through the accordion bathroom door.

"Why don't you ask Samantha to eat your nachos with you? You obviously would rather be in *her* company!" Regretting the childish statement almost instantly, I hovered over the tiny sink and shook my head, looking at my sad reflection in the square IKEA mirror. I moved in closer to look at the picture wedged in the crevice of the mirror's edge: Jason and I standing on the rocks in Ogunquit, Maine, his tan arm strung across my shoulders, a childish grin planted on my face. *Happy times.*

"It's not like that. How many times do I have to tell you? Sammie is like a sister to me."

"*Sammie? Sammie!*" I let out a shriek, surprising myself with the height and power of my voice. "Now you have a pet name for her? Now you call her *Sammie*?" I had torn open the door, the cheap hinges jerking out of the base. I could feel my face growing red, much like it used to when I'd throw temper tantrums as a child. Fists in the air, I barreled toward him, halting as I saw his eyes turn steely, his body rigid. He instantly turned into a human tornado, whipping his wildlife books across the room, flipping the coffee table, hurling my makeup vanity into the wall, lipstick and eye shadow flying everywhere and leaving a smattering of color on the cheaply painted white walls. It ended with one loud thump as he bashed his beefy fist into the glass of an 8" x 10" photo of the two of us on the wall, sending blood dripping down the USMC tattoo on his forearm.

"Is this what you want, Abby? I don't know what to say to you to make you understand Sammie and I are friends and we will always be friends! There is nothing you can do to change that!" He ripped open the door and was gone.

I crumble on the floor in the center of the room, breath heavy in my chest. My tears of anger turn into fearful sobs as I cower like the delicate little deer on the back of the wildlife book that is face down in front of me. I've seen his anger before, I've seen him grow silent in a crowded room, and I've seen his nervous eye twitch in public places. Going into the relationship, I was aware that he was a war-damaged veteran with PTSD, but I'd never seen the anger like I saw tonight. I look down at my trembling hands. The room around me looks like it got tipped over and shaken, all of its insides misplaced and damaged. Nacho cheese clings to the walls, bits of chips scattered underneath the upside down coffee table. I hear some rustling in the corner of the room. Felix, Jason's ferret, climbs up the side of his cage and places his front paws on the bars.

"Hi, Felix. Are you hungry, little guy?" I twist open the container of his food and unlatch the door as Felix's long body stretches toward me to reach for my hand full of pellets. Jason taught Felix to eat out of his hand, and most of the time it's the only way he'll eat. He pops his front paws up and rests them on my palm before he gently nibbles at the pellets. His whiskers tickle my hand and his tiny grunts are surprisingly soothing to me. In the two months we'd had Felix, Jason had bonded with the furry little creature like it was his child. I had opposed getting Felix at first, mostly because of our lack of space, but Jason had convinced me. We'd been heading to L.L. Bean for a new camping tent when we passed a sign outside the PetSmart next door: "*Ferrets make great pets. Find out how you can save one today.*" Instantly intrigued, Jason pulled me into the store, darting toward the roped-off section lined with more than a dozen ferret cages. When Jason had dashed toward the cage that held a white ferret with red eyes, a thin man with a name tag that said "Ferret Specialist" approached him eagerly while I occupied myself with a cute brown ferret in the adjacent cage.

"Do you have any questions, young man?" The Ferret Specialist rested his hands on his hips. His pants, held up by a thin red belt that matched the embroidery on his shirt, hung low on his slender frame. *Paul* was written in cursive along the top of his front breast pocket.

"What happens to these guys if you can't find homes for them?" Jason asked as he stuck his finger in the cage, letting the white ferret sniff him.

"Well, they go to the ferret rescue and live there for a while. But our goal is to find each of them a loving home. An owner that can give them the kind of attention they need."

"So, do they need a lot of attention? What do you feed them?" The questions shot out of Jason's mouth like rapid fire.

"Well, they like to play like cats do, but they also get attached to their owners like dogs do," Paul said as he unlatched the cage and retrieved the white ferret, its body hanging on him like a slinky. Its beady red eyes looked right at Jason as if he knew whom he had to win over. "Would you like to hold him?" he asked as he held the ferret's neck and lower body out toward Jason.

"Sure." Jason grabbed the ferret easily, as if he had done this before. The ferret snuggled up and burrowed in his neck, the long body dangling across his forearm.

"Look. He likes me." He had turned toward me with pleading eyes, showing off his ferret necklace. "Can we get him, Abs?"

"Where are we going to keep him?" I had asked. "Look at this one. Don't you think he's cuter?" I pointed to the brown one in the cage by me.

"No, I like this guy because he's different. He is the only one here with red eyes."

"Yeah, people tend to veer away from the albino ferrets. They find them *scary*," Paul interjected and threw up a set of finger quotes.

"Pleeeease. I'll take good care of him. He needs a home."

"Fine." It didn't take much begging, as I've always had a weak spot for animals.

After we'd spent nearly a hundred dollars on all of the ridiculous ferret supplies and filled out the adoption paperwork, we walked out of the store with our very first pet. Felix became our baby in no time. I cradled Felix in my arms and let him sniff my mouth, his little nose moving like a beating heart.

Only two hours have gone by since the fight, but it feels like a decade ago. Time drags on as I think of other things I could've said, could've done to calm him down or prevent his outburst. I simply cannot get over his friendship with his ex. Luckily there are only pictures to prove Samantha's existence, and I haven't had to see her in person. Thank God she lives far away. But even Samantha's distance and the fact that she's married don't put me at ease. There's something about the way Jason responds to Samantha, as if his every decision has to be passed by her, like she's one of his internal organs.

Jack Johnson's voice pulls me out of deep thought as I see my cell phone lighting up on the bulky black chair in the corner, the only piece of furniture that's not upside down or on its side. The ringtone tugs at my heart as I recall the day Jason programmed it in my phone. *Because this song is sweet like you.* An unknown number dances to "Inaudible Melodies" across the screen.

"Hello."

"Hello, this is Dr. Wallis from Brookside Hospital. I am calling because you appear to be the last number dialed in one of our patient's phones."

"Um, okay. I'm not quite sure I understand."

"As to be expected, since we don't typically make these calls. But we couldn't find any other emergency contact for the patient. We only have a license that was found at the scene of the accident. Do you know a man by the name of Jason Barnes?"

"Yes, Jason is my boyfriend. What's going on?" I start to boil with impatience.

"It appears that Jason has been in a major rock climbing accident. The call came in at 9:15 this evening." I look over at the alarm clock on my makeshift nightstand, the bright red numbers glaring at me. That was one hour after our fight. One hour after I had to nag him about his ex. "A hiker made the call when Jason was found lying unconscious on the ground in Heartbreak Park. An EMT responded immediately."

"Is he going to be okay? Can I see him now?" My words scramble together as I clench the phone.

"Ma'am. You are certainly welcome to come and sit in the waiting room, but unfortunately we're not allowing visitors in his room at this time. Ma'am—"

"Abby Jacobson. Please call me Abby."

"Abby. Because of the way he landed, the angle at which he hit his head, we have had to place him in an induced coma for a couple of reasons. We are trying to prevent any more swelling of the brain and we are also trying to prevent him from waking up and thrashing around, which could possibly lead to another blow to the head."

"Dr. Wallis. Does this mean Jason might not make it?" The words barely escape me before I have to take a break and swallow, trying to make the lump in my throat disappear. The emotions hit me at once like I'm the target on a dump tank. I'm just waiting for another sentence from the doctor's mouth to make me fall off the edge and land in a tank of dirty water.

"We can't say for sure, Abby. We will certainly keep you updated as soon as we know more. Can we assume that you are his emergency contact?"

"Yes," I answer quickly, contemplating who else would be on Jason's contact list. In our two years together, he's seldom mentioned his mother, and his father seems to be non-existent. He did mention a little sister who lived in Colorado. When it comes to holidays and birthdays though, the cards and gifts have always been from Samantha and her dad.

"Abby, would you happen to know his Social Security number? We need to process his paperwork."

"Um. Actually no, I don't. But I can get it." The first thought that pops into my head is to contact Samantha. She seems to have all the answers concerning Jason. The bitter reminder of this makes my heart race.

"Oh, and one other thing. There was also a bike at the scene of the accident. We had a great responder team on tonight who was courteous enough to take the bike to the hospital and put it in storage. Since you're his girlfriend, I'm guessing you have access to his belongings, so if you would like, I'll have security take you to storage when you arrive. I'll have them keep an eye on it until then."

CHAPTER THREE

Samantha

RELIEF COATED MY DAD'S FACE as I crossed the threshold of the hospital room. Regardless of how often we see each other now, I still get excited. Since we reunited years ago, my dad has made a huge effort to make up for lost time. He makes it mandatory to visit us in Philly once a month, whether by car or plane.

"Daddy!" I melt into his embrace. Always one to get straight to the point, Dad doesn't waste any time before he starts reiterating the hospital rules in his deep, crusty voice.

"We have to go in the room one at a time. They'll have to clear you as family first." *I'll always be family.* "His mother is in there now. Hopefully you can go next. His dad isn't here; he doesn't know if he can leave work to make the trip." *Typical — to overlook his dying son for four hours' extra pay from the minimum wage job at the 711.*

Twenty minutes roll by like the wheels of a slow-moving vehicle on a dirt road; nerves tear through my body and a constant banter of fear rattles my brain. An old episode of *Full House* plays on the TV in the waiting room as Dad and I make small talk.

"How is Alex? Does Courtney miss me?" Dad attempts a joke to ease the moment.

The small waiting room is brimming with people. I watch a little girl dig through a battered laundry basket full of toys in the corner of the room. After intense scrutiny, she settles on a My Little Pony and charges toward her father, who is seated across from me. Her dad scoops her up in his arms and adjusts her little body on his lap, cuddling her as she focuses on the toy. I look at them fondly, but I can't help but be jealous of all the younger years that I missed spending with my father. Fear seeps out from behind the man's smiling eyes as he looks up at me and catches my stare. A wave of empathy crashes over me as I think about what has led them to take up residence in this waiting room. I can't help but wonder if his wife is the one who is hurt. I sneak a look at the man's left hand and see a plain gold band wrapped securely around the ring finger that the little girl is marching her My Little Pony across. I silently send a prayer up to God that the girl doesn't lose her mommy. She tries hard to avoid eye contact with anyone else in the room, but her eyes are peeled off the toy and she looks up at me abruptly as if she can read my thoughts. I smile at her, and a tiny little grin starts to tug at the corner of her lips before her shy gaze is jerked backed down at the toy. I realize that everyone in the waiting room is thinking about the same things—fear of losing someone, emptiness, and memories. I think of how many comforting hugs have been passed in this room, how many tears of heartbreak have rolled onto these chairs, and how many lives have been changed with a few simple words.

Besides work, my last time in a hospital waiting room was when Jason first got back from Iraq. All the family members had gathered in the waiting room, balloons and flowers gripped tightly in hands as they anxiously awaited their marine to get cleared to finally come home. At the time, I was so happy to see Jason and know he was safe that I never anticipated the changes that would eventually warp our future. The family members had passed the time by exchanging stories about their marine's injuries. Whenever a marine was released into the waiting room, we would all get up and clap. The injuries ranged from a broken arm to missing limbs, but every marine had the same look on his face: eyes fixed in a blank stare, devoid of any emotion. Blank expressions clung to their faces as their family members cheered, embraced and cried.

When it was Jason's turn to make his entrance, I stood up, my heart pounding and my palms drenched in sweat. He looked around the room, awkward and confused as the remaining family members cheered. When his eyes met mine, instead of showing recognition, he simply stared and limped toward me robotically, clumsily lean-ing on a cane with each slow step. Unlike our usual bear hugs, I embraced him gently, afraid of breaking him even more. He leaned on his right side as he patted me lightly with his left hand, as if we were acquaintances going in for that first awkward hug. He reached into his pocket and pulled out a bag of ranch-flavored corn nuts. A small smile escaped his mouth as he told me he saw a vending machine full of them in Germany and knowing they are my favorite, had to stop and get them for me. The simplicity of his gesture made me cry right then and there. While he had managed to survive a Humvee collision with small injuries compared to the other passengers, a piece of his personality and life seemed to have died.

My memories and thoughts are suddenly interrupted as Jason's mother walks out of the secured hospital room and into the waiting room. Emma Jane, a southern woman obsessed with cooking ridiculously fattening food and attending church daily, walks into the room in an outfit similar to what I last saw her in seven years ago: a jean jacket with Mickey Mouse embroidered on the right front pocket and a pair of high-waisted jeans. Bleach-blonde hair falls in messy curls past her shoulders with an inch of dark root showing at the scalp.

"Oh, Miss Samantha, it's so good to see you! Unfortunately under such poor circumstances. Our Jason has gotten himself hurt once again."

Her nonchalant tone makes me sad and angry—sad that Jason never had a chance at a good upbringing but was raised by a delusional mother who kicked him out on the street when he was eighteen. She was sweet as a southern belle to your face, but the moment you were out of sight she was formulating tangled lies of gossip. The woman could not be trusted, which is why she spent her life jumping from man to man instead of raising her two children. Men and money came first, and Jason and his sister spent every night alone eating cereal for dinner and sitting around their TV-less house. Television was the devil, according to Emma Jane. I never understood her logic: Television was the devil, but doing cocaine off the back of her child's history book in the next room was perfectly acceptable in her eyes.

Jason had all the potential to succeed, and while others gave up on him, I stood strong and supportive like a column he could grab onto. At the peak of our relationship, before life trampled us, I used to be fascinated by his focus. He would spend hours breaking apart math problems and investigating life's mysteries—mysteries others wouldn't think twice about—researching them and picking them apart. When he was intently interested in something, his eyes took on the fascination of a toddler discovering clouds for the first time. He was never bored. He could sit in a small square room alone with nothing and still find some miracle of the world to focus on, some way to be amazed.

He would never make a living in a normal job. Most people would call that laziness, but I knew he just didn't want to give in to society's standards—he wanted to be his own, unwavering self. I think he could've been a doctor or a prominent researcher if he hadn't been so stubborn, and maybe today he would be laughing at the rest of the world.

"Emma Jane, would it be okay if I go in next to see Jason?"

"Well, Miss Samantha, of course you can go next." Assessing me from head to toe, she responds in an overly friendly tone, given the situation. She is holding Jason's backpack and the few articles of clothing he must have had on before the nurses and doctors stripped him and went to work on his injuries.

"And maybe we can go down to the cafeteria afterwards and catch up—I want to hear all about that architect husband of yours. I hear he's providing real well for you." With a seductive wink, Emma Jane sits down, shuffles through her gold-tasseled fake Coach bag and pulls out an issue of *Cosmopolitan*. Knowing Emma Jane's propensity to act like a twenty-two-year-old sorority girl, I didn't question her *Cosmo* subscription at age fifty-seven.

With sweaty palms I press the security intercom so that I can get cleared to enter the ICU. A middle-aged nurse who introduces herself as Allison leads me into Jason's room.

"Jason is a fighter," Allison says as she secures the tubing that dangles from the machine by his bed. "His body has undergone massive trauma in the past twenty-four hours. I've been telling all of his visitors to hold his hand and talk to him. Sometimes the patient can sense the comfort." Allison has a calm and patient demeanor and a set of sad brown eyes like a golden retriever. I get the feeling that she has taken care of a lot of young patients like Jason and has seen more than her fair share of death. I so badly want to barrage her with questions about his status, but I know that she has about as many answers as the rest of us. Fear of the unknown consumes the mind. Different outcomes play a game of Ping-Pong in my head as I trail Allison like a puppy dog.

The room is drenched in a sterile antiseptic scent, waking up all of my tangled senses. The sight of Jason on the bed helpless creates a dark hole in my heart. Memories dash through my mind, but all that seems to be clear is the ocean water in California—a vision of Jason holding out his hand saying "trust me" as he leads me into the overpowering, six-foot waves.

As I shuffle closer to the bed, a lump grows in my throat, a twisting pain in my gut. Tears begin to pour from my eyes. I no longer feel weak for crying, for letting my emotions run free. An explosion of emotion wells up in my heart as a memory seeps in: *Your eyes look beautiful when you cry*, Jason used to always say. Too bad he couldn't see me now.

Hospitals never scared me before. I'm used to being in one at least forty hours a week. I can handle seeing fractured bones, and I can handle being in the room when a doctor tells a patient and his family that he may never walk again. But now I understand what it's like to be on the other side—the side that isn't just a job, but life, love and fear all combined in one. The side where one word makes all the difference.

My side usually consists of using high-tech machines and science to pick apart bones–bones used for movement in a patient who I only know by an ID number. I never thought about all that surrounded the bones of my patients—a heart that loves a child with everything it has, a mind that makes decisions for his survival, a hand that holds another's in times of need. Now it's my turn to see someone I love so hurt and helpless. If anything, maybe this will make me a more empathetic technician.

Jason is covered in a loose-fitting gown splattered with tiny blue shapes. He lies there so still, eyes closed, immobile—the hand gestures that are so closely related to his character are absent. He's always used his hands to convey his emotions. They're the hands that held his rifle in combat, created magnificent meals, held his beloved books, wrote letters home from Iraq. The memory of those letters is still bitter and fresh in my heart even though it was years ago.

I sit on the rigid hospital chair beside his bed, silently scolding the hospital for not having more comfortable furniture while people are visiting their loved ones for possibly the last time. Then again, maybe the hospital staff doesn't want the visitors to get too comfortable when they have to say goodbye. Seeing his face makes me think about the day he left for Iraq.

It seldom rains in southern California, which is why the balmy, wet air had struck me that day as a sign that something was about to go terribly wrong. I wound and dipped along the winding road of Camp Pendleton, taking the turns more slowly than ever before. Although I had driven this route a thousand times in the past two years, I felt the need to go more slowly, to prolong saying goodbye to Jason. As soon as I pulled into the entrance labeled "Location of Departure," a million emotions invaded me all at once, and the tears began to trickle, ever so gently down my cheeks.

"Alright, this is it." Jason, far too happy to be going off to war, said as he leaned in for one sweet, subtle goodbye kiss. Opening the back door of our tiny VW Golf, Jason retrieved his pack and hauled it on his back effortlessly as I met him on the passenger side of the car. I remember the sound of the wet, rocky dirt crunching beneath my feet. Knowing Jason all too well, I tried to avoid a sappy emotional goodbye scene. Instead, I gathered a last bit of strength and wrapped my arms around him. Burying my face in his freshly issued desert camouflage uniform, I allowed a few tears to slip out, leaving them behind on his collar as if to send him off with a piece of me.

"I love you. I'll be fine. Remember, this is what I was trained to do. This is what I signed up for." He enveloped my face in his strong, callused hands.

"Just don't die, okay? Promise me that. Promise me."

"I promise you. I love you always." *I love you always:* the four words we so conveniently passed back and forth since we first started dating. The four words that served as a goodbye on all phone calls and somehow managed to cure all our disagreements.

"I love you always." I reached for the driver's side door as Jason gave me a wink, turned on the heel of his combat boot and headed off to the lineup with the rest of the adrenaline-filled marines. I had watched as he walked away, the hop in his step making him appear carefree, as if this were just another day. Each step had significance, as if each time his foot hit the ground might be the last time. Rather than walk with a heel-to-toe stride, he bounced on the balls of his feet, launching forward as if he were pushing himself closer to his next obstacle. Like a bird scouting for food, his head was always erect, searching to ingest more of life's miracles. I used to call him "Kangaroo" because he was so bouncy and full of energy.

As I started the engine and prepared to see him one last time, I couldn't help but notice the family next to me: a pregnant wife looking at her husband as he held their toddler and said goodbye. The little boy wore a "My Daddy Wears Combat Boots" sweatshirt and smiled as his daddy kissed him and enveloped him in one last hug. I felt like a coward, feeling such pity for myself. And here this woman was, about to have a baby while raising a toddler alone. As if being a single mom weren't hard enough, this woman would wake up every day and wonder if her children's father will come home in one piece, if he'll ever teach that little boy how to play baseball in their backyard or cradle their newborn baby in his arms.

"What doesn't kill you makes you stronger," I mumbled to myself as I took a deep breath and pulled out of the gravelly lot.

Kenny Chesney serenaded me as I carved my way through the dark early morning roads of Camp Pendleton on my melancholy voyage home. As I had passed the boot camp barracks, I saw new recruits running along the road in flawless formation. Naive to the world and filled with adrenaline, these marines hadn't even experienced the simple milestones that come with being young—first love, that first wild year of college—yet there they were, training to kill. I think back to the moment I first met Jason, fresh out of boot camp with his jarhead haircut and dog tags dangling in front of his hunter green PT shirt. Unavoidable beads of sweat trickled down his tan skin in the Mississippi heat as our eyes met while we crossed paths on the flight line track. Both runners, away from home for the first time, both caught up in the military lifestyle, it was inevitable that we would connect.

I had been on a mission to complete four years in the Air Force while plucking away at college classes with the hopes of freeing myself, and my father, from college debt. The Air Force was the kindest of the branches and was more academically oriented, or at least that was what I had been told. And what better way to get out of that small town in New Hampshire than to enlist? I had the candid goal of hitting the books, staying single and becoming an orthopedic surgeon.

I'd always been fascinated with bones, which is why my mother bought me one of those skeletons they use as learning tools in science classes. I remember being very little and finding such fascination with which bones connected to which. One Christmas, my aunt Kathleen came over with the game Operation. The hours passed as she and I tried to use steady hands to grasp the tiny plastic bones. Every time one of us would hit the buzzer, my mother would shout in aggravation from the other room where she was swilling vodka and chain smoking. In the long run, my mother's lack of patience made Aunt Kathleen and me experts at the game because we were so scared of upsetting her and leading her into a drunken rage.

Jason's only intention for joining the Marine Corps, on the other hand, had been to find a family—a group of people he could relate to, people who were not like his mother. On his eighteenth birthday, Jason awoke to Emma Jane thrashing around the bedroom he shared with his fifteen-year-old sister.

"Jason, you're 18 now; it's time to make the family some money. You can't live here anymore. John is moving in, and he is bringing his son Colton."

Jason had torn the covers from his body as he sat upright in his wire-framed twin bed. He knew this moment was coming; he just wanted to hold on as long as he could for the sake of his baby sister. Emma Jane had been putting his stuff by the dumpster over the past few months in preparation for her most recent boyfriend to move in and for her to tell Jason that he was eighteen and it was time for him to be a *man*. The less he had in the house prior to his eighteenth birthday, the easier it would be for her to kick him out that day—tossing all attachments aside for Mr. Right Now, who at that time was John Copper Waite. A mechanic down at the local auto body shop, John spent his days doing cocaine off the back of an old rusty muffler while the newly hired fifteen-year-olds did the oil changes and ran the shop. He paid them in beer or what little cash he had. John was no shock to Jason; he was used to this by then. In fact, John was the better of the parade of men that Emma Jane brought to the house. Most of them were so wasted they couldn't speak when Jason entered the room. At least John still had his entire set of teeth (although slightly decayed) and acknowledged that Jason was alive.

While other new recruits needed an abundance of persuading to join the military, all it took Jason was the pictures of the various destinations that the military could take him. *Anywhere is better than here*, thought Jason as he signed the papers at his high school's job fair on the last day of school.

There were four rectangular tables covered with pamphlets exhibiting the benefits of each individual branch, and Jason didn't hesitate when he approached the table with the erect, intense-looking man in his early thirties. With a rigid haircut and jagged features, Sgt. Anderson had greeted Jason with a stern yet welcoming gesture. From that moment on, Jason was a model marine, following orders and volunteering for duties no one else wanted. Compared to his life at home, the Marine Corps was a cakewalk.

Jason and I had eased into our young married lives together, with the exception of an occasional bout of jealousy that's typical of young love, a fight about Jason's overly flirtatious gestures or an argument about my obsessive need to fill our calendar with charity work—as if working around the clock to defend the country wasn't enough charity for a twenty-year-old marine and airman. It was young love coated in the batter of real-life worries, unlike the typical "away at college" romance most of my high school friends experienced. We loved hard and fought even harder, always hoping it would get easier when our time in the military was up.

We had always dreamed of having the freedom to choose where to live, where to work and where to travel overseas, the desert not being one of our top choices. However, as time wears on all of us in relationships, our fights became much more frequent after Jason returned to the States.

"Jason." I lean forward, taking his hand in mine. Warm tears cascade down my cheeks, each drop symbolizing a memory. One lonely drop lands on his cold hand as I rub it into his cracked, callused thumb.

"Jason, it's Samantha. I always imagined we would see each other again under different circumstances." I speak softly, feeling awkward in the silence of the empty room. The beeping machines answer me back to remind me that he's here, he's alive. My eyes are glued to him as the memories we've shared, good and bad, trickle in and out of my mind. I think back to all the changes I saw in him after Iraq. Maybe he wouldn't be lying here in a coma if I had pushed harder to get him the help he needed.

"You always said you'd live into your nineties. I know you aren't ready to die yet," I plead. "You always said you had nine lives, and if I remember correctly this is only your third."

His accident in Iraq had been his first run-in with death, and the time his Honda Civic spun out on the slick California freeway was his second. Tears spring to my eyes as I hold his hand tighter and begin to sing one of our favorite songs, Kenny Chesney's "I'm Going to California":

> *She lived at the end of a little dirt road*
> *In a house where secrets go untold*
> *Barefoot in a cotton dress*
> *Dark hair in a tangled mess*
> *And a head full of crazy dreams*
> *She said*
> *I'm goin' to California*
> *A place where the sun always shines*
> *I'm goin' to California*
> *And I'm leavin' everything behind*

Suddenly, the right side of Jason's body starts to convulse as the monitors beep loudly, piercing my ears. Two nurses run in with alarmed expressions.

"What happened?" Allison darts for the machines on the opposite side of the bed. Her movements appear calm, but her expression is filled with questions.

"I—I don't know what happened; he just started jerking the right side of his body. I was just touching his hand, that's all," I stammer as flustered words spew out of my mouth.

"Dr. Bennington, please report to room 204!" the second nurse demands into the phone.

"Ma'am, I'm sorry but you're going to have to leave. Take a seat in the waiting room, and Dr. Bennington will brief you as soon as we know what's going on." The second, less patient nurse ushers me to the door, practically pushing me through the narrow exit.

"But is he okay? What happened?" I stutter in a daze, backing out of the room.

"Ma'am, the doctor will brief you when we stabilize him. For now, get a cup of coffee and try to relax."

Relax. Such an awful word to say to someone in a hospital. I make a mental note to never say that to my patients.

Before I have a chance to protest, the nurse ushers me into the waiting room. Seeing the urgency, my dad stands up abruptly.

"I—I don't know, Dad, I don't know what just happened. He just started jerking his right side." I ease into the seat next to him as he grabs my hand to soothe me.

Twenty-five slow minutes later, Dr. Bennington walks into the waiting room. Adjusting a pen in his pocket, he marches directly toward me.

"Mrs. Barnes?" He looks down at me, implying that I am Jason's wife, hand extended.

"Um, no. I'm not Mrs. Barnes. I'm um, his ex-wife. I'm Mrs. Colton. Samantha." I stumble on my words and stand up to shake his hand. Eyes darting around the waiting room, Emma Jane is nowhere in sight to take over her son's health matters.

"Well, regardless, can I have a word with you in my office? I'm guessing Jason's mother is elsewhere right now, and since you were in the room when he reacted, it might be more beneficial to speak with you at this time." Dr. Bennington squeezes his chin with his thumb and index finger, sad blue eyes peering around the room for an absent Emma Jane.

"Doctor, is everything okay?" My dad stands up. I can tell he is on the defense by the way his hands launch up to his hips as soon as his body is upright.

"Based on the resemblance, I am guessing that you are Mrs. Colton's father?"

"Yes, sir. Dale Brighton." He extends his hand and shakes with an overly firm grip.

"Well, Mr. Brighton, it's a pleasure meeting you. If you don't mind, I'm just going to steal your daughter for a moment to discuss Jason's health."

"Yes, Doctor, that is quite alright—anything we, I mean *she,* can do to help." Dad sits back down as he gives me an approving wink.

Dr. Bennington leads me down a narrow, brightly lit corridor on the opposite end of Jason's hospital room. Opening a door to a room that looks nothing like a typical hospital setting, he motions for me to take a seat in front of his mahogany desk. Colorful pictures of family serve as wallpaper on all available surfaces. If I didn't know better, I'd think the office belonged to a professor, not a doctor. Books on a variety of subjects fill a shelf next to his desk, and seashells are strewn on a side table in front of a portrait of two little girls lying on the beach side by side, hands cradling their pink faces with bright smiles.

"Samantha, I want to explain to you what I think may have happened to Jason in there."

"Okay," I reply, tucking a loose strand of hair behind my ear.

"Jason has been in a coma for nearly five days now. My staff and I have tried several methods to create brain stimulation, to no avail. We are experts, and we have over seventy years of combined experience working with brain trauma patients—which is why I'm ninety-nine percent sure he was reacting to something you did or said when you were in that room. He recognized your voice. Can you tell me exactly what type of physical contact you made, even the most minor of details? Or is there anything you said before his stimulation that may have caused it?"

I shift in my seat, trying to recollect all the details of my brief visit to his room.

"Well, I um, just held his hand. Maybe I squeezed it a little too hard?"

"But were you holding his hand instantly before he jerked?"

"Well, I was holding his hand and singing a song. It was a song that uh, well, we used to sing together."

Dr. Bennington's deep-set, kind blue eyes dart back and forth before locking into mine. He rests his clipboard and takes a seat behind the enormous desk. He has a kindness and understanding that suggest medicine isn't his only background. Maybe it's the family pictures scattered about the room, or the way he sits down and listens as I speak, with no impatient tapping of fingers, loss of eye contact or glance at the clock to show he has other places to be and patients to see. This comforts me, and words tumble from my mouth about Jason's past, about the changes I saw in him after Iraq.

I tell him about the night I found Jason plastered to our front deck in a low crawl position. Sound asleep, I'd awoken to low, hovering whispers. I had looked over to see an empty space in bed beside me, so I walked toward the whispers. The sliding door on our third floor deck overlooking the small pond was wide open. Our wind chimes danced in the spring breeze, the sound drowning out his voice.

I'd craned my neck around the corner of the open sliding glass to see Jason flattened against the wooden slats on the deck floor in a low crawl position. His upper body was lifted slightly on his elbows, and he held an invisible rifle against his shoulder. "Enemy fire, enemy fire! Get down, Lance Corporal Wilkins!" His words had come with a hushed, eerie force. I stood there watching briefly before I attempted to wake him from his nightmare.

Most of his words were mashed together in inaudible clusters, but the name *Lance Corporal Wilkins* stood out from the slurs. He repeated it multiple times, and it was lucid compared to the rest of the slurs. My thoughts scrambled together as I tried to remember him talking about a fellow marine with the name, but nothing came to mind. I had tiptoed across the deck, the wooden slats creaking beneath my bare feet. "Jason, Jason," I whispered, afraid to wake the neighbors. He blinked a few times before showing a hazy recognition of where he was.

"Where am I? What's going on?" He had looked at me like a toddler who lost his mother in the mall.

"You're home, baby. Let's go back to bed."

Dr. Bennington's eyes seldom blink as he listens intently to me. I clasp my hands tightly and tell the stories of Jason's PTSD episodes. My words flow easily in Dr. Bennington's presence. I tell him about the time I woke up to Jason's hands gripping my neck, his body hovering over me to pin me down as he mumbled angrily and incoherently. His eyes had stared eerily through me as if he were somewhere else, frightened and angry at the same time. My screams had eventually broken his trance, and he'd fallen sideways onto his side of the bed while mumbling—more to himself than to me—that he'd thought I was the enemy.

"Samantha, the things you're telling me are very common for returning vets. Post-traumatic stress disorder is far more common today than we'd like it to be. It sounds like you did all you could do to try to get him help." Dr. Bennington leans back in his chair, dancing his fingers delicately on the smooth dark wooden arms.

"I've been his only family. That's why we've remained such close friends after we split. His family is pretty much non-existent, and I can't stand not to be there for him. He's like the brother I never had. Minus the marriage part." Half a smile sweeps across my face as I try to lighten the mood.

"And that's the best thing you can do for Jason right now. He needs a solid support system, friends who will be there with him consistently and not just pop in and out of his life when it's convenient. Stability, in more ways than one, is key for him at this point."

Towering over me, Dr. Bennington pushes himself up from the chair, gesturing me to the door with his massive hands.

"So, I have your contact info. I'll keep you updated on Jason's progress."

"Thanks." I grip the gold doorknob and start to walk back into the sterility of the hospital.

"Oh, and Samantha? We don't get to choose our family. We choose our friends. Remember that."

"Very true." Nodding gently, I turn and head back to the waiting room.

Talking to Dr. Bennington was like spending an hour in therapy. I spoke, he listened, and I left feeling as if I had accomplished something. I toss my tan canvas bag over my shoulder and head back into the waiting room. My dad is sitting in the corner chair, an outdated *Field and Stream* magazine spread open in front of him. His green eyes look up in surprise as he springs out of the chair, his lanky body unfolding itself as he walks toward me.

"Nothing changed. Dr. Bennington just wanted to know a bit about Jason's past."

"You were in there for an awful long time."

"Yeah, well, Jason's past isn't something that can be summed up in a few minutes of small talk."

"True," he acknowledges as he pushes his sandy brown hair out of his eyes and looks around the empty room, hands planted on his narrow hips.

"Let's go get a cup of coffee in the cafeteria. I hear they have that flavored stuff you like so much." Dad loops a long arm around my shoulders and leads me to the cafeteria just off the main lobby.

We slide our trays down the metal counter, dressing up our coffees while admiring the selection of snacks that are on display just begging to be purchased.

"So, how is Alex doing?" My dad slides himself into the booth, his knobby knees bumping the table.

"Good. He's been busy with work. His firm is working on establishing a location for the newly designed recreation center."

"Very good. Very good. How does he feel about you being here?"

"He's fine with it, Dad, you know that. He understands."

As I raise the steaming hazelnut coffee to my lips, my eyes dart around the cafeteria and land on a brunette at the fountain soda station. She's stunning. Long black ringlets cascade down her delicate white lace shirt. She looks around nervously and tugs at a chunky teal necklace that rests on her collarbone. Her legs are shapely, but they look exceptionally thin in her black leggings. A pair of edgy black biker-like boots with shiny buckles cover the bottom half of her pants while her top half looks innocent, all dainty and sweet in contrast.

Like watching a train wreck unfold, I can't stop staring at her. She looks sad. A tiny heart-shaped set of deep red lips curve slightly downward. A small nose is centered on her face, a dozen freckles sprinkled across it like an afterthought. And the roundest set of blue eyes is planted below perfectly angled eyebrows, like two blue sapphire gems. Her makeup looks as though it's been painted on by a professional artist, shimmery gray eye shadow skimming her upper lid and black eye liner curving upward, cat-like, at the edge of each eye.

"Is Jason still seeing the therapist regularly?" My dad plants his pointy elbows on the table, adjusting the cuffs of his red and black plaid flannel shirt.

"He says he is. But once again, Dr. Coyle is trying to be a drug pusher instead of a listener."

"Typical." My dad's eyes gloss over. I can tell he's thinking back to his first days back from Vietnam. He never talked to me about what happened, not a word, but I could tell he understood Jason, and maybe that's why they got along so well.

Never one to show much emotion, Dad tries to redirect the conversation by talking about updates he's making to his house. I can't help but be distracted by the elderly lady rolling through the checkout line. She bumps the corner of the cashier stand with her wheelchair and gets stuck, reminding me of the time Jason and I were biking along on the hilly streets that surrounded our apartment complex in California. Side by side, we'd pedaled away while chatting about mindless things. Suddenly, in the middle of my story about a lazy co-worker, Jason swerved his bike to the side of the road, dropped it on its side, and went sprinting toward a little old lady who was struggling to get up the hill in her wheelchair. By the time I caught up to them, Jason was pushing her up the hill and talking with her about her great-grandchildren like they were old friends. I became the third wheel as I pedaled slowly beside them, my legs burning from the resistance of the hill.

He pushed her all the way to the top of the steep hill to the senior home where she lived. Before saying goodbye, she made sure to tell me what a gentleman my husband was and lectured me on the importance of holding onto a good man. Her name was Ethel, and Jason ended up going back every week to visit her. The two shared stories over tea and stale nursing home cookies. He entertained her by telling her about his hobbies, and she told him stories about when she and her husband were young and in love. He told me she always ended their conversations by saying, "These are the best days of your life; enjoy every moment."

He was so good at making rare friends. Jason would find the good in just about everyone. I silently scold myself for the times I teased him for making friends with weird strangers. This is what he was good at; he thrived on making people happy.

"We better get back to the waiting room; I don't want to miss any of Dr. Bennington's updates." I push myself up from the table, feeling like I've been in this hospital for months, not hours.

Walking back to the waiting room, I link arms with my dad, feeling his bony elbow jabbing into my side. We walk in synchronized step, both tall and lanky, two people cut from the same cloth. In grade school I used to silently curse my father for giving me his straight build, all muscle and sharp angles, not a feminine curve in sight. While my friends were transitioning from training bra to big girl bra, I was perfectly fine in an unsupported cheap sports bra, just enough to conceal my tiny protruding bumps. Now, I thank God for sparing me my mother's vivacious curves. She was all chest, hips and rear. I couldn't imagine running with the extra weight and space of a size D chest and a full set of hips. It would be like carrying another human on my trail runs.

As we approach the waiting room, I see the familiar face from the cafeteria, the sad girl with big blue eyes. She sits alone, hands nervously trying to settle into a comfortable grasp, legs crossed. It's not until she looks up and locks eyes with mine that it dawns on me. *Abby*.

Chapter Four

Abby

THE PAST TWO DAYS have gone by in a fog. I've walked around in a cloud of sadness. I've learned how to create a bed out of the uncomfortable rigid chairs in the waiting room. I line up three in a row and curl up on my side. I'm not family, so I don't have the privilege of sleeping in the family room on a cot. Jason's mom, whom I haven't actually met yet, has had that luxury, even though this is her first appearance in his life since I've known him. Without her approval, I can't get past the ICU doctors to see Jason, so I'm holding onto what morsel of patience I have left. Even though I've shared a bed with him every night for the past two years, sat across from him at our tiny dinner table for every meal, and taken him to all of his appointments at the grungy VA hospital, I am sadly still not considered family.

Just two weeks ago, Jason had called me his family. I had come home from work to Jason greeting me anxiously. As soon as I stepped through the threshold of our apartment, he grabbed me and turned me around, making me promise to close my eyes. "Keep them closed," he said as he took my giant purse off of my shoulder and guided me to the corner of our tiny apartment. When he was satisfied with my location, he gave my shoulders a little squeeze and said, "Okay, you can open them." The first thing I saw was a splash of colors. My paint containers sat perfectly lined up on a shelf on the wall. Next to the shelf, my current project sat half-finished on a brand new easel in the corner of our apartment. A bright red stool sat perched in front of the easel. All my painting supplies were neatly organized on the adjoining wall in various compartments, all neatly hung.

In one fluid motion, Jason flipped the stool over and held it upside down in front of me. *You have a beautiful talent. Share it with the world. I love you. Love, Jason.* The letters were written messily with a black calligraphy pen.

"Sorry—I'm not the least bit artistic, so this probably looks a little messy to you, but I tried," Jason had said. He winked and flipped the chair back to its correct position.

"Jason, I can't believe you did all this for me. It's all so organized and new." I look around, still taking in all of my supplies, neatly arranged. I spot a brand new set of my favorite brushes, still in the package sitting on the ledge of the easel. "Oh my God, are these vintage brushes? Jason, these must have cost a fortune!" I spin around and face him, my excitement spilling into a smile that spreads across my face.

"A true artist needs the best supplies." He looked at me, his serious tone almost scary. "Sit." He pushed on my shoulders, lightly pressing me onto the stool. "Now, I want you to promise me you'll work at this easel every day." A flash of color on the wall catches my eye. A piece of purple yarn creates a triangle, and dangling from it is a bright pink frame with black matting and small bright pink writing listing several quotes:

> *Every child is an artist. The problem is how to remain an artist once he grows up.*
>
> —Pablo Picasso

> *Twenty years from now you will be more disappointed by the things that you didn't do than by the ones you did do, so throw off the bowlines, sail away from safe harbor, catch the trade winds in your sails. Explore, Dream, Discover.*
>
> —Mark Twain

> *Go confidently in the direction of your dreams. Live the life you have imagined.*
>
> —Henry David Thoreau

> *The mind is everything. What you think you become.*
>
> —Buddha

They were the quotes Jason had been reciting to me since I told him that I wanted to be an artist with my own studio. I was speechless.

"Jason, I can't believe you did all this for me." I felt a tear well up as I turned around to face him.

"Well, it would've been better, but I didn't have a lot of room to work with here." He waves his hand, motioning to our tiny studio apartment.

"This is more than I ever imagined." I stand and wrap my arms around his neck. He grabs my waist and moves me slightly back so we're eye to eye. A crooked smile takes up half of his face before he kisses me on the nose. "Just promise me you won't give up, okay?"

"Okay. I promise."

Apparently the saying "blood is thicker than water" only applies to hospital visitation rights, because his mother has certainly not earned any other rights in his life. I used to get mad that Jason had never taken me down south to meet his mother. I was afraid he was trying to keep me a secret from her. He kept making excuses about her being busy or traveling for work, but over time, he confessed that she embarrassed him. He never mentioned why, just that he would rather not get me involved in stupid family drama.

Another day of visiting the sub-par cafeteria. I don't go to the cafeteria to eat though; I just go for a change in scenery. I can't eat. The only thing I've been able to keep down is a few spoonfuls of chicken noodle soup. My nerves fight off any possibility of an appetite. Once again I'm sitting in the waiting room, staring at *Full House* reruns and sipping my third Diet Coke of the day. I've already gone through the pile of outdated magazines that sit on the table beside me. I silently wonder if any of the articles that I read are even valid anymore. Most of them are at least a year old. I'm guessing the article on ADD in *Psychology Today* is completely inaccurate now. But I'll do anything to pass the time—I feel like I've been walking in quicksand the past few days, stuck and unchanging.

I'm suddenly jerked out of my thoughts to the sound of voices around me.

My eyes dart up to the sound of a familiar voice. I see a young girl and a man approaching the waiting room. It's obvious they're related; if the identical features didn't give it away, their matching gaits do.

I know it's Samantha because I've seen pictures. When we were moving Jason's stuff into my apartment, I discovered a tattered old scrapbook at the bottom of the military-issued pack he used to carry his clothes in. I hid it under a pile of car supplies in my trunk. I was curious to see what she looked like, but scared at the same time.

One rainy night, after my shift at the restaurant, I pulled the scrapbook out from underneath the pile of jumper cables and car-cleaning supplies. A torn piece of plastic was taped to the front, covering an index card that said "California 2001" in purple cursive. Samantha had clearly made the scrapbook, as it was outlined with bright flowery '60s stickers. I gave it one last thought before I opened it and was sucked into Jason's past like time travel.

Hesitant to have an image of Samantha to attach to Jason's stories embedded in my memory, I finally peeled open the cover. The pages were filled with traditional couple pictures, young and clearly in love: the two of them splashing around on the beach; his arms wrapped around her waist at the top of a mountain; sitting around a bonfire side by side, both of their faces covered in marshmallow and laughing; both of them on bikes on a dirt trail, big grins planted on their perfectly tanned faces. The last page was one of them standing on top of a mountain, snowboards sticking out of the ground on either side of them. Jason had a massive black and blue mark on his right cheek, below a puffy red eye. Knowing Jason, he probably fell on one of the trails while attempting a new trick. *They were so active together,* I thought. *The most we do is walk down to the local pub.* I closed the book, relieved and sad at the same time. She would no longer be just "Samantha" to me. She would be the pretty blonde who had made Jason happy.

I look up, and the obligation of having to acknowledge her presence strangles me.

Her eyes slowly move toward me as she peels herself away from her conversation with her dad. "You must be Abby." She strides over toward me, hand extended, like it's a job interview: She's clearly my boss, and I'm the eager employee, awaiting her direction.

"Yeah." I can't bring myself to make eye contact. An internal battle ensues in my mind as I try to force myself to be nice, telling myself Jason's injuries are far more important than my feelings toward his ex. I take a deep breath while limply shaking her hand. I study her features, quickly drinking it all in. Even though she isn't quite beautiful, she has a face I could stare at for hours. I memorize her wide-set blue eyes, the shape of almonds. Her skin isn't as tan as it was in the photo album, but there are a dozen tiny freckles scattered on her nose, probably leftover from all of her days in the California sun. Her lips are clearly her standout feature. Bright red and plump, they sit on her face with a perfect protruding pout rising up to meet her short, blunt nose. She's all sharp edges where I'm rounded curves, all athlete where I'm spectator. I turn toward her father to relieve some of the awkwardness I feel.

"This is my dad, Dale."

"Hi, Dale. Jason has told me so much about you." I intentionally act as if Jason has never said a word to me about her. While at times I've been known to have an attitude, I've never been one to allow jealously to crash through me like it is now. She doesn't look hurt. It's clear that I'm the one who is on the receiving end of the pain here. The three of us sit down in the waiting room and attempt small talk before Emma Jane, a tall, blonde tornado of a woman, whirls into the room.

"Well, well, Miss Abby!" The amazon woman waltzes over to me, her tone much too chipper for an ICU waiting room. As I look around at the other visitors, all eyes are on Emma Jane as if she's a clown at a child's party and we're all waiting for her next trick. She pulls me up into a hug, gold bangle bracelets clanking down her arms, the stench of cheap perfume emitting from her. She smells like she rubbed suntan lotion on herself then sprayed Baby Soft on every inch of her body afterward. She looks nothing like Jason except for the shade of blue in her eyes—the silvery blue I saw the day I met him outside Sebastian's Café on Brentwood Street.

I'll never forget how my life changed when I heard the bells jingle on the entrance door. I looked up from the Classifieds section of the *Brookside Monitor,* and my eyes followed this blue-eyed stranger as he made his way to the counter. I had carefully spied on his friendly conversation with the barista as he handed her cash and turned away with a cup of coffee cradled in his hand. He caught me watching him and politely gave a nod as he walked by my table and out the door, toward the sidewalk bike rack. I remember the hop in his step, as if he were just so happy to be alive. As he was riding away,

I saw something shiny drop from the seat of his bike and bounce onto the pavement and into the street. Instinct tumbled through me as I ran out, grabbed the tiny bike lock key and began to chase him.

"Hey!"

"Yeah?" His neck pivoted as he came to an abrupt stop, pulling onto the sidewalk where I was neurotically chasing him down the street.

"You lost this." His eyes zeroed in on the key as I held it out to his right hand.

"Thanks, I guess I shouldn't go too far without that."

Hands in my jean pockets, I rocked forward on my toes. "Nice bike." The words came out before I realized the ridiculousness of them.

"Thanks. Trying to help save the environment a little." He winked and scanned me from head to toe. "So, how do I reward you for saving my key so I can continue to save the environment?"

"No reward necessary."

"Hey, wait a minute, didn't I just see you in that coffee shop? You had your head buried in a newspaper?"

"Yep, that was me. Job searching. Always a fun way to spend a Saturday afternoon." Biting my lip, I pulled my nervous hands out of my pockets and folded them across my chest. From the time I was about seventeen, I had a surprising confidence around men. I inherited my mother's dark locks and blue eyes, and I've always been told that's a lethal combination—maybe because I don't appear as free-spirited as a blue-eyed blonde, nor as feminine as a curvy brown-eyed brunette. I was the rare combination of both worlds. With a twirl of one of my long shiny locks, I could capture the undivided attention of any one of my masculine victims, like a spider weaving a web. I still had a modest nature about me though, so men weren't turned off by a snobbish attitude.

I had recently gone on several dates and learned how to play the game quite easily, but there was something about Jason that was different. The longer I looked into his eyes, the more my nerves flitted and flopped around in my chest, as if he had some power over me.

"Well, if you are due for a break from your job searching, I'd love to join you and finish my cup of coffee." Raising his coffee cup in a toasting fashion, he started to turn his bike around toward the café. "It's probably not a smart idea to drink and ride anyway."

We walked back to the café in the crisp fall air, bright leaves crunching below our feet, and talked until we were dehydrated from all the coffee and the barista hinted that he was closing. I think about how happy I was that day, how different things are today.

"Hi." I rigidly join Emma Jane in a hug, slightly uncomfortable with her immediate affection.

"Emma Jane, this is Abby." Samantha hops up from the chair as if on cue. "Emma Jane, would it be okay if Abby and I go into the room together?" Before I have a chance to speak for myself, Samantha takes over the conversation.

"Why, of course you two can go in the room next. I just stopped by to pick up my overnight bag anyway. Ain't no sense in sticking around, so I'm going to stay with a friend in town." Emma Jane gestures to her huge pink bag nestled in the corner of the room between the magazine rack and a wooden chair.

"Thank you." I put on my most polite smile as Samantha motions for me to follow her out of the waiting room and into Jason's room. I've been dreaming about my first moment alone with Jason for the past three days, and I sink into a sea of disappointment when I realize Samantha will be joining me like a third wheel on our date.

Chapter Five

Samantha

ABBY AND I WALK DOWN the hallway in silence. I can feel the discomfort percolating in the air. Being around Jason's girlfriends is nothing new for me, so I slide right into my routine of the normal introductory banter.

"So, are you from New Hampshire?" As always, I initiate the conversation.

"I was a military brat," she responds hesitantly after a minute of silence. As if she's being forced to elaborate, she continues. "My dad's career in the Army had us traveling all over. When he retired, he said he'd always wanted to live in New England, so this is where we ended up. Been here ever since." She maintains perfect posture as we walk and keeps her eyes forward, clearly not wanting to warm up to me.

"Nice. I know Jason loves New England. Always been a fan of the cold."

"Yeah, well he likes a lot of places. We both like to travel, so we have plans of going other places together." Her sentence is cut off as the nurse lets us into the room.

I offer her the chair alongside the bed. I sit in the chair that's catty-corner, keeping my distance.

"Hi, baby." She grabs his hand then looks up at me awkwardly as if I'm crashing the party. She leans forward to gently caress the bandages that are hugging the swollen side of his skull. Her voice crackles slightly as she looks away. I can see the fear erupt in her eyes as it registers just how serious his injury is. Everything about him appears swollen, as if his body has been injected with air. I know from working in a hospital that swelling is not a good sign. His face is sallow; the usual California tan he was born with is absent, leaving his cheeks various tones of gray. In the short time he's been restricted to this bed, I can already see a loss of muscle mass. Jason always had a naturally athletic build. He certainly doesn't have the height of a basketball player or the lithe frame of a runner, but his muscular build makes him at least good at every sport he attempts.

"I'm sure the swelling will go down and he'll be back to our, *your,* Jason again." I catch myself too late. She picks up on my verbal stumble and looks me directly in the eye for the first time. I can feel the anger wafting off her body.

"This is your fault, you know." Tears make their way down her pink cheeks. She's suddenly transformed from sad and quiet to angry. "I was mad at him for being friends with you, and he got angry and left. If you would've just left him alone and minded your own business, he would've never left and gone rock climbing."

"Abby." I inch closer to her, afraid she'll burst into a rolling boil of anger. "This could've happened at any time. Jason is a daredevil. Trust me, I've seen him miss death by an inch several times."

"Trust YOU?" Her entire face transforms into a deep shade of red. "YOU are the last person I trust! For the past two years you have tried to control my and Jason's relationship, and for whatever reason he listens to you. Don't you have a life of your own?" She rockets herself to a standing position, one hand on a hip and the other extending a set of perfectly manicured fingers, darting in different directions as she inches toward me. I back up, actually scared that she might pounce on me. The last time I got into a girl fight was when I was in fifth grade and Melissa Wallace told everyone on the playground that my mom was a drunk. That didn't end well, so I backed up and kept quiet. When she is done screaming, she speed-walks past me and out of the room, her shoulder nudging mine as she flies past.

"Is everything all right in here?" A nurse pokes her head around the doorframe with a raised eyebrow.

"Yeah, everything is fine." I plop down on a chair and let out a long sigh.

CHAPTER SIX

Abby

AFTER MY OUTBURST, I march out of Jason's room and wind down a series of hospital corridors. My anger is still tearing through me like a tornado and my head is so clouded with bad thoughts that I can't figure out where I'm going. I walk down the hallways in a panic as I pass through various different departments. Everyone seems too busy running around in scrubs to notice me, and I'm afraid if I ask someone how to get out into the waiting room, my anger will come out in my voice and they'll see the tears that have continued to pour down my face like an endless flow of water twisting down a river. I normally hate confrontation, but it was as if someone took over my body and released all of the pent-up anger I've had for the past two years. In the midst of it all, I can't help but be a little proud for standing up for myself for once. As my anger starts to dissipate and my head becomes clear, I somehow find my bearings and make my way back to the waiting room.

Hoping to avoid Samantha and her dad, I keep my head down and head to the ladies room to touch up my face, which I'm sure is now covered in streaks of mascara. Before I make it to the bathroom, I see a pair of hot pink heels and I'm colliding into Emma Jane.

"Oh, honey. What's the matter?" She gently rests her hands on my shoulders as I look up shyly, a piece of hair covering one tear-drenched eye. "I think you need a cup of coffee and a break from this waiting room."

Before I can answer, she steers me out of the room and into the cafeteria. Words are tripping over themselves, trying to escape, as

I explain my outburst to her. We slide into the booth closest to the sandwich station; the overbearing smell of red onion is so strong I can taste it. I look over at the chef who is rhythmically slicing and displaying a variety of meats in the tin containers.

"Honey, I don't blame you." She grabs my hands in hers. "Samantha has a way of controlling Jason. Look at me—I'm his mother and he no longer talks to me because of her. I don't know what it is with that girl, but she has pitted him against me, and it looks like she was trying to pit him against you too. All I ever did was try to be the mother that she never had."

"She doesn't have a mother?" I'm taken aback by this news. I always knew she was close to her dad, but I didn't know her mother wasn't around.

"Well, it's not my business to talk about it really." Her eyes scan my face. "Abby, I've heard so much about you from my Jason." Emma Jane leans in and pushes a strand of my hair behind my ear, revealing one of my diamond studs. She leans back in her seat and gasps. "Oh my, those are the most beautiful diamonds I have ever seen! Does my son have a talent for picking out jewelry now?"

"Actually, my dad gave me these for my eighteenth birthday." I feel my face growing red. My pale skin has never allowed me to hide my embarrassment. "My mom told me he saved for months for these earrings. He had his heart set on buying me them for years and just couldn't wait until my birthday. According to my mom, he would walk by the base jeweler window every Saturday to make sure they were still there. That was when we were stationed in Texas. We moved a lot because my dad was in the Army." The words spill out of my mouth, sentences smashed together in an attempt to keep conversation and avoid silence.

"Sounds like you're a daddy's girl," Emma Jane says as tears fill her eyes. "Sorry, this is so embarrassing. It's just that I've always wanted to be a daddy's girl."

Her eyes look down at the bottle of Diet Coke that she lets lightly fall from hand to hand. "My daddy left my momma when I was just a little thing." She holds her hand out level with the height of the table, indicating how tall she was. "Then Momma just lost it. She left us with our ill grandma, who couldn't take care of us. Before long, well, we were being tossed from foster home to foster home." Her gaze leaves mine and looks off over my shoulder.

"Oh, Emma Jane. That is horrible. I'm so sorry you had to go through all of that."

"Yeah, well what doesn't kill us makes us stronger as they say. And it made me a better momma to Jason. I always made sure he was my top priority. Never let that little boy outta my sight until he packed up and joined the Marine Corps." She folds and unfolds her hands as her jewelry clinks against the table. "And then, well, he found Samantha and she kind of took over his life. But I'm sure you know that already. She has a tendency to manipulate our Jason into doing what she wants. She always left me out of things and never invited me over for the holidays or for visits when the two of them were married. All I wanted was what was best for him. It's all a mother ever wants. But she swooped in and took over his life. And to think she has all that money of Jason's that he worked so hard to save over the years." Her eyes stare off as if she's lost in thought. "This is the first time I've seen him in years. Even after their divorce, she had a hold on him. I'm sure I'm telling you everything you already know though, right?"

"Actually, Jason and I fought about Samantha right before he stormed out and got into his accident." As the words fall out of my mouth, the reality of them hurts my heart, but it feels like a relief at the same time. I'm finally able to talk to someone who understands. I tell Emma Jane about our fights over Samantha. Everything that I've been battling for two years comes pouring out of my mouth, like a river opening up to a sea. For once in my life I let the tears collide with my words and I let Emma Jane see my vulnerable side. She darts up and slides into my side of the table, pulling me into a warm embrace and just letting me sob. My parents were never physically affectionate people, so Emma Jane's embrace feels like a soft touch in my steely world.

"It's okay, Abby Girl. Everything is going to be okay." She smoothes my hair as I fall deeper into her embrace.

"You just called me Abby Girl." I look up and see a blurry vision of her through teary eyes. "That's what Jason always calls me." I swipe my dripping nose with the back of my hand, and I immediately become a child in her arms.

"Well, Jason and I always thought alike." She winks and delicately pats my eyes with a tissue she's retrieved from her purse. "A mom can never have enough tissues and wet naps on her. And a girl can never have enough makeup on her. Let's go get you cleaned up and touch up that makeup before we head back to the waiting room."

After digging around, she pulls a clear plastic container out of her purse filled with eye liner, mascara and about a dozen different shades of eye shadow and lipstick. Draping an arm over my shoulders, she leads me to the ladies room and sits me down in the handicap stall while she arranges her makeup case on the sink, pulling out the high-end makeup I've always dreamed of using. MAC, Lauren Mercier and Clinique products line the sink as she applies them to my features, dabbing and swiping while humming and twirling with each new application. "You know, I always wanted to have a daughter I could do this with, but Jason's younger sister Cara was always a bit of a tomboy. She would always trail behind Jason climbing trees and catching frogs." She pauses, looking down at the blush pallet for a moment; moisture inflates her already big, round eyes. "But everything happens for a reason, right? And that's why you're here with me now." She dabs my nose one final time with the blush brush and uses the handicap hand rail as leverage to lift her body from a squatting position. She plops the makeup cases one by one in the container as I assess my face in the mirror. It's a little more makeup than even I'm used to, but I figure there's no harm in making her feel good for a day, so I leave my makeover in place and pretend to like the bright pink pucker she created with a variety of liners and shades of lipstick. She loops her arm through mine and we walk together toward the waiting room.

CHAPTER SEVEN

Samantha

I CHOSE TO WORK in a hospital because I thrive in a busy atmosphere, and there's never a shortage of patients in this world. I see a sequence of patients on a typical day, all with varying injuries and personalities. You would think the job of a radiology technician gets boring, but I find the difference from one bone structure to another absolutely fascinating. Adding to that are the millions of cells that make up the skin, organs and features of my patients, making every one of them completely unique.

It confirms my belief that we are all created with distinct attributes. Like snowflakes, we all have unique points and edges surrounded by a center that drives us to follow our individual passions and desires.

I can tell Abby and I have different centers. I can also tell Jason chose her for a reason. He loves her in a way he could never love me. I've spent countless phone conversations being his verbal punching bag when he would vent to me about girl after girl gone wrong. Before giving it any time, he would give up on these girls for the simplest of reasons. Tabitha wasn't laid back enough, Erica hated to travel, Melissa watched too much TV. He would always somehow magnify his girlfriends' smallest flaws into issues that were simply unbearable to live with, and he'd always walk away as though he never knew them. Abby is the only one who he fought for, the only one who kept him interested, so there must be something special about her. After I witnessed her fiery explosion in Jason's room, I realized our tempers are one trait we have in common. "Hey, Dad.

Do you mind if I step out for a bit? I need to get some fresh air." I look over at him intently surveying an old *Men's Health* magazine— anything to keep him from having to make small talk.

"Sure. Do you want me to join you?"

"Nah, just need to stretch out my legs and go for a run. Is the house key still in the same spot?"

"You bet." He winks at me like he's sharing a deep, dark secret.

The good thing about running is that you can do it anywhere at any time in almost any weather. My dad's house is so close to the hospital, I decide to walk there. The streets of Brookside welcome me back like an old friend. Even though I didn't spend my childhood in Brookside, I've spent enough days after my dad and I were reunited to have some knowledge of the back roads and shortcuts of the small city.

I stroll along Main Street and peek into every window like a tourist taking in the streets of Paris for the first time. Nostalgia floods me as I approach the storefront of Sebastian's Bakery. While a lot of Brookside's small businesses have come and gone in these storefront windows like strangers passing in the night, Sebastian's has always remained faithful to the locals. Having traveled around the country a bit, I know Sebastian's pastries and coffee aren't the best I've encountered, but their customer service is phenomenal and keeps the locals coming back—sometimes two or three times a day.

My love of coffee has driven me into a love for cafés, and over the years I've developed a rating scale for every café I frequent. Each place I set foot in is measured by four categories: Coffee flavor and selection are first and foremost, and customer service is second. (I've never understood why someone would hire a curmudgeon to serve people their morning doses of caffeine and sugar.) I place food in the third category, simply because I typically order only coffee—unless, of course, I'm meeting a friend for lunch or brunch. And the last category is atmosphere: It can make or break a café, and Sebastian's atmosphere most certainly makes it.

The welcoming storefront lured me in the first time I walked by it years ago. Unlike most other places along Main Street, Sebastian's has outdoor seating that allows dogs. Small white bistro tables and ice cream parlor chairs are clustered inside the roped off-section. Several "Dogs Allowed" signs dangle from the red rope, and black and white checkered water bowls are strewn along the edges of the table legs. Water seeps onto the sidewalk from the dogs' sloppy snouts. To some this may not be appealing, but to me it's heaven.

As I pull open the door, the entryway bell alerts the dogs that are lounging by their owners' feet. A black terrier sits at attention, tilting his head and looking at me through big round black eyes that are partially covered by overgrown bangs. Even though it's no longer morning, the smells of pastries and coffee wake up my senses as I walk into the cozy café. Artsy red scribbling on the black chalkboards behind the counter alerts guests of Today's Specials.

Sebastian's knows how to keep their old, stubborn locals coming back by keeping their old-school staples on the menu, but they've slowly incorporated a modern feel to the place to bring in a fresh, young crowd too. I think it's the secret to their success. It's the middle of the week, but guests are lined along the pastry counter, eager to order their lunches and get back to work. The barista dances to the sounds of Sinatra in the background while grinding beans and pumping various blends into the recycled paper cups. She plucks away at each customer's order and sends them off with a bright smile. I think about my small dream of being a barista, surrounded by the enchanting smells of freshly ground beans every day while creating a variety of different coffee concoctions, sampling them along the way.

After the barista hands me my hot cup of dark roast with a pump of sugar-free caramel and sends me off with a chipper goodbye, I make my way to the creamer station. I tilt the carafe so it only drops a little splash of half and half and watch my coffee turn from black to a creamy shade of beige. Before I look up, I get the sensation that someone is watching me. I tilt my head back and feel my first swig of caffeine surge through my body while I catch Abby's eyes so intently focused on me that I can almost feel them drilling a hole through my own eyes. I'm thankful when she averts her eyes back to her laptop, clearly caught staring at me. But that doesn't stop the awkwardness I now feel. The café is busy enough that I could make my way through the crowd, pretending I didn't see her, but I feel the need to be the bigger person. I turn my body sideways and shimmy my way to her table.

"Hey, Abby. So you've discovered the legendary Sebastian's Café?" I stand over her as discomfort pierces me, making me stand awkwardly with a hand on one hip while sipping the overly hot coffee between nervous breaths. I can feel the liquid burning the back of my throat but I try not to show my pain.

"Yeah. I live here so I know it. In fact, this is where Jason and I met." She looks up at me, holding my eye contact for a solid fifteen seconds. "But I'm guessing he already told you that." She keeps her eyes glued to mine, as if she can see my thoughts. I've always have believed steady eye contact is a sign of confidence, and she's bubbling over with it now. I can't help but wonder what's on the laptop screen in front of her. I wonder what her hobbies are. I wonder if she's the type of girl who travels with a flock of girlfriends or if she flies solo in the friend department. Maybe she's the type of girl who only keeps a handful of male friends. I've always been a bit envious of those girls who travel in herds with their matching, interchangeable wardrobes. Those girls always intimidated me, passing by in the high school hallways like they had a big secret kept among just them.

I always danced among all the various groups in high school, but I kept two close friends by my side through the years. Jocelyn and Mark were my high school sidekicks, but we drifted apart when I left for the Air Force. We were inseparable from seventh grade until the summer after graduation, transforming and molding together over the years like three chameleons. Jocelyn and I were the first ones that Mark came out of the closet to. While we had our suspicions about his sexuality over the years, it was touching when he chose us as the first that he told about his preference for men. I make a mental note to use one of the social media accounts that Courtney has set me up with to track them down.

"Listen, Abby. I'm on your side here. I'm not trying to get in the middle of anything." I think about sitting in the chair opposite her but decide against it.

"I've gotta go." She slams her laptop closed, flattening a well-manicured hand on top of the cover. I stand there in silence as she gathers her belongings and flies out of the door, leaving the couple at the table next to me looking in my direction as if they're watching the climactic scene in a soap opera.

By the time I make it to my dad's house I'm buzzing from the dark roast and the run-in with Abby. I slide the key out from behind the secret compartment in the hanging birdhouse on the back porch and let myself in. Sitting on my sloppy twin bed, I lace up my running shoes and hit my dad's neighborhood streets. I love running in new places, and I've always been a firm believer that running while you travel is the best way to explore a new city. My dad lives in a classic suburban neighborhood, and the hills alone make for a much harder run than my flat trail runs in Philly.

As I make my way through the winding streets, I pass a gathering of protesters outside of the state building and a cluster of small businesses including a movie store, a pet shop and a hair salon. The autumn air is warm enough to run in, yet provides a nice air conditioning that dries my sweat almost instantly. I've run in all climates, but the air in the fall is splendid. Some of the neighborhood trees have started to transform from summer green to assorted shades of reds and oranges.

I push up a hill that leads to the local schools. The elementary, junior high and high schools are clustered together and snaked through a nook in the land. From the top of the hill, the view is magnificent. Large colonial homes carve out the streets below and make the town appear much larger than I realized. I love running by the schools because several trails wind between the buildings and lead into the woods. I imagine they provide a nice getaway for students skipping class or seeking an afternoon rendezvous with their high school sweethearts. I'm guessing that was not the intent during the planning stages of building—having married an architect, I now think of all these things.

Armed with my mace and my phone, I take a sharp turn onto one of the trails. Not knowing where it will take me is the best part, and I know I can always turn around. The trail winds and dips as I leap over large rocks and pass a cluster of teens smoking cigarettes. I hold my breath as I pass their cloud of smoke—no sense in running in the open air if I'm inhaling second-hand smoke.

I force my burning legs up the slow and steady incline and follow a slanted wooden sign with "Heartbreak Park" carved out in sloppy cursive. I turn the name over in my mind several times before I remember that this is where Dr. Bennington said Jason was found after his accident. The trail slowly transforms from dirt to cement and opens up into a beautiful, picturesque park. Picnic tables are scattered on large slabs of grass. More efficient signs stand at the entrance of several paths that lead to lakes, playgrounds and ponds. I take my chances and follow the sign that directs me to "Monty's Wall." I pass a family of four having lunch at a picnic table, a mother pushing her newborn in a stroller and twin boys pushing their scooters and trying to dodge each other. Monty's Wall turns out to be a massive flat rock that sits at the highest peak of the park.

I stand at the bottom of the rock, my neck bent back like a flexible straw. I assess the slight grooves carved out in the smooth, flat surface. The one time I went rock climbing in California gave me enough experience to know this rock isn't meant for a novice climber. I look around to see that I'm standing in the center of a circle of several other rocks with varying inclines and ridges, but none of them compare to the herculean rock that stands in front of me like a giant looking down on his prey. I know Jason well enough to know this is the rock he braved before he ended up in the hospital. Before he went to Iraq he would've had the sense to use caution during his stunts, but after he returned he threw all caution out the door as if his life weren't worth the extra care and packaging.

I'll never forget the day he brought me to Silverado Canyon, armed with his new rock climbing gear. It was the middle of summer in southern California, so the sun was already beating down on my bare arms as he had me step into the harness. This had been his latest obsession, so we only had one set of gear. Knowing Jason, I had expected him to outgrow this hobby as quickly as all the others. Our garage had been filled with the aftermath of his varying interests over the years. Mountain bikes, skateboards, scuba diving gear and other toys clung to its walls and quickly started to barricade the entrance. And every sport had at least one corresponding book sitting on the shelves he built, covering the last remaining space. He'd read them cover to cover, inhaling all of the details and putting them into action. My frustration would escalate every time I stepped into the garage to retrieve one of my belongings and ended up tripping on a surfboard or some other toy that made its way into clutter.

I'm not sure if it was because he was lonely or because he truly enjoyed being around me, but he always insisted that I tag along on his adventures. Looking back, I find myself being thankful for his persistence because the experiences have allowed me to contribute to conversations I would've never imagined having—especially at work, when patients come in with broken bones from a similar adventure.

That day, Jason had strapped me in securely and stood firmly at the bottom of the rock, far enough away so that the ropes angled out and allowed him some leverage to stabilize me in case I slipped. I followed his instructions carefully, pressing my body tight to the rock, and obligingly placed my feet and hands in the grooves that he rattled off from below. My body was used to running, not pulling up my own weight on a vertical ledge, so when I tried to hold on to the top two grooves with my hands, my back muscles gave out and I fell back. My heart raced while my body plummeted toward the sandy ground. Suddenly I felt the harness tighten and my body jerked upright, nearly smashing back into the wall. I looked down to see Jason leaning backward, struggling to keep me afloat with the ropes.

"Let me down NOW!" My fear had turned into anger as I found myself furious with him for putting me in harm's way once again.

"Come on, just give it another try. You almost made it to the top," he had insisted.

"No! Let me down!" Tears were starting to form in my eyes, some from anger at him and some for fear that he really wouldn't let me down. He had all the control in this situation. Luckily another couple approached the rock and began prepping their gear so Jason had no choice but to let me down, fearing the wrath of the stranger's glare and concern. After my feet were on solid ground I tore off the gear and ripped through the path that lead back to the main road, kicking dirt up behind my angry stomping feet.

"Sammie!" he yelled, a giggle lacing his voice.

"WHAT is so funny?" I turned, propping both hands on my hips.

"I think it's funny that you get so worked up over this. I had you secured; I wasn't going to let you fall."

"Oh really, you think it's just hilarious that I'm scared of falling off of a forty-foot rock and onto the ground? Possibly dying?"

"Stop overreacting. You weren't going to die." He swiped the sweat from his forehead with the back of his hand.

"I am so sick of your stupid life-threatening hobbies! Just because you have no fear doesn't mean I have to live life like that. I happen to value my life!"

I remember that fight like it was yesterday. I look down at the ground and kick a lonely stone with the tip of my running shoe. I turn my palm over to reveal a tiny scar from where a sharp rock had sliced through my skin when I was trying to leverage myself that day.

Every one of these incidents seems to have left a mark on me, whether physical or mental. And they only got worse when he returned from Iraq.

CHAPTER EIGHT

Abby

MY OFFICIAL RESIDENCE MIGHT as well be this hospital, because I have been living here for days now. Every morning I am woken up by a chipper Emma Jane, who always strolls in with some fresh gossip magazines. She seems to disappear every evening after visiting hours and returns the next morning at sunrise, sometimes before. I never ask, but I wonder where she's spent her evenings for the last couple of weeks. I'm guessing she has a friend in town.

"Good morning, Abby Girl." She strolls into the waiting room, setting her bottle of Coke on the table after taking one big gulp.

"Hi, Emma Jane." I roll myself up from my makeshift bed made of chairs and drop my feet onto the floor. Before my eyes can even adjust to the sensor light that switched on, a stack of magazines falls into my lap and I'm trying to keep up with the story about Lindsay Lohan's recent arrest that she is reciting to me. Emma Jane always seems to be going a mile a minute, jumping from one subject to the next. As sweet as she is, she can be rather exhausting to be around, especially with my current mental state and the unknown that lies ahead.

She strides toward the blinds and opens them with one quick motion. A cascade of sun floods in and covers the carpeted floor like a stain. "Rise and shine, sleepyhead."

One of my biggest pet peeves is morning people. Jason is a morning person, and I consider it one of his biggest flaws. Often times before the alarm clock even goes off, he pops into a sitting position and catapults himself out of bed. I, on the other hand, am a firm believer that the snooze button was one the best inventions ever, and I shamelessly press it numerous times before surrendering to the day. Jason assumes everyone else in the world is a morning person right along with him—he tries to hold conversations with me while I'm clearly concentrating hard on getting my last two or three minutes of sleep.

Sometimes I think it's out of loneliness that Jason has always wanted me to wake up with him. Annoying as it's been, I know he's happiest and at his best first thing in the morning, before the hours of the day move over him like a boat over water, creating a wake that leaks out the memories of the past—memories he's never seemed to want to share with me.

"Do you think Dr. Bennington will have any updates today, Emma Jane?" I look up at her hopefully.

"I don't know, Abby Girl. We may have to ask Princess Samantha. She seems to have cast him under her spell."

I did find it a bit odd that Dr. Bennington seemed to direct all of his updates toward Samantha. The other day he even asked to speak with her directly—maybe because Emma Jane wasn't around and she's second in command, which infuriates me even more. They must think of me as just another one of Jason's short-term girlfriends. In my paranoia, I wonder if everyone here knows I'm the one who caused him to get into this accident. I imagine all of the nurses and doctors talking behind my back, saying what an ungrateful witch I am to fight with Jason and drive him to a life-threatening accident.

"Earth to Abby. Earth to Abby." Emma Jane's snapping fingers pull me out of the soap opera I created in my mind. "Let's go for some breakfast in the café. I only have a little while before I have to meet a friend in Westford." As she pulls me up to my feet, my homemade fleece pillow falls off my lap and onto the floor. Jason made me the bright pink pillow during one of his crafty phases. I reach down and grab it by the tag he sewed on the corner, which lies in between little black paint brushes and smiley faces. *Made with love for my Abby Girl.* I press the pillow up to my nose and take one long inhale, memories surging through me like water escaping a dam. I cover it with the rest of my belongings in the corner of the waiting room and trail behind Emma Jane, who has already started her beeline for the cafeteria.

The cafeteria is filled with hospital workers, rushing through the line and settling at tables to eat a quick breakfast before starting their day. Some look as if they are just getting off an overnight shift with wrinkled scrubs and hair in disarray. Others are bright-eyed and ready to start the day. We inch through the line, sliding our brown trays along the metal rails and eyeing the selection of breakfast food. I've never been in a hospital long enough to test cafeteria food and always assumed its poor reputation was true. But for the first time in days, I'm salivating over the wide selection of eggs, bacon and sausage staring up at me. This must be my body's way of telling me that I need to eat.

Emma Jane fills her tray with a selection of muffins, pastries and two different types of juices. She looks like someone who is either indecisive or feeding a family of four. The chef assembles an English muffin sandwich with bacon for me and pushes it across the counter, nearly sliding it off the plate and onto my tray. The bacon is crisp and the egg is made just the way I like it, neither too runny nor overcooked. The cashier rings up Emma Jane's carbohydrate buffet as she fumbles through her pockets.

"Oh my. What on earth? I had my cash in this pocket just minutes ago." A look of worry soaks her face.

"It's okay, Emma. I'll get it." I slide my tray closer, signaling to the cashier that I'll be paying for both.

"Oh, Abby. Thank you so much. I owe you. I just don't know what happened to my cash. I had a whole wad of it one second and it disappeared the next." Her voice elevates so the whole line can hear us.

"Don't worry about it, Emma Jane. Really."

"That's what daughters are for, aren't they?" She winks at the cashier, who smiles back impatiently.

We eat our breakfast at one of the last available tables. Emma Jane talks as I inhale my sandwich, disproving the stigma of hospital food: this is one of the best breakfast sandwiches I've ever had. Emma Jane reaches across the table and wipes a flood of yolk streaming out the side of my mouth.

My hunger starts to disappear, even though everything I see reminds me of Jason. The eggs in my sandwich remind me of the breakfasts he's made me, each with something unique on the plate.

Even though I am not a mother of a child, a pet or even a plant, Jason has always made me a Mother's Day breakfast in bed. He always sets a single pink rose on the edge of the plate with a note coiled around it: *To the future mother of my children*. I've always thought it was sweet even though I had been undecided about having children all my life. As a little girl I always had a hard time with girlfriends because they always wanted to play dolls and I was more into setting up little neighborhood businesses. I'm not sure if it was something that was innately built in me or if I learned from watching my parents' constant financial struggle, but I had the most successful lemonade stand on the street. When we moved around it was like I had a little traveling business, always setting up my world-renowned lemonade stand on our newly inhabited street and introducing my sugary summer cocktails to the neighbors.

Emma Jane slathers her muffin with butter and drenches her scone with grape jelly. She piles the doughy creations into her mouth so fast that I'm only halfway through my sandwich when she gets up from the table.

"I'm done! I've got a busy day ahead of me, so I gotta head back and get my visit with Jason out of the way." She piles the remaining pastries into her purse, dressing them in the thin paper napkins from the table.

"Oh, uh, okay." I swipe up the remaining yolk from my plate and shovel the rest of the English muffin into my already full mouth. As I get up to clear my tray, I notice that Emma Jane leaves hers behind. She looks down at my hands. "Don't waste your time throwing that stuff away. That's what these poor hospital workers are paid to do," she says loudly, yanking the tray from my grip and setting it on a large table that is occupied by a group of workers. Embarrassment floods my face as I shuffle behind her, trying to keep up, hoping the workers don't catch a glimpse of my face. I'm surprised by her rudeness and suddenly don't want to be associated with her.

I'm still trailing behind her, catching her words as she throws them into the air theatrically as we approach the waiting room. Samantha is sitting in the corner chair, *my chair*, a book held up in front of her face as if she's reading in front of a group of first graders. She lowers the book to her lap and adjusts the trendy reading glasses on her head. I feel a secret satisfaction that she has to wear glasses and I don't, making her that much more flawed than me. An avid reader myself, I try to catch a glimpse of her book, but she catches my eye before I can make out the author's name.

"Hi, Abby. Emma Jane." She looks up quickly, grabbing her coffee cup from the end table.

"Hi, Samantha." I can hear the contempt in Emma Jane's voice as she angles herself to face me, turning her back to Samantha. "So, Abby Girl, maybe we can go out shopping this afternoon." She grabs my hands in her grip in an overly friendly gesture, her voice booming throughout the small room. Out of the corner of my eye, I see Samantha pick up her book and go back to reading. I suddenly feel uncomfortable in Emma Jane's presence. There is something wavering about her tone and disposition. One minute I'm trailing behind her trying to keep up, and the next she's making plans with me like we're best friends hanging out on a Saturday afternoon.

CHAPTER NINE

Samantha

FIVE MINUTES AFTER EMMA JANE enters Jason's room, she's bounding down the hallway clutching a cell phone to her ear. "Yes, I'm on my way, Billy. Just make sure you have cash to pay the cab when he drops me off." She flips her phone shut and bends her towering body in half so she's at eye level with Abby.

"I've got some business to take care of, Abby Girl. If you decide you want to go shopping later, give me a call." She kisses her on the forehead like she's tucking in a toddler for the night. Abby looks confused, and I start to feel bad for her. Emma Jane has woven a web around her innocent world.

After Emma Jane is out of sight, I drop the book in my lap and take another sip of coffee. For the first time, it's just the two of us in this waiting room, the awkward silence dancing between us. "Hey, Abby. I was going to go see Jason next, but you can go in if you want. I'll just say it's me through the intercom so they see me on camera. I'm sure you want some time alone with him."

Abby tries to hide it, but I can see her eyes transform from somber to excited when the words slide out of my mouth.

"Yeah, um, okay. That would be great." She looks down to break the eye contact we made.

"I don't know why hospitals make all these stupid rules anyway. I'm sure Emma Jane will put you on the family list if you ask. I happened to catch her when she was having a moment of kindness, so she put me on the list." I try to make it sound like I'm not closer to Jason, that Dr. Bennington didn't trust me more than Jason's own mother.

Sometimes doctors break the rules, and that's what Dr. Bennington did after our meeting. He placed me on the visitor list even though I'm not blood. I don't tell Abby that though; it would just be another stab in her side. There's nothing wrong with a little white lie.

"We won't get in trouble, will we?" Abby suddenly looks like a little girl getting caught sneaking a lie past her parents. I realize how young and insecure she really is. She hides it well though, with her confident swagger and threatening eye contact, her edgy makeup, always applied to perfection.

"What's the worst they'll do? Kick us out of the hospital?" I walk toward the intercom, making certain I'm seen on camera as the one trying to gain access. After the door buzzes, I motion for Abby to run in front of me as I head back to my book and coffee.

Twenty minutes later I'm jerked up from my Erica Appleton novel to the sound of the security door slamming shut. Abby walks toward her stack of stuff in the corner and shuffles through one of the bags, her head bent downward. When she finds what she's looking for, she bolts upright and heads toward the waiting room exit. Something small and shiny falls from her. I leap up, racing toward it and scooping it up. "Abby!" I catch her attention before she exits.

"Yeah?" She turns around slowly and I see that she's crying. Tears fill her blue eyes like sea water reaching for the shore. I look down at the object in my hand. A clear glass heart hangs from the end of a silver chain. I turn the heart over in my hand and see a tiny piece of rice floating inside the heart, bearing minuscule writing that says "Jason" on one side and "Abby" on the other. It floats inside the water-filled heart like a buoy in the sea. I hold it out to her, hoping she didn't see me examining the necklace's contents.

"You dropped this." The necklace dangles from my hand like a peace offering.

"Oh, it must've fallen off of me." Her hand darts up to her neck as she feels for the missing necklace, smoothing her pale skin.

"Looks like the clasp broke." I survey the circular clasp, trying to flick the jammed trigger.

"Oh no." She reaches for the chain, her eyes welling up with more tears.

"Hey, I know a great little jeweler in town who could fix this in a second. He's an old friend of mine."

"Really?" Her eyes dart from side to side, finally settling on mine.

"Absolutely." I look down at the massive white watch on my left wrist. "And he's opening in about ten minutes. I have my dad's car so we can pop over there before he gets busy."

"Well, I guess I don't really have anything else to do right now." Abby looks around the hospital room for a distraction.

The five-minute drive to O'Malley's Jeweler feels like hours. The silence sits between us like a silent stranger. I try to make small talk with Abby, but her abrupt answers don't allow any conversation between us, and I start to feel like I am interviewing her rather than talking with her.

The good thing about a small city like Brookside is that you almost never have to struggle to find a decent parking spot. I pull into a metered spot on Main Street and search for some quarters in my dad's tidy console. Brookside's wide streets are so different from the crammed and crowded streets of Philadelphia. For this reason, I have invested in a monthly public transportation pass that allows me to avoid having to attempt jamming my car into a tiny spot along the side of the street outside the hospital where I work. While Alex and I are one of those rare couples who don't fight often, we have had a few squabbles about my stubbornness when it comes to learning how to parallel park. I openly admit that I get very defensive when it comes to my driving ability, and that's because of the several dents and dings I've acquired due to my poor perception of space.

"Shit!" My so-called organized father has Band-Aids, pens, a map and a few rubber bands scattered in the shallow dish of his center console, but no change except for a few pennies and nickels.

"Here, I have some quarters." Abby digs into her deep purse.

"Thanks." We get out of the car simultaneously and feed the meter enough for twenty minutes. "This shouldn't take long."

O'Malley's is tucked away in one of the narrow alley-like streets that join Main Street and School Street. Brian O'Malley and I went to high school together and dated for about a month freshmen year, ending things so I could go back to my on-again-off-again relationship with Alex. When Brian was only sixteen, he was handed over the family business when his parents got into a fatal car accident. His high school social life came to a screeching halt. Every day after school he would come directly to the jewelry store and work until close, trying to finish his homework between customers. I'm guessing his teachers felt bad for him and let him slide by, because he'd often fall asleep in class or show up with half-finished assignments. Our group of friends would hang out at the store on some school nights to keep him company, but he still had to miss out on a lot of the things most high school kids consider essential. He was too busy keeping the business running to attend school dances and football games, but we all did our best to keep him in the loop during our evening loitering sessions in the store.

"Where is this place?" Abby looks at me as if I have plans to kidnap her.

"It's a hidden gem." I lead her down the narrow street, dodging the potholes bubbling up from the cement.

I make a quick right turn into the storefront that says "O'Malley's Jeweler," a bright green shamrock serving as the apostrophe in the name. The hours of operation are sketched into the door in worn gold cursive. I hold the door open for Abby like she's my date. The familiar bell rings over the door, bringing me back to high school. Brian is bent over on the other side of the counter, tidying one of the jewelry displays.

"We're not open yet."

"Then why is your door unlocked?" my sarcasm shoots back.

He jolts upright at the sound of my voice. "Sammie frickin' Brighton!" A head of light brown curls bounces with his quick movement. Brian was always known for his curls, and instead of being self-conscious about them, he embraced his genes by growing out Afros and dreadlocks when we were in high school. On one rare occasion he dyed his curls completely red so he looked like Carrot Top. I can see a touch of gray coiled into some of his bouncy tendrils, but miraculously the color doesn't appear to age him one bit. He's still slender and long-limbed like a runner but with just a bit more softening around the waist than he had in high school.

"That's Samantha Colton now." I cough, motioning down to my wedding band.

Brian races from behind the counter and sweeps me up into a warm bear hug.

"Well, it's about time you two got married. You could've saved everyone a lot of pain and just tied the knot in high school. Hey, wait—weren't you married to some marine?" I feel the tension burning off Abby and change the subject quickly.

"Bri, this is my friend Abby." He takes the hint and directs his attention to her as she holds up the broken necklace. "Could you do me a favor and fix her clasp?"

"Well, it's been a while since a lady has asked this much of me, but I'll see what I can do." He gives a seductive wink at Abby, who cracks a blushing smile for the first time in my presence. Brian goes to work on the necklace as Abby browses the counter.

"So, where has life taken you, Bri?"

"Well, I got married to a nice Southern girl who moved here for college years ago and never went back." He reaches into his back jean pocket, pulling out a two-fold leather wallet and tossing it my way as his other hand stays busy with the clasp. I flip through the worn plastic photo holders to see a life of happiness. Brian with his beautiful wife and two adorable daughters. Two heads of blond ringlets turn to look up at him in awe as the photo was taken. He and his wife look so happy that they could be on the cover of a *Family Circle* magazine. I'm suddenly flooded with happiness for him because if anyone deserves this, Brian does.

"Brian, they are absolutely beautiful." I look down at the two little girls and can't help but feel twisted with sadness, knowing I'll never have this. It will always just be me, Alex and a dog. I'll never have the chance to take part in molding someone's life or showing them the beauty that the world has to offer. I'll never see what Alex and I could've created, a blend of our traits and features.

"They certainly keep me on my toes." Pride pulls the corner of his mouth into a big bright smile, still showing the warmth he had in high school. "So, what about you? Do you and Alex have a herd of little ones yet?"

"Nope, we haven't taken the big step yet. Alex is so busy with his current project, I think we're going to push it off a bit longer," I respond, hoping a customer walks in to divert his attention from me and my life. It's always such an awkward question to answer—partly because I don't want to make the other person feel uncomfortable when I ramble on about my medical condition, and partly because deep down I'm holding on to a magnitude of anger about it. Instead of telling the truth, I just blame our lack of children on busy work schedules or house projects, or in this case Alex's career.

"You know, you'll never be 100 percent ready for kids. But I'm sure you've heard that a million times." Brian holds up the necklace in front of him, satisfied with his completed task. "Abby, your necklace awaits!"

She looks up, smiling for the second time today. He motions for her to twirl around. "If you could just lift your hair for two seconds." Abby combs her mane with delicate fingers, piling it at the back of her head and exposing her neck. A pair of bright yellow dangly earrings swing from her ears and make a clicking sound. I watch as Brian gently clasps the necklace, resting it on her skin. There's a certain finesse about his touch that makes it obvious that his life is filled with women. Brian rests his hands on Abby's shoulders, turning her around to assess the necklace. "Perfect. Good as new."

"Thank you so much." Abby feels for the necklace on her collarbone, using her two fingers to turn the heart over. "How much do I owe you?"

"Absolutely nothing. If you're a friend of Sammie's, you're a friend of mine." Brian motions for me to come toward him as he embraces me in another friendly hug. "Tell Alex I said hi and I forgive him for stealing you away from me in ninth grade." Brian winks as I let out a boisterous laugh.

"I'm sure he'll be relieved to hear that."

"Oh, wait a second, I have something for you." He releases his grip and bounds toward a door behind the jewelry cases at the back of the store. Silence hovers in the air between Abby and me for the two minutes that Brian is gone.

After what seems like hours, he returns holding a beige suede jewelry box. As he stands before me, he snaps open the cover, exposing a gold chain bracelet with charms dangling off the links. "Um, before your mom's accident she had dropped this off to be cleaned." He hesitates. "I've had it ever since, hoping you would happen to stop by when you were in town."

Words tangle in my throat before I'm able to speak. I use my pinky to lift the bracelet up as a dozen tiny charms dangle before me. I survey the bracelet as nostalgia wipes away any anger I had toward my mother. A Hollywood star sags from the chain and into my palm. It must be from the days when my mom dreamed of being a Hollywood starlet. I see a gold heart with the word "Love" written in cursive across it, and I wonder if it's from my dad or some other flame from her past. I glide my fingers over the charms one by one, tracing my mother's past like a historian. The heaviest charm of all is a gold baby carriage with the word "Mom" inscribed on the side. Sadness hugs me like an old friend as I rub my thumb over the lonely word.

"It's cleaned and good as new. I figured you would want it." The words stumble out of Brian's mouth.

"Thank you, Bri. Thank you so much." I drop the bracelet back into the box and pull him into another tight hug, hiding my face in his shoulder as a couple of tears make an escape. I hug him long, partly because I'm touched that he has kept this all these years and partly because I'm trying to conceal my tears from Abby.

"And don't be a stranger. You know where to find me when you're in town." Brian holds up his hand in a paused good-bye wave as Abby follows me out the door.

The drive back to the hospital is awkwardly silent, but Abby has made it clear that she isn't big on conversation with Jason's ex-wife. I turn the radio up as Madonna serenades me, promising to "strike a pose," and I pretend I'm by myself. I've never been extremely outgoing, but silence when riding in a car with someone has always made me feel on edge. I've read enough psychology books to know that the need for unnecessary conversation is a defense mechanism for one's insecurity. My mother always had a string of thoughts unraveling from her mouth when we were in the house together, and when she was silent I knew something was wrong. Maybe that's why I feel such a need to make small talk with Abby, who is still essentially a stranger to me at this point.

Much to my surprise, Abby reaches out and turns down the volume.

"Do you have something against Madonna?" I say playfully.

"I just, well, I just wanted to say thank you. For this." She fondles the necklace, looking down at her lap. A cluster of chunky yellow and black bracelets shimmy down her forearm and rest on her delicate wrists.

"No problem. Brian is a good guy. Probably one of the nicest guys I know."

"Yeah, but you really didn't have to go out of your way and all that." She looks up briefly before looking back down at her tangled hands resting on her lap.

"It's not a big deal. I wanted to get over to visit him anyway."

"So?" Abby looks out the window and hesitates. "What happened?"

"With Brian? Ohhh, we were an item in high school briefly, but—"

"No, I mean what happened with your mom?" She breaks apart my high school memories in an instant as I'm pulled back to the dark times after my mother's accident. I grip the steering wheel tighter, my palms suddenly sweating.

"Oh." A pause lingers between us before I gather my words. "She got into an accident after I finished high school. She died." The words are stuck in my throat and are awkward when they finally surface.

"I'm sorry. I—I didn't know."

"That's okay. I don't talk about it much. Jason doesn't really even know what happened." I catch myself bringing Jason up and try to change the subject. "But the past is the past. That's why Brian is such an inspiration to me. He lost both of his parents, and he managed to turn his life around for the better and not hold any grudges on the world."

"Were you close?"

"Me and my mom? Well, it was just the two of us for as long as I can remember, so we kinda had to be close." I hesitate to release all of my family drama on Abby, as I'm sure she's already overwhelmed with what's going on with Jason.

"What about your dad?"

"My dad wasn't around for years. It wasn't by his choice though. My mom turned him into the bad guy and took custody of me, even though he was far more fit to be a parent." A wave of sadness crashes over me when I think about all the years I missed out on with my dad. "The mother is always right by New Hampshire law, so my dad didn't have much of a choice in the matter."

"Wow, you and your dad seem so close for not having all those years to bond." She tucks a strand of hair behind her ear, and for the first time, I can see that she is relaxed in front of me.

"Yeah, my dad and I are kind of like soul mates. I do have some memories of him from when I was real young, before my mom had full custody. And all of those memories seem to be my happiest ones. Poor Alex had to go through the ringer when he asked my dad's permission to marry me."

Before I can tell if she even wants to hear my story, I keep going. The words gush out of my mouth like rain pouring down a gutter spout. "Since my dad really wasn't around when Alex and I were kids, he never knew him, so Alex really had to start from scratch with their relationship. We were both living in Philly at the time, and we flew home for Christmas. Christmas was always small on my side of the family—usually just me and my dad, after my mom died. Occasionally an aunt or an uncle or an old military friend of my dad's would stop by. So, it was just Dad, Alex and me. My dad and I had cooked our traditional bacon-topped turkey dinner with mashed potatoes, and I made my mom's famous gravy." I catch myself rambling. My internal voice tells me to speed it up. "Anyway, after dinner Alex asked me if I wanted to go for a walk in the neighborhood. Since New England winters don't really kick in until January, it was still just cold enough to be winter but we weren't quite shivering. My dad's house was only a couple of blocks away from Plummer Street, which is the street Alex and I grew up on. I had noticed where Alex was headed, but I figured he was just aimlessly walking."

I look over at Abby in the passenger seat and realize that she is intently focused on my story, so I use that as approval to continue.

"Alex's parents had moved to Florida quite a while back, so I knew we weren't stopping to see them. As soon as we stepped onto Plummer Street, light droplets of snow started falling. It was as if Alex had ordered it for the occasion. I remember Alex getting a little bit nervous; his right hand kept fiddling around in his pocket. When we got in between the houses where we grew up, he dropped to his knee in the middle of the road. He dropped so fast that it startled me."

A little giggle escapes my mouth.

"I thought he had slipped and fallen or passed out. One minute we were walking and the next he was eye level with my belly button and looking up at me. He held out a box wrapped in paper with little dogs wearing Santa hats. He sat there, halfway between the house I grew up in and the house he grew up in, in the middle of the road. And I'll never forget the words he said: *Marriage is about compromise and love. If I offer to meet you halfway through this crazy life, will you meet me halfway?* I was so taken aback by the sudden proposal that it took a little while to sink in what he was asking me. Of course I said yes. I think I maybe even shed a few tears. It was so absolutely like Alex to propose to me in such a way that was sweet, yet sensible at the same time."

I find myself getting a little teary as I think back to that day. I remember the taste of pecan pie on his lips when I gave him that first kiss after his proposal.

"After I put on the ring and calmed myself down, my dad came walking from behind Alex's old house. He had a thermos of hot chocolate and a jar of Fluff and served it to us in honor of the first time Alex and I had met. Before we knew it, the neighbors started to trickle out to their front porches shouting words of celebration. Most of the neighbors were still there from our childhoods, so they were like family to us. We heard a lot of 'It's about time!' or 'Finally!' Alex's parents even surprised us and were waiting at my dad's house for us when we got back. So, every Christmas, no matter where we are celebrating, we always have hot chocolate and Fluff after dinner. Sometimes we sneak a little liquor into the hot chocolate."

I look over at Abby and end the story with a wink. I notice that her eyes are watering a little. She swipes a finger underneath her lower lashes, catching a tear and wiping it on her jeans ."I get so emotional over these kinds of stories. I'm such a sucker for a good proposal story." A touch of embarrassment transforms her cheeks from pale to pink as she changes the subject quickly. "Do you have any siblings?"

"Nope, it's just me. My dad never remarried either, so not even a stepfamily. I think that's why he's so close to Jason. He's the son my dad never had." I add this to try to relieve some of her jealousy of Jason's connection to my family. "What about you? Are you close with your family?"

"Yes, very close. I couldn't imagine losing one of my parents." She looks over at me as I put the car in park in the hospital parking lot. Moisture surfaces in her eyes, causing a reflection of tiny gold flecks against the lucid blue. "They don't really approve of Jason though."

"Well, I don't think a lot of parents would approve of Jason. He's hard to understand. But you seem to be doing a pretty good job of grasping who he is and why he is that way."

"Yeah, I guess so."

I angle myself to face her. "Listen, Abby." I pause as I watch a young couple walk across the parking lot with a bouquet of pink roses. "I'm not here to take Jason away from you. I love him like a brother and nothing more. To be honest, I feel really bad for him. When I start feeling bad for myself with losing my mom and all, I think about all he has gone through and how strong and kind-hearted he turned out to be. Yeah, he certainly has his fair share of quirks and oddities, but overall he is one of the kindest people I have ever met. My dad and I are his family. I know that the whole ex-wife thing is hard to grasp, but really, I'm very happily married to Alex. I just want you to understand that."

Abby blinks the moisture from her eyes; her long lashes reach for her cheek. "I do. I understand."

By the time we walk into the hospital entrance, some of the tension between us seems to have dissipated. I'm hoping that Abby can focus on the bigger picture here and the fact that Jason's health is the most important thing. I'm sure he would hate to wake up to a catfight between his girlfriend and me.

As we make our way through the twists and turns of the hospital corridors, my eyes become locked on the gift store. Blue and pink teddy bears line the window, peeking out at us as if begging to be purchased.

"Hey, feel like going in the gift store to see if there's anything that we could get for Jason's room?" My fast walk comes to a screeching halt as I peer in the window to see what else they have to offer.

"Sure, why not?" I see a glimpse of hope pass over Abby's expression as she spots some 'Get Well' balloons in the corner of the store.

The store is a decent size for a hospital. We make our way through the various aisles, plucking random gifts off of the shelves, assessing them, and putting them back. The small florist station in the corner leaves an everlasting floral scent on all of the items.

"Hey, check this out. I think Jason would really like this." Abby's voice pulls me out of my shopping haze. I see her eyes focused intently on something in her hand two aisles over from me.

"What ya got there?" I look down at a silver contraption in her hand.

"It's a bottle opener and flashlight in one!"

"Wow, he certainly hasn't changed, has he?" I think back to all of the little tools and contraptions he used to collect. Some he would order from QVC; others he would find at random yard sales and flea markets. Most of them would get stowed away never be seen again, but every now and then he would surprise me as one of his handy tools came to the rescue when we were in a rut.

"He's obsessed with trinkets and tools. I don't know what half of the stuff is. I'm constantly cleaning out this drawer in our apartment that has a collection of these things." She taps the palm of her hand with the tool, as if shaking out its contents. "It's actually really frustrating, but…" I can see the thoughts pass through and surface as if I'm extracting them from her.

"But I think you should get it. It's something he can mess around with when he wakes up." The end of my sentence tilts upward as I try to sound hopeful. "Hey, and look over there. They do engraving. Maybe you could write something on it?" I point to a little stand in the corner of the shop that has a sign for "Free engraving with purchase of $20 or more."

We wait in line behind a picky elderly woman who is getting a money clip engraved for her ailing husband. It takes her a good ten minutes for the sales clerk to explain to her what 'font' means, and another twenty for her to actually select a font. This gives Abby plenty of time to decide what she wants engraved on the tool, so by the time we reach the counter we are prepared.

"And what can I do for you two young ladies today?" The middle-aged sales clerk appears relieved to be dealing with younger, sharper customers.

Abby gently sets the tool onto the glass counter top. "Ahhh, I must say this is the first time that I've ever seen one of these purchased, let alone engraved." He picks the tool up, smoothing it in his callused hands. "I gotta say, I honestly thought we were going to get rid of these. But hey, glad we kept them around, for your sake. Now, what would you like engraved on this, um—" He turns the tool over in his hand, searching for a name to call it.

"It's a bottle opener and a flashlight in one," Abby shoots back in a high-pitched voice as if she is trying to sell the item on an infomercial. I may actually start believing her, she's so good at making it sound appealing. "See?" She takes the tool from the sales clerk and shows him how it works.

"Ahhh, I don't see how we've survived this long without such a tool." He winks at the two of us. "So, what would ya like this bottle opener, flashlight in one to say?"

"Jason, I love you forever. Love Abby Girl." She rattles off the words, proud of her selection.

I take a risk and give her a tiny squeeze on her arm, letting her know I'm here for her. She looks up and offers me a genuine smile. I think I may finally be breaking down her walls and getting somewhere with her.

CHAPTER TEN

Abby

EACH DAY IS THE SAME: coffee in the morning with Samantha. We take walks on the hospital grounds in between visiting Jason. We don't actually visit him; instead we sit and watch him in his unchanged vegetable state. The first few days I was immensely sad; now I'm simply frustrated and angry. Nothing is changing and the doctors don't seem to know what's going on. The swelling in his brain is the same, still amplified like a balloon on one side, refusing to go down.

Normally I would think of the glass as half-empty in this situation, but Samantha has urged me to think of it as half-full. She's been a great source of comfort, almost like the sister that I never had. On our afternoon walks she tells me stories about Jason when he was younger. Nothing ever romantic or physical, just stories about his personality or silly things he'd do.

Once there was a family of raccoons living on their apartment roof in California. The mama raccoon left the babies, so Jason climbed to the top of the roof and lured them in with a piece of cat kibble. He wore kitchen-cleaning gloves up to his elbows and carried each hissing raccoon down one by one. He ended up with a few scratches, but it was worth it when the raccoons were taken to a safer place by Animal Rescue. Samantha pointed out the scratches to me when we were in his room. If he only knew that his ex and I were poking and prodding at him while he was asleep.

The nurses think we're an odd combination, and I can only imagine what they say to each other when we aren't around. I feel the way they look at Samantha and me. Their eyes scan our opposite features and different builds and try to figure out what Jason's type is. I guess Jason wasn't lying when he told me he didn't have a type. We had been walking through the mall one snowy winter day. I had agreed to brave the storm with him and venture out to the mall to cure his cabin fever.

"I need to move, Abs. These walls are closing in on me."

He had jumped up from the bed and bounced on his toes in front of me, pleading. We'd been lying in bed for most of the day, going back and forth between watching TV and reading our books. He'd been reading a book called *Finding Your Authentic Self*, and I was flipping through art magazines.

"It's terrible out though." I lazily rose from the bed and sauntered across our small apartment to the one window we had. I twisted the blinds open to see giant snowflakes swirling in the wind and turning into water droplets the second they hit the window.

"It's not THAT bad. Aren't you a true New Englander?" He twisted his body right to left, stretching out his muscles.

"Actually, I was born in Hawaii, during my dad's brief tour at Hickam Air Force Base. So, no, I'm technically not a true New Englander, and I'd prefer to be lying in the sun on a beach somewhere right now."

"Well, I consider myself to be a true New Englander even though I was born in the South, and I'm telling you as a regional expert that it isn't that bad out and I promise to get us there safely. I don't even like malls, but I just need to get out and stretch my legs. Don't you want some new scenery?"

"Fine." I pulled my coat off of my art stool and slipped it on quickly, before I changed my mind.

We slowly carved our way down the streets, following a plow that was paving the way for us. The roads weren't as bad as I had thought they would be, but my stubbornness prevented me from admitting this to Jason. While the mall wasn't far, it took us a long time because Jason was extra cautious, probably more afraid of my scolding him for going too fast than of the roads themselves.

We got a parking spot close to the main entrance since the storm kept most normal people at home. Jason swaddled me in his arms and pulled me close as we trekked through the snow. "See, isn't this romantic?" He twisted his neck and kissed me on my forehead.

I gave him a stubborn look and watched the snowflakes cling to his eyelashes. "Yeah, yeah."

"Ahhh it feels so good to move my legs." He held my hand and speed-walked through the mall, stopping to twist and stretch every few minutes.

"Hey, can we pop into Macy's for a second? I want to see if they have any more of these jeans in my size." I pointed down to yellow paint splatter on the boot cut, worn jeans that I was wearing.

"Sure, but do you really think I believe you when you say that it will only take a second?"

"Well, you should. You know I'm not a fan of clothes shopping," I say, admitting my aversion for finding clothes that fit me right. My curvy bottom rarely fits right in the jeans they make for girls my age. They're always too tight on the rump and too baggy in the waist. I have a complete hourglass shape—voluptuous in the chest and rear, and tapered in the middle. Today's designers don't cater to my pinup build; instead they make clothes to fit the straight and narrow. The pair of jeans I was wearing that day was a diamond in the rough. I had found them two months earlier, surprisingly in the juniors section of Macy's. One leg at a time, I had slid into them seamlessly and watched them mold to my body just right. It was probably the one time in my life when I actually enjoyed shopping for clothes, because it ended in a victory. I had to find those jeans again.

As we passed the MAC makeup counter I forced myself to look away from my true shopping passion. I'd trade clothes shopping for makeup shopping any day. Trying on new makeup is like having a brand new canvas to work with. When it comes to clothes, I wear mostly black or white simple styles and put all the focus on my jewelry and makeup.

"Step away from the counter." Jason tugged my elbow teasingly as he saw my eyes dart toward the MAC makeup.

"I can do this. I can walk away," I joked back, facing my addiction head on. After we dodged the perfume ladies who were pleading to spritz us, we made our way into the juniors section. Because of my build, I'd been shopping in the women's department since I was fifteen, and I knew full well that I looked completely out of place in the juniors department, but I had to find those perfect jeans. Jason and I stood in the middle of a sea of skimpy clothing, categorized by color. A section of sparkly black tank tops emblazoned with words like "Hottie" and "Sexy" sat adjacent to the piles of folded jeans.

I darted toward the cluster of denim in the corner of the store as Jason trailed behind me. The two of us stood confused in the center of the various shelves of jeans, overwhelmed and out of place, as if we are at a comic book convention.

"What about these?" Jason grabbed a pair of low-riding dark blue skinny jeans off of the shelf, letting them unfold like an accordion.

"Are you kidding me? Look at these hips..." I looped both thumbs through the belt holes and pulled the waist out slightly. "Do you honestly think I'll look cute cramming these hips into those spandex-looking things? Not to mention the butt crack that will be exposed as a result."

"I happen to like your butt crack." He folded the jeans back up and tossed them back on the shelf just as a sales clerk approached us from out of nowhere.

"You must be die-hard shoppers if you made it out in this storm." She planted herself next to Jason and smoothed her perfectly manicured hand over a pair of dark boot cut stretchy jeans.

"Eh, it's overrated. The media always makes these storms out to be worse than they really are." Jason adjusted the worn navy blue beanie on his head, pulling it down his forehead so the color made his eyes stand out even more than they already did.

"Exactly! Right?" She grabbed his arm and flipped her long blond hair over a bare, tanned shoulder. She was wearing one those shirts that fall effortlessly off of one shoulder, as if she were not trying to be sexy. As if the shirt *accidentally* slipped and exposed her skin in just the right place. Her pin-straight blonde hair fell beyond her shoulders and rested perfectly on her bosom, as if it was meant to be used as coverage. She had the type of hair that swung in all the right places when she walked and long bangs that swept across her forehead. My hair, on the other hand, is so thick that it sits in the same place for hours, incapable of that carefree swing. I instantly felt intimated around her. It didn't help that she was blonde. My brunette color runs so strong that even today's hair color technology can't give me the blond highlights I've wanted since I was a little girl, longing for "yellow" hair like Christina Aguilera.

"My name is Brittany. I'd be happy to help you find something."
She continued to look at Jason, forgetting I was there, clearly forgetting we were in *women's clothing*.

Jason had looked down at his arm where she grabbed it and sidestepped so he was closer to me. He looked away like a shy little boy.

"So, what brings you here today?" She focused her eyes on him, as if he were the one shopping even though we were surrounded by lace and ruffles.

"*I* am looking for a pair of jeans that are identical to these." I emphasized the "I" and smacked my hands against my thighs. I usually prefer to dodge sales clerks, but I found a little cattiness seeping out of me that day and wanted to mark Jason as my territory.

"Hmmm... well these look like last year's model," she had said in a pretentious tone, stepping behind me to check the tag on the back of my jeans. "And I'd say you were, what—a size eight?"

She looked at me from head to toe, clearly critiquing my curves as she placed her hand on her size two waist. Her eyes darted back and forth between me and Jason, summing up our physical rating in her head. Jason is a 10, with an athletic build that looks like it could be on the cover of a *Men's Fitness* magazine. My face has always been my best feature as I've never had the desire to even attempt to lighten my curves with exercise. I am naturally lazy when it comes to movement. My painting hand is probably the only athletic thing on my body.

"Yep, size eight," I had said proudly as I thought about knocking her itty bitty frame over and stepping on her face.

"Best-looking size eight around." Jason wrapped his arm around my waist and pulled me in close to him. "Gotta love a girl with curves in all the right places." He kissed me on the cheek, putting a show on for the sales clerk. I was glowing inside, so proud that he was sticking up for me, even though he probably didn't even realize he was doing it. She looked defeated, like a beauty pageant contestant who just found out she got runner-up.

"We may have some of last year's models out back, but it's doubtful." She was suddenly bored with us. "I mean, I could check, but—"

"Yes, check please." I had cut her off in a demanding tone. I like to consider myself a nice person, but I've never been one to let others walk all over me. Being a military brat, I was constantly surrounded by new people, having to assert myself that I am no pushover.

She looked disappointed after she found out she had no chance with Jason, and she sauntered back to the stockroom, trying her best to sway her bony hips side to side. Ten minutes later she walked toward us slowly as if she were just drifting through the store, in no rush to help us. The brand new pair of size eight jeans hung over her forearm.

"Here. Looks like we had last year's model in your size after all." Her voice had taken on a blasé tone as if she had lost interest now that she had no chance with Jason.

"Why, THANK YOU, BRITTANY!" I had said, overly upbeat and sarcastic. "I'd also like to use this coupon." I pulled out a store coupon that I had plucked out of the flyers the weekend before. I grabbed Jason's hand as we made our way to the checkout counter and made a point to flirt with him in a way that was tacky and extremely awkward for her. Jason flirted back, unaware that two girls were about to pull hair and claw at each other over him.

"So, she was totally your type, wasn't she?" I had asked as we walked out of the store.

"Who?" He looked at me dumbfounded.

"Brittany! The girl who was practically humping your leg five minutes ago."

"The sales girl? No way. I don't have a type, but even if I did, she seemed far too boring for me. Hey, can we go into REI? I want to see if they have something I need for rock climbing." He led us into the store as my insecurities about Brittany disappeared from my mind. Even with all of her blonde, tan perfection, Brittany was boring to Jason, and that made me feel much better.

CHAPTER ELEVEN

Samantha

I KNOW IT'S NOT TYPICAL to tell your ex-husband's girlfriend stories of your past together, but Abby has been asking a lot of questions about Jason and why he is the way he is. I feel like it relieves some of the guilt she has about his accident if she knows that he has come close to death on more than one occasion. Her round blue eyes concentrate on every word that comes out of my mouth, as if she is a child being read her favorite book. She has features that are naturally innocent looking, and if it weren't for the artsy, often dark makeup that she wears, I would think she was younger than she is. Her makeup gives her face an edge.

"The day that he got back from Iraq, we were driving on the freeway when his Honda Civic spun out of control after another car slid into us from the slippery rain. He was going too fast, and I cursed him as we were spinning. All of sudden we came to a stop facing oncoming traffic. It was as if the world suddenly slowed down and all of those cars came to a perfectly peaceful stop. I was sure we were going to end up slammed by those cars, but it was as if something or someone held us and shielded us from it."

"So, he did daredevil things when he was with you too?" she asks me timidly.

"Ha! Are you kidding me? He's been this way since he was born! You see this scar here?" I turn his left palm facing upward to reveal the thick pink band of scar tissue. "That's from our trip to New Orleans. He was trying to climb a metal rail to take a picture of the above-ground graves. He slipped and grabbed a sharp metal post on the way down."

"I always wondered what that scar was from. I was too scared to ask." Abby's eyes dart towards the ground, as if she's ashamed.

"Abby, I know Jason has issues. I know his anger is a problem."

"I've been taking him to Dr. Cohen every week." Hope pierces through Abby's eyes as she says this.

"Yeah, unfortunately Dr. Cohen isn't much help. I think he needs to see a doctor who actually cares." I try to tone down my response even though the mention of Dr. Cohen's name makes me boil with anger.

"Well, if—I mean *when*—he wakes up, I will research better doctors for him." Abby goes back to staring at Jason, her hand softly wrapped around his. "What happened to him over there?" she asks without making eye contact.

"Honestly, I don't know. He never talked about it when he came back. I just know that he left one person and came home another. He'd always been a daredevil, but his stunts became more often and more careless. We weren't right together before he left, and then he came home and that just escalated the process of us splitting up. You know, he really loves you, Abby. I wouldn't say that if I didn't truly believe it."

"I know he does. And I'm a fool for being so stupidly jealous."

"Yes, you are. You are a ten; I'm only an eight. And you are five years younger, so in the grand scheme of things you are a far bigger catch than me," I say with a wink. "And considering he's like my brother, you have absolutely NOTHING to worry about!"

"Thanks, Samantha. You're not so bad yourself. I think he's going to be in for a big surprise when he wakes up and sees the two of us all buddy-buddy, huh?"

"There have been more bizarre things that have happened."

The nurse walks in, interrupting our bonding and gives us the signal for "Time's up."

"Well, I guess we better head back to the waiting room." Standing up together, I drape one lanky arm over her shoulders, giving a tiny squeeze. "Everything is going to be okay. Oh, and do you want a helpful piece of advice?"

"What's that?" Abby looks confused.

I lean in, whispering in her ear. "Don't trust a word that comes out of Emma Jane's Botoxed lips."

"I think I already figured that one out on my own. She's not the saint she makes herself out to be, is she?" A look of relief settles on Abby's face as we walk back into the waiting room.

CHAPTER TWELVE

Abby

SAMANTHA IS NICE. I don't know why I ever worried about the two of them. If they were the last two strangers on earth, I couldn't picture them together. She is so conservative and soft-spoken, where Jason is loud and uninhibited. I suppose I could see them young together, before life got real. Maybe they fit together like two puzzle pieces—where she had spaces and indents, he extended himself to fit into them smoothly, if only for a few years before their shapes grew and formed into different configurations.

"Good morning." I look up as Samantha folds herself into the booth in the hospital café, our official meeting spot.

"I snuck in some good coffee from my dad's house. Godiva, my favorite." She slides a plastic to-go mug over to me, suspicious eyes darting around the cafeteria as if she's committing a crime. "Cream and two Splenda, just the way you like it."

"This is a tiny slice of heaven." I take a sip of the smoldering rich coffee, robust flavors of hazelnut dominating my taste buds. "You've spoiled me; I'll never be able to drink this hospital mud again."

"Alex calls me a coffee snob. And I certainly cannot deny it."

For a moment the two of us are just friends exchanging trinkets of our lives and we forget why we are here. Jason is our common bond. She has his past, and I am hanging on to what he may or may not have of a future.

"Speaking of Alex, I talked to him this morning. I'm going to go back to Philadelphia for a little while." We both know why her eyes divert as she says *a little while*. We have no idea how long Jason is going to be in a coma, if Jason is ever going to wake up at all. Life goes on. People work and have relationships and houses to take care of. People who are not me, because Jason was—*is*—my life. All I have now is a few pieces of decent artwork, a tiny studio apartment and a boyfriend who is in a coma that he may never wake up from.

"The only flight out that was somewhat affordable leaves this afternoon." She looks down like a child who just got caught doing something naughty.

"I completely understand, Sam. As much as I'd love for you to spend countless hours at this hospital with me, I know you have a life to get back to. I'm thankful that you made the trip up at all." A smirk crosses both of our faces. "Well, I wasn't very thankful that you were here at first, but you've grown on me."

"This is the tough part about living far away from home. Sometimes I feel like I'm constantly saying goodbye to people I care about. Sometimes I feel so guilty that I'm not here with my dad. He's getting older and I'm all he has, ya know." I can see a tear start to surface in the corner of her eye.

"Well, if you ever decide to move back, you will always have a friend to have coffee with." I lift my cup, trying to hide my sadness.

After Sam leaves, her absence leaves an emptiness in me. When she was here, I felt like I had someone on my side, someone who knew Jason the way I did. Now that she is gone I feel so alone. The only thing getting me through the days is my daily visits with Jason. As long as he's in the same state of being, I'm approved to spend time in his room. I've tried to brighten up his room by making colorful "get well" signs with my art supplies. I hung a big bright green poster board from the TV that he doesn't use. Letter cutouts cling to the green surface, so bright that they appear to be shouting *GET WELL!* I'm no longer hoping he gets better and wakes up; I'm demanding it. Beneath the letters is an inspirational quote in cursive, the words delicately sprawling across the sign: *There is no medicine like hope, no incentive so great, and no tonic so powerful as expectation of something better tomorrow.*

Although these annoying inspirational quotes only frustrate me now, I put them up for Jason's sake. He always loves a good quote. I look at his face, drained of color and animation. I haven't seen his fuzzy hair in weeks. I've always loved picking at his fuzzy head of hair—long enough not to look military-issued, but short enough not to look too sloppy. He tried so hard to rid himself of the marine image by growing his hair out and wearing baggy clothes. Whenever someone would ask about his past, he would always avoid the five years that he was in the Marine Corps, skipping over that time of his life as if he was playing a game of hopscotch. I think he actually convinced himself that those five years didn't exist; he blocked them out of his head as if they were a bad nightmare. I could always see a trace of his military ways though, as if that time had left a permanent mark on his habits and way of life. Jason never slept later than 5 a.m., and he would pop out of bed as if he was alarmed by something, sitting upright on the edge of the bed, his back erect and his legs at a perfect ninety degrees. I look over at his closed eyes, his lids puffy and swollen like two protruding marbles.

I get angry at myself as I think about how I used to get annoyed with his early morning alertness. I would give anything to see those bright eyes right now, those silvery blue eyes that sparkled against the backdrop of white, never showing any signs of red or distress and never tiring of life. He always kept a slight trace of stubble behind on his face as another way of looking opposite of the once clean-shaven marine. The nurses must've shaved the stubble off so they could have a cleaner surface to work on, because his jaw, chin and cheeks are free of any trace of hair, bumpy and red from a touch of razor burn. Why didn't they ask me to shave it for him? I would've done a better job. He would be furious if he knew they not only shaved his stubble, but left patches of red bumps behind. I grab his hand; it sits cold and slack in my clammy grip as I stare at his face and think about how different and alive it looked the day I painted it just a few months ago.

"Sit still!" I had scolded. But Jason was always moving. You could never get him to settle down. It was a combination of his mind going a mile a minute and his body struggling to keep up.

"You mean to tell me that you don't have my face memorized?" he teased as he plucked dandelions out of the grass. We were at Brookside Park on one of the hills by the playground. It was in the prime of summer so we were surrounded by moms with kids shouting and playing, but we were in our own little world.

"I'm not one of those creepy girls who stares at you while you sleep, so no, I don't have your face memorized." I reached out and tilted his chin slightly to the right after he rolled onto his side, cradling his face with his left hand. "Okay, perfect. Stay just like that!" I said as he looked off over my shoulder. I'm not going to ask what you are looking at, but just keep looking at it. This is perfect."

"Can I at least still talk?" He twirled the dandelion with his right hand while maintaining his stare behind me.

"Do you think I honestly have a choice of whether you talk or not?" I shot back at him, acknowledging his inability to keep quiet for more than five minutes. I was curious to know what he was looking at, but I didn't dare ask, because knowing Jason, he would tell me a very long, drawn out story. He wouldn't be able to help himself. He would break his pose and use his hands to help get his point across, undoing his perfect position for my painting. "You can talk, just don't move," I lectured as I swept my vintage brushes across the canvas, outlining his sturdy jaw and temples.

"Do you want to know what I'm looking at?"

"Yeah, kind of. But it won't be worth it to know if you can't tell me without moving."

"I promise, I'll move my lips only."

"Okay. Shoot," I said bluntly, switching brushes and swirling my smaller brush in a silvery blue to create his eyes. My art store doesn't make a color that matches his eyes exactly because they're the most distinct shade I have ever seen—a blue so deep and pure like the ocean on a sunny day, but with tiny silver flecks that shimmer against the blue. They're the shape of two round Junior Mints, but the outer lids reach down toward his cheekbones, shading the corners of his irises slightly and creating an innocent puppy dog look.

"So there's this couple over at the playground. They're pushing their little boy on the merry-go-round. He looks like he's about five, and he has Down syndrome."

"That is so sad."

"It's not sad at all." He started to move, but I put my hand out to stop him in his tracks. "Sorry." He fell back into position.

"But seriously, it's not sad. That kid is probably happier than most kids. He's probably happier than you and me. Think about it—he's free from worrying about what others think about him. We just assume he's the one with the problem, but maybe it's us. We're the ones who live day to day consumed with what others think of us, trying to fit into this mold that society decides for us. He doesn't know he's 'different' from everyone else. Maybe the joke's on us; maybe he thinks we're the ones who are weird because we sit here and stew in our own misery, judging others because we are insecure with ourselves. Look at him; he looks so happy."

After I put the finishing touches on one of his eyes, I craned my neck back toward the playground. The little boy was holding on tightly to the merry-go-round bars, a big smile planted on his face. His curly reddish-brown hair bounced as he leaned back, clearly enjoying the ride.

"I guess you have a good point. He does look happy." I started on his other eye, filling in the shade of blue and silver that I had to create on my pallet. Jason is always thinking outside the box, always looking at people and situations from different angles. While others would argue with him and think his opinions are a bit out of the ordinary, I usually agree with them. There will never be a dull moment in our lives together. His mind is like a set of tentacles, reaching and grabbing for new possibilities and thoughts that go against the norm.

"You see what I mean, Abby Girl? We are a narrow-minded bunch of humans. And selfish to think that we are normal. There is no normal. Don't even get me started on life on other planets," he said as he tilted his head down, looking at a blade of grass that he was gliding his fingers across.

"I won't. Trust me." I reached out and lifted his chin back up with my forefinger. "Keep looking over my shoulder."

"Yes, ma'am."

I shaded in the stubbly area around his chin and darkened his eyebrows so they were almost identical to his actual eyebrow shade. He has thicker-than-necessary eyebrows, but he refuses to get "man-groomed," claiming real men don't get groomed. I blew off the excess dust and dandelion dander that had gathered on my textured canvas.

"Are you done yet? I can't sit still for much longer," he pleaded like a toddler antsy to move.

"And voilà! Your portrait is complete!" I held out the canvas so it was on display in front of us.

"Wow. Abby Girl. You are amazing." He stared at the image before him in awe. "That really looks like me, doesn't it? I mean I'm not quite that good-looking, but it really looks like me." We both fixated our eyes on the face not quite looking back at us but looking toward the right as if off in the distance. The facial structure looked strong and masculine, but the eyes soften the ruggedness, giving an innocence to the picture. He was contemplating life, weaving thoughts in his mind about the world, just as he does in reality. He rubbed his index finger and thumb against his stubbly chin.

"Do you have any idea how much people would pay for these pictures, Abby? You are just as good, if not better than any of those artists who have shops down on Main Street." He took my free hand in his. "Please. Please promise me you will do something with this talent. Don't waste it. God gave it to you for a reason. People would kill for a talent like this."

"I promise." I dabbed a speck of the blue-silver paint on his nose, teasing him.

"Hey! Is that what I get for complimenting you?" He reached for the pallet of colors but I jumped up and started to dodge him. He caught me, wrapped one arm around me and gently swiped the bright red that I used to paint his shirt collar down my nose.

"Red! Why red? You could've at least used a more subtle color."

He wrapped his free arm around my waist and pulled me close. "I chose red because it's the color of love."

I realized just how closely matched up the color of his eyes were to the blue-silver sitting on the tip of his nose. A smile broke across his face.

"And because it matches your lipstick." He guided my head closer to his and kissed me, our noses skimming each other and the colors blending.

CHAPTER THIRTEEN

Samantha

WHEN I GET BACK TO PHILLY, everything is exactly as I left it. Alex is working a lot of hours, Courtney is still bouncing from one guy to the next, and Chauncey is still the neediest dog around. For the last few weeks, the world has gone on without me while I watched the walls close in on Jason and Abby's life. She is the new me. It could have just as easily been me in her sad, scary world, holding on to Jason's life with a grip so tight that it leaves her feeling numb and powerless.

I know how this feels because I've put myself in her shoes over and over since I found out Jason was in a coma. Jason could've died when he was my husband, which would've shattered my world, and that's why I feel so guilty that I let him go, throwing him into the arms of another innocent woman who has to deal with this. I've made myself appear strong for Abby's sake, but inside I'm a mess. I feel so responsible, as if I, as a perfectly capable parent, gave my child up for adoption. When I gave up on Jason, I passed along his problems to another person, creating a rippling effect of sorrow, loss and confusion.

Alex has been working on a big renovation in a low-income neighborhood, so he's been getting home late most nights. I've been using the time to run away my stress about Jason's coma.

After a particularly hilly run, I'm feeling extra energized, so I decide to tackle cleaning the attic. Knowing full well I'm about to be covered in dust and dander, I bypass the shower and dive right into my project. I climb up the steep, narrow stairs effortlessly, since my legs are already warmed up.

Alex and I made a pact to go through our individual things and keep our attic organized all year long. When I was in New Hampshire he spent most of his evenings organizing his belongings. I look over to the corner that Alex designated as his. Boxes are lined up neatly, each labeled in his neat handwriting with a red Sharpie. The wall behind is covered in baseball hats, five rows perfectly lined up and looking forward like spectators at a sporting event.

My corner of the attic is in complete disarray. Beat-up boxes are piled high and uneven, like a game of Jenga. A mountain of garbage bags filled with old clothes surrounds the boxes, creating a cushion for the boxes to land on if they topple over.

I let out a giant sigh and plop myself down on the clothing bags that are now acting as a bean bag chair for me. I lean forward and slide one of the giant Tupperware containers toward me, eager to see what lies inside. The snap on the lid is broken so it flies open easily, displaying a random blend of memories. Photos are scattered everywhere, serving as bookmarks for the other objects. I shimmy out a stack of photos that's jammed tightly between my old high school yearbook and a collage photo frame of me and my dad. I fan the photos out on the hardwood floor as a smattering of memories spreads out before me.

My pictures must have been mixed up during one of my moves because they aren't grouped together chronologically. A photo of my mom holding me as a baby is flush against a photo of me graduating from boot camp, looking serious and proud. I spread the photos around as if I'm dealing a deck of cards.

A photo of Jason and me stands out among the rest. It must've been around Christmas because he's wearing a Santa hat and we're standing in front of our little Charlie Brown tree. I remember how adamant he was about having some sort of a tree even though we were living in a tiny apartment at the time and both of us worked every single holiday when we were in the military. I'm holding a big rectangular clothing box. That was the year that he got me a really expensive snowboarding jacket. I remember how mad I was that he spent our money on that bulky thing with far too many pockets.

"Jason, I already have a jacket that's perfectly fine," I'd insisted.

"I know, but if you want to snowboard with me you'll need the very best. And see, this pocket can hold extra snacks that you may need on the trail," he said as he unzipped a deep pocket that expanded along the inner lining of the front right side of the coat.

"But the jacket I already have is only a year old and holds everything I need. Seriously, I can't even imagine what you spent on this," I said as I looked at the price tag Jason had left behind. The small print was priced $589. I had hoped he was going to tell me, *"But it was fifty percent off."* I had been so angry with him for spending that much on something I already had, when we were barely getting by on our miniscule military paychecks.

"I don't want it. Take it back and put the money in our checking account. When are you going to realize we need every penny we make? We're never going to get out of debt if you keep buying stupid, useless crap!"

My anger and fear of being broke had taken over my holiday spirit. I threw the coat down on the floor, grabbed my keys and flew out the door, leaving Jason alone on his favorite holiday. I had been so worried about money back then, so afraid we wouldn't have enough to survive while he was always buying pieces of equipment for his countless hobbies.

I drove to the park where Jason and I had picnicked often. Even though it was December, it had been a particularly warm day, even by Southern California standards, so the park was filled with families walking and playing. I sat there and tried to push my financial worries out of my head. I tried to let go of my obsession with saving money. Couldn't I have just accepted the stupid jacket and shown appreciation for it? He had obviously spent a lot of time shopping for it and bought it special for me.

After about an hour I had calmed myself down and promised myself I'd go back home to Jason and apologize for acting like a spoiled little brat and accept his gift to me graciously. I trudged up the stairs that led to our second floor apartment, excited to hug Jason and thank him for the gift and apologize for being a brat.

"Hey," I said softly after I quietly opened the door and sat next to him on our beat-up futon.

"Hey." He was flipping through the few channels we had and staring straight ahead at the television.

"So, I thought about it, and I'm sorry I acted like a brat. I really like the jacket. And it was really thoughtful of you to buy it for me. And

I can't wait to wear it on our snowboarding adventures. I already thought about what I can put in the pockets. Maybe some—"

"It's too late, Sam." His words came out void of feeling and emotion.

"What do you mean? What's too late?"

"I gave the jacket away. That way someone who really needed it would appreciate it. It's gone." He continued aiming the remote at the TV.

"Who did you give it to?" I stared down at the empty box on the floor, no longer upset over the loss of money, but more upset with myself for not just appreciating the gift in the first place.

"I brought it to the homeless shelter. That way someone who needs it will end up getting a really nice jacket for Christmas."

"Oh." I instantly felt stupid. Here I was complaining about our lack of money when there were people who couldn't even afford to eat. I looked down at my hands, saddened by my lack of gratitude. Jason reached over and grabbed my folded hands. He smiled at me as if nothing had happened, as if I hadn't thrown a fit. "That was really nice of you," I said shyly. "And I really did like the jacket."

"I know." He gripped my hand tighter and pulled me down so I was leaning back on the futon with him.

I drop the picture into the pile and let out a sigh. The memories flood back through me and create a tinge of guilt.

I organize and discard things relentlessly for three hours straight. After I've gone through nearly everything, I slide the freshly categorized boxes to my corner of the attic, against a small stack of boxes that I just didn't have the energy to get to, and notice a slice in the bottom of one of the smaller boxes. As I blindly feel around inside the box, a smooth wooden surface glides across my fingertips. I peek inside, and recognition comes over me: the jewelry box. I tip the box on its side, and all its contents slide out, revealing themselves in front of my crossed legs. I slide the small cherry-wood jewelry box closer to me before I lift the lid.

All of my old jewelry is on display in the box. Rings are lined up in the small felt crevices like soldiers standing at attention, dangly earrings fill four square cutouts, and necklaces hang from little metal hooks the inside the jewelry box doors. A cluster of turquoise beams up at me as I remember my brief obsession with the stone. I glide my index finger along the tops of the rings, feeling the stones' different textures.

My finger stops on the engagement ring Jason gave me after we had been married. He had saved up for months to get the unique pear-shaped diamond. Jason was not interested in following society's rules that put extra pressure on people to be showy, and I know he got this ring only because I wanted a diamond so badly. He had said that he chose pear-shaped because it was different, like me. He had told me later that he had been putting twenty dollars aside here and there until he had enough saved up in a cigar box that he kept under our bed. I shimmy the ring out from between its felt crevice home and slide it on my ring finger, flush against my set of rings from Alex. It slides on smoothly, as if there hasn't been a gap of time since I've worn it, as if to say that I am still that same person who married young so many years ago. The shape of this diamond is so different from my simple princess cut one from Alex, as if my personality has transformed over the years, morphing from one shape into the other. I feel a sense of relief as I take Jason's ring off my finger and drop it into the zipper-front pocket of my hooded sweatshirt.

CHAPTER FOURTEEN

Abby

DEEP DOWN INSIDE I KNOW I should be preparing myself for a life without Jason in case he really does die and leave my life forever. But I'm in denial. I dive into my painting to escape from my frightening reality. In between visiting Jason, I lock myself in our tiny apartment and paint pictures of him and only him. A picture of him holding Felix, one of him skateboarding, one of him reading a book in the park, the sun ricocheting off his face. I emphasize his silvery blue eyes in every picture. Even though I haven't seen those eyes for weeks, I have them embedded in my memory.

An empty photo box is tipped over in front of my easel on the floor, and pictures of Jason are scattered before me. I never realized how many photos I had taken of him, and I'm thankful to have memories of him moving and living that I can hold on to forever. About thirty photos of a lone Jason look up at me as though he's trying to tell me something, trying to hang onto his life.

I find myself talking to him while I paint, and I have this fantasy that he'll answer me, that he'll walk in the door and we'll finish our lives where we left off. My back is facing the door while I paint, and I often find myself craning my neck to see if he's behind me, watching me. I have visions of him walking in the door and surprising me with a bouquet of my favorite flowers, pink roses. *You are such a girly girl,* he has always said about my love of pink roses. He's right; I am all girl. I love colors and makeup and perfume. I love stocking up on the flowery scented lotions around the holidays, and I love scheduling days at the spa and salon. I love reading fashion magazines and romance novels, and I veer away from anything that would cause me to break a nail or smudge my eyeliner. Jason is the only one who has gotten me to go against my girly ways and realize that there is more to life than frills and flowers and that dirt and sweat can sometimes be fun too.

Not long after I met Jason there was one of those local carnivals in town—the kind that have the creaky rides and travel from town to town. They had this small section for people who wanted to play a mini game of paintball, mostly kids of course. He gripped my hand and pulled me toward the ticket booth.

"Two please," he had said proudly as he slid his cash across the counter.

"What? Jason, I can't play paintball." I tugged at his hand and gave the ticket attendant a look of apprehension, but she wasn't feeling sorry for me.

"Abs, yes you can. Come on, it will be fun. You're not going to get dirty. You may get colorful, but not dirty," he insisted as he gave the attendant a nod, confirming that we were going ahead with the game. She craned her neck to motion for the next customers to come forward, clearly not amused by our bickering.

"But doesn't the paint hurt when it hits you?" I asked as he secured my vest after doing his own.

"Maybe a little, but nothing you can't handle," he said with a wink as he pulled me toward the rack of guns. "Hmmm... let's see. Looks like this one will be just right for you."

He pulled a gun off the rack and stood it up beside me to measure it against my height. I trusted his gun calibration even though I had no idea how a person's height has anything to do with what size gun they should be assigned. He handed it over to me with a sturdy grip, clearly having had experience holding this type of weapon. As I accepted it daintily I nearly dropped it on my toes.

"Geez, this thing is heavy!" I screeched as I fumbled to catch it as it slid in my grip.

"You've gotta hold it with a purpose." He heaved his gun up with the precision of a color guard soldier and stood erect as if he were about to perform a 21-gun salute. "And never, EVER, take your eyes off your weapon."

He gripped his gun in one hand and adjusted mine with his other hand. "This, my dear, will be your best friend for the next—" he looked down at his military issued watch—"crap, nineteen minutes. We gotta get started before our time is up."

I held my gun as instructed and followed him into the mini paintball course. Dark green netting was hung and drooping in various clumps around the roped-off section serving as hideouts.

"Take cover!" Jason yelled as he ran toward one of the bunkers made of two pieces of platform wood leaning against each other. I stood there helpless at first, but I was so afraid of getting smothered by a paint bomb that I dove toward one of the green tents. After a few seconds of silence, I slowly raised myself to a crouching position and extended my neck so I could see where he was. A couple of little boys went sprinting by covered in blue and red paint and shrieking delightfully.

"I've got you where I want you, Miss Jacobson." Jason's eerie voice penetrated me from behind. I jumped up and started to sprint toward the other bunker, but I was stopped by another little boy who sprang out in front of me. Just as I turned around to see where Jason was, a splatter of purple paint exploded against my right arm. In shock, I looked down to see the color dripping down my arm and morphing me into what I imagined looked like Barney the big purple dinosaur. Before I could object, I aimed my gun toward Jason, who was now darting toward another bunker. I pulled the trigger as a spray of blue thumped him on his right butt cheek. I began chasing him like a little kid playing a game of tag. I laughed uncontrollably as I pulled the trigger three more times, turning Jason into a human rainbow. Our nineteem minutes were up in what felt like an instant.

"Darn! I was really starting to have fun!" I said as our buzzers went off and we started to walk into the safe zone.

"Oh, there are plenty of other things we can do around here that are fun," Jason said as he tugged on my arm and pulled me toward a bean bag toss game. I had looked down at my nails. The once perfect shade of red was now covered in splatters of green, blue and purple, but I didn't care.

My cell phone ringing startles me out of my memories. I glance down at my phone on the floor and see Samantha's name dancing across the screen. She's the only one I want to talk to lately, the only one who understands. And it helps that when I talk to her, I feel closer to Jason, as if she is my only connection to him anymore.

"Hi Abs, how are you doing?"

"Eh, I'm okay; I've just been sleeping a lot. How are you? I take it you made it back to Philadelphia safely. I'm sure Alex is happy to see you."

"Yep, safe and sound. Yeah, it's good to be back, but being so far away makes me worry even more. Any updates from Dr. Bennington?"

"No, it's the same thing every day, Sam. I just don't know what to do anymore. I feel like I'm just sitting in limbo waiting for something to happen. He still hasn't responded to any of their tests. It's been weeks, Sam, and everything I read online makes this sound bad. Really bad."

"First of all, stop reading things you find on the Internet. It won't do you any good. Don't give up hope, Abs. Miracles happen every day, and Jason is one hell of a miracle." Samantha's voice cracks as she changes the subject. "Are you eating at all?"

"I'm not going to lie to you, I have no appetite. Every time I eat, it seems to come right back up." I fondle the tassels on the afghan in my lap. "I'm sure you wanted to hear that though."

"Yeah, depression does that to you. Just please promise me you'll try to eat. Or I'll send my dad over there to check on you!"

"Yes, ma'am," I say sternly while making a mental note to call the restaurant and figure out my schedule for the upcoming week. "Speaking of food, I have to call the restaurant manager and find out what shifts I have next week. I forgot that I actually have a job and somewhat of a life outside this apartment. I'll call you soon. Have a good week."

"Goodbye, Abby. Call me if you need anything at all."

While waitressing isn't my dream job, I don't mind working at Ronic's Bistro. The upscale French restaurant has surprisingly been a great income for me. Serving New Hampshire's wealthiest five nights a week, I make as much as my friends in their post-college nine-to-fives. I'm still just barely making enough to get by on my own, but the schedule is flexible and it allows me to spend my days taking art classes and searching for jobs that will lead me to a career in art.

I started my fine arts degree a couple of years ago, but it's not the easiest degree to find a job with. If my dream of becoming a famous artist doesn't come true, I suppose I can always be a teacher. Realistically, I'd like to open a studio that teaches art to children with disabilities.

Jason is my biggest cheerleader when it comes to my art, and I selfishly feel like I will fail if I don't have him as my support. My mom always urged me to go into something practical like nursing or finance. Maybe it was because she had such instability in her life after my dad got out of the military. I struggled against my passion for art until I met Jason. I fought it like an enemy, trying to tame my need to create colorful landscapes and facial features and trying to find office jobs interesting. I did a couple of temp jobs as an administrative assistant and I was bored out of my mind. Going into work and sitting in a cubicle all day was like jail to me, free of color and emotion. Just the thought of all of those file cabinets and the modular partitions that separated one prisoner from the next makes me ill with boredom.

After I met Jason, I started to dive deeper into my passion, and a flame was ignited in my heart and mind for both him and the art. He has always treated my desire to build an art career to be a reachable goal. He never treated me like a starving artist, which technically I am.

"Ronic's Bistro, this is Elliot." It's refreshing to hear Elliot's voice on the other end.

"Hi E, it's Abby."

"Abby! How are you, Abs? Take as much time off as you need." His feminine voice sings to me.

"Actually, I'm calling to get my schedule for next week. I'm ready to come back to work." I make my way toward the wall calendar hanging on the bulletin board above the mini refrigerator.

"Really? Are you sure you're ready? We've got plenty of coverage, Abs. Of course we miss you and we want you here, but—"

"I promise you I'm ready to come back. I need the cash, and I need to get out of this depressing tiny cave I've been dwelling in. It will keep my mind busy while Jason..." I can't get myself to finish the sentence.

"I get it, Abs. Okay, let's see, how about you start your usual shift on Monday the 31st?"

"That's perfect," I answer, trying to conceal my sadness, thinking about how long Jason has been in a coma. My eyes scan the rest of the month and I notice the tiny red heart circling Monday, the 3rd.

"Hey, E. I, uh, gotta go. I'll see you next Monday."

I hurriedly hang up the phone, frozen in realization: I was supposed to start my period nearly four weeks ago. In the chaos of the accident, it completely slipped my mind. Now I'm in an instant panic, trying to recalculate our sex life.

Jason and I had always been very safe; I've been a faithful birth control pill taker. But there were those antibiotics that I had to go on for the horrible sinus infection I had. I rewind my entire life over the past few weeks, all the events playing in a rapid sequence in my head, images darting in and out, trying to recollect when this could have possibly happened. Based on my calculations, I could actually be two months pregnant already.

The nearest drugstore is only a ten-minute walk from my apartment, but my impatient nature takes over and before I know it, I am sitting behind the wheel driving the short distance. The sooner that I have an answer, the sooner I can get on with my life. As luck would have it, the longest red light in town decides to change colors right as I'm about to breeze through. I sit in silence and play out all the possible scenarios in my head. When red switches to green, I turn and twist through the remaining streets to get to my drugstore destination.

I grab four different brands of pregnancy tests and make my way to the counter, adding random things along the way to hide my obvious urgency. A bottle of hairspray, a king size Hershey bar, a giant bottle of water and a thank you card sit on top of the tests in an attempt to camouflage them. I don't know why I even care—I'm twenty-five years old, not a teenager hiding from a parent. Still, it's always embarrassing to purchase anything from the "awkward aisle," as Jason has always called it. He avoids it at all costs, conveniently making a detour into the snack aisle whenever I have to go into the feminine section.

The teenage boy behind the register eyes me up and down as he scans the items, making me feel more uncomfortable than I already do. I take my long receipt of coupons and fly out of the store. I start tearing open the boxes on my drive home, reading the directions at stoplights. One line equals not pregnant; two lines equals pregnant. Easy enough.

I take the last sip of the giant bottle of water as I enter my apartment. Tossing the boxes on the bathroom floor, I take one test after the other and line them face up on the back of the toilet. I wait the designated three minutes, stepping side to side in my tiny bathroom. I promise myself not to look at the tests until the alarm goes off on my watch. I catch a glimpse of myself in the mirror and notice how thin and pale I look, my eyes permanently bloodshot from all the tears that have invaded my life over the past few weeks. My heart begins to accelerate the second that the alarm sounds. I take one long deep breath and look down at the back of the toilet to see eight blue lines staring back up at me.

Chapter Fifteen

Abby

One Month Later

THANK GOD I WORK for one of the few restaurants in the state that provide decent medical coverage for their employees, because these doctors' appointments are adding up fast. I always imagined pregnancy to be nine months of torture and pain. I imagined my body being taken over by this baby who would take up residency. I was never the type to want children, unlike most of my friends. I always thought of them as extra baggage on one's journey through life. But now, much to my surprise, I enjoy feeling the growth in my body, and I never feel lonely; sometimes I feel as if Jason is here with me. Now that I'm approaching my second trimester, my doctor says I'm officially in the safe zone, so I've started to talk to the baby, holding full-blown conversations as I go through my daily activities.

"So, baby, how about we go get one of those delicious coconut donuts at the coffee shop where I met your daddy? Your daddy is the most handsome man I have ever seen. I hope you have his eyes." I stand sideways in front of the full-length mirror assessing my growing belly as I talk to my new friend. I call her "baby" now, as I am convinced it's a girl but haven't decided on a name yet.

I've shared the news with my family. They're happy, but they can't help but show their concern for the single mom I'm possibly about to become. My parents have never been happy together, but their strict religion has led them to avoid divorce at all costs. They have fought over money as long as I can remember. My dad's military pay was never quite enough for my mother's expensive taste, which is why she went through their small savings in a short amount of time, leaving them just barely able to get by from Dad's retirement pay and part-time gig at the local hardware store. I knew better than to ask them for help with my art classes, which is why I've been attending part time while working for the past eight years while all of my friends are using their four-year degrees at fancy office jobs. My father has always taught me to be grateful for what I have, and I always have been.

Maybe that's why I admire Jason so much—because he had less than I had, and never seemed to let it get him down. He's always able to make something out of nothing. One summer when all of my friends were planning their expensive getaway vacations, Jason created a beautiful escape for us.

"Abby!" Jason had come bursting through the door as I lay in bed watching old sitcoms.

"Get dressed, preferably in layers. I'm not sure what the temp is going to be like where we're going."

"What are you talking about?" I lazily flipped through the channels, ignoring him as he tore through the dresser drawers and filled a small duffel bag.

"I'm taking you on a weekend getaway. Now all you have to do is get dressed; I have everything you will need in this bag." He extended his arm, helping me up from the bed.

I questioned him for the entire ride through the White Mountains. We carved our way through the winding roads as the green trees opened up like arms above us. The smell of nature energized me as I dangled my arm out the open window. Finally, after a couple of hours, he pulled into a small woodsy parking lot.

"You deserve a weekend getaway. I know it's not as fancy as your friends' trips to the Caribbean, but this will have to do for now." Jason leaned in for a quick kiss before getting out of the car and racing over to my side, opening my door and leading me to a little area carved out in the woods. The small plot of land was private and overlooked a rocky crevasse. The only sound was water cascading rapidly down the rocks, landing into a pool that was created by nature.

"You did this for me?"

"I was out hiking one day awhile back and found this secret little spot."

Jason started to set up his old two-man tent, filling it with various blankets and sleeping bags that created a sweet, cozy little nook. We spent most of the day lounging on the smooth rocks, absorbing the sweet summer sun while talking about silly things like old cartoons, cereals we loved as children and our favorite subjects in school. Mine was art, his was science. For two days we had forgotten about the rest of the world, thrown all of our worries away and melted into each other.

Jason has an amazing ability to make something out of nothing; I just hope I can do the same for his baby. I start to feel doubt creep in as I think about the struggles I may have to go through if Jason dies and I have to raise this baby on my own.

Just hearing the word "dies" in my head makes my heart hurt. *Jason* and *dies* pulsate in my mind so many times throughout the day. My heart breaks for this baby, who may have to go through life with no father, only a mother who knows absolutely nothing about raising a child. He loves children and has the necessary knowledge, since he basically raised his little sister. His upbringing was the opposite of mine: I grew up as an only child in a home padded by the loving triangle of my mother, my father and me.

I imagine how Jason's smile would light up his face the first time our baby smiles or walks or says his or her first word. When his smile is triggered, it peels open his mouth at the corners, revealing a big, bright set of white teeth. And once he starts smiling, he has a hard time stopping. He's one of those people who smiles at every stranger he passes on the street, leaving a print on that person's day like an old photograph that keeps reappearing over time. His smile is so good at covering up his pain; it even had me fooled for a while.

CHAPTER SIXTEEN

Samantha

I SLIP BACK INTO my normal life in Philadelphia. The weeks go back to normal, except that they are lined with my sadness about Jason's state and the unknown. Alex catches me zoning out during dinner or while I'm doing a household chore; often times I'll look up to him watching me and I'll feel a tear crawl down my face. The possibility of losing a friend so suddenly is the hardest thing I've ever had to face, but I'm sure Abby's pain is twice as suffocating.

The weather in Philly is rarely perfect, and this Saturday is no exception. Alex and I lay cuddled on the couch watching reruns of *Seinfeld* as the rain blows angrily, hitting the window in big chunks every few minutes. Chauncey lies in his usual spot, at the bottom of the stairs in the main entryway of the house. He's positioned like a guard dog, but the truth is that he would just roll over and accept belly rubs if an intruder actually tried to get into our house. Luckily our house in Philly is far enough into suburbia that we don't have to worry about the crime associated with living in a city—just dogs, bikes, kids and the occasional screaming house-wife. My phone vibrates on the glass coffee table and jerks me out of my *Seinfeld* trance.

"Ha, I knew you couldn't go a day without your phone." Alex gives me a flirty kick from his side of the couch, winking a brown eye, long dark lashes nearly touching his cheek. Abby's name blinks on my screen. We've been chatting every day, but it's mostly me calling her to check in on Jason's status, so I feel a little anxious when I see she's calling me. I instantly fear the worst.

"Hi, Abs." I pick up quickly, as if I've been waiting for the call.

"Samantha. Do you have time to talk?" Her voice comes through hasty and determined.

"Of course. What's up?" I walk backwards out of the room, using sign language to indicate that I won't be long. Alex rolls his eyes playfully and goes back to *Seinfeld*.

"Are you sitting down?"

"Not yet, but I will be in three, two, one." I take two steps at a time on the stairs and plop myself on the chaise lounge on the second floor landing. "Okay, I'm officially sitting down. What's up?" I try to sound calm, but I'm so afraid she's going to tell me Jason is gone forever.

"I'm pregnant." Abby says the words so fast that it sounds like one long word.

"What? Wait. Huh?"

"I'm thirteen weeks pregnant. I was actually pregnant before Jason's accident; I just didn't know."

"So that explains the constant nausea you've been having. Oh my God, Abby, this is a miracle!" The excitement in my voice is so prevalent that Chauncey wakes up, saunters up the stairs and sits down in front of me, head tilted in speculation.

"I'm glad you see it that way. Sam, I can't take care of a baby alone. I can barely take care of myself. I have only enough money to get by week to week. I just spent half of my paycheck on all these stinking pregnancy tests!"

"Just take a deep breath. We have six more months to think about this and make a plan." I gently tug at Chauncey's ear hair, rubbing the fine, wavy red fur between my fingers.

"I'm freaking out, Sam. I mean, yeah, this is amazing. It's like I'll still have a piece of Jason with me if he. . . how could I have not known though?"

"Well, Abs, everything happens for a reason, and I'm sure with you being all caught up in the past few weeks, it was the last thing you had space in your thoughts for. If Jason were awake now to hear this news he would be so happy. He loves kids."

Another reason that Jason and I were not right together: I would've never been able to satisfy his need for children. Two years ago, after trying to conceive for a year, the doctors detected that I had a condition known as blocked fallopian tubes, which raised my chances of not being able to have children. The news came as a shock to me and Alex, but it hit me exceptionally hard, as I always wanted to be the mother that my mother wasn't. I wanted to pass along my love to a child, love like I never received. We've managed to accept it, but it still passes my thoughts at least once a day. Chauncey reaps the benefits of our inability to procreate, as he's showered with our love like a child. Lucky dog.

"Yeah, I'm sure I'll make it work. It's just such a shock right now. The good news is that I'm healthy and all is good." Abby hesitates. I hear her breath on the other end. "I just never thought I'd be twenty-five, working at a restaurant, pregnant possibly without a spouse. My life is completely off track. This is NOT what I planned."

"Ha! If you would've asked me where I was hoping to be now ten years ago, my response would be so different from what you see today. Life is not a sheet of MapQuest directions that you follow; there are bends and turns along the way." I can't help but giggle at myself. "That's about as much wisdom as I can provide today."

"Thanks, Sam. You always make me feel better."

"Well, I like you, Abs. Jason certainly has good taste in women, doesn't he?" I attempt to lighten the mood. "And maybe the baby will give you something to focus on while he is recovering. Ya know, take your mind off things."

"Yeah, I guess so." I can hear Abby's smile through the phone. "I just feel so guilty that I'm feeling some joy over this baby, *his* baby, while he's in a coma and may never wake up. What if he never wakes up, Sam? What am I going to tell this baby? How am I going to do this on my own?" A clump of questions starts to unfold all at once.

"Listen, I know this is hard to hear, but you have to take this one day at a time, Abs. Just breathe and focus on making sure that baby is healthy." I think about how hard it must be for Abby to transfer her love from Jason to the baby for the time being.

An hour has passed before I know it. Abby and I talked about everything from work to baby names to—of course—Jason. I tried hard to keep her on a positive track, to avoid the giant *what-if* that constantly lurks in the back of our minds. By the time we hang up, my ear is hot from pressing the phone up against it. I lazily walk down the stairs, massaging the knot in my neck from tilting my head toward the cell, Chauncey following close behind. I hear the snores before I turn into the living room. Alex is sound asleep, blanket tucked in up to his chin, one foot hanging outside our tan couch throw.

"Hey, sleepy bear." I gently smooth the hair on his head and kiss his forehead. I'm suddenly overcome with sadness as I think about how I'll never be able to have his baby. I'll never be able to cradle a miniature Alex in my arms. His eyes suddenly spring to life as he grabs me in one swift scoop and pulls me on top of him. He teases me with kisses before I pull him up the stairs and into our bedroom.

CHAPTER SEVENTEEN

Abby

I'M FAT. I'M FAT, and I know this because my jeans no longer fit. I'm officially out of regular jeans and into the stretchy-waisted maternity ones. As if I didn't have enough difficulty shopping for regular jeans in the first place, the maternity section takes my pain to a whole new level.

I nearly had a breakdown in Target the other day because the maternity clothes and the plus-size sections are right up against each other, as if they are shouting to the world I'm pregnant, therefore I am FAT. I had left the store feeling more defeated than when I entered, having accomplished absolutely nothing. After I expressed to the plus-size sales clerk that the two departments need to be differentiated more clearly, I stormed out of the store having purchased nothing except for a box of Fruit Roll-Ups. Pregnancy has made me mean, and I instantly felt bad and sad for yelling at the sales clerk. I ponder my various hormonal outbursts as I flip through old magazines and sit in the waiting room at my doctor's office with all the other mothers who look just as uncomfortable and miserable as I am. I have an ultrasound scheduled today. I think about all of the television shows that I've seen where the mother and father watch their baby flipping around on the monitor, the look of bliss and amazement in their eyes. But there will only be one set of eyes watching this baby flip around quite possibly for the rest of his or her life.

"Miss Jacobson?" The nurse looks around the room searching for me among all the women in varying stages of pregnancy, all

carrying differently and portraying different side effects. A redhead
smiles at me through her melasma-covered skin; one exceptionally
large woman is leaning on her side because of what appears to
be debilitating back pain. And a girl who looks to be as young as
sixteen looks so incredibly scared. This is one good thing about
doctor's appointments: They relieve some of the loneliness I feel
during pregnancy and somehow make me feel better. I get up
slowly, pushing myself forward using my legs for leverage. Every
move I make is exhausting these days, and it takes all my effort to
walk to the nurse.

"Good afternoon, Abby. How are you feeling?" We walk down
the carpeted hallway. I move slowly in her wake.

"I'm good. Just ready to have this baby already." I smooth over
the pale blue maternity shirt that molds to my growing belly.

"Well, unfortunately, you have a ways to go still. Just try to relax
and enjoy the ride of pregnancy, and always remember that it's up
to the baby when he or she decides to enter the world. According to
your chart here, you don't want to find out the gender?"

I was so sick of people telling me to relax. The love of my life has
been in a coma for nearly four months. How the hell am I supposed
to RELAX?

"Yep, I like surprises."

"I wanted to be surprised with my first one, but my husband,
being the planner that he is, just had to find out." The nurse smiles,
clearly thinking back to her younger years. I know she means well,
but I can't help but be envious that her baby had a father, her baby
had two parents and a stable home life, and my baby's father has
been sleeping for months now. I smile politely, stopping myself
before I get carried away in a downward spiral of depression.

After my vitals are taken, Dr. Sharma sneaks into the room
quietly, as usual. A stunning gold and red necklace peeks out from
behind the opening of her white lab coat. After my first appointment
with Dr. Sharma, I went home questioning why she didn't have
the colorful red dot on her forehead like the other female Indian
doctors at the hospital. After a quick Google search, I discovered
that the dot symbolizes marriage. For some reason, the fact that
my kind, gentle doctor was not married made me feel a little better
about my situation.

"Good afternoon, Abby. How are you feeling today?" She walks toward me, setting her clipboard on the desk. Her big, round brown eyes are unmoving as she listens for my response intently

"I'm good. Just starting to get uncomfortable."

"Well, that is to be expected." Her voice is soft and calm, as if she's a storyteller in a first grade classroom. Since I have known Dr. Sharma, she has not raised her voice or displayed an ounce of impatience or anger—not even when I tried to joke with her about drinking a daily shot of Jack Daniels. She simply smiled, and probably judged me internally. Everything about her is calming; sometimes I feel as if I'm going to fall asleep in the middle of the exam.

I stare up at the ceiling above the exam table while she gets down to business. There's a poster of a happy couple, each holding a hand of their toddler as they walk down a beach. All three of them look happy and content, as if life really is a beach. I feel a twinge of jealousy as I stare up at them. Part of me is mad at Dr. Sharma for placing such an unrealistic picture up on her walls. What about the mothers who may end up alone and single? Do we not deserve enough to be on the walls?

"So, are you still against knowing the gender of baby?"

"Yes."

"Okay, well luckily baby Jacobson has its legs crossed, so we can't see the genitals. You are free to take a peek at your little one." Dr. Sharma glides the machine over the surface of my belly.

I drop my head to the left and settle my eyes on the screen. The alien-like head curls into its tiny limbs. One hand is pressed closely to the head, a thumb shooting upwards as the rest of the fingers curl into a tight grip. The legs are crossed as if my baby is sitting politely in my womb.

"Looks like he or she is giving you a thumbs up."

I thought of the irony of that. As if the child would be applauding me for being the cause of her father's accident. I think back to the night of our fight, the last night that I saw Jason coherent, as a salty tear trickles out of my eye closest to the bed.

"Yeah. It does, doesn't it?" I say with a little sniffle.

"You have a healthy and happy baby in there, Abby. Just keep doing what you are doing, and baby Jacobson will enter the world safe and sound." Her face is stoic as she jots down some things on her clipboard and adjusts her glasses.

I take the long way home, winding along the carved-out back roads that Jason loves so much. This is the first time I've taken these roads since before Jason's accident. I think about what would've happened if I wouldn't have gotten so jealous that night. Maybe we would've eaten the nachos together, watched a movie and fallen asleep in the safety of each other's arms.

I'm pulled out of my daydreaming trance as a sign to the right grabs my attention: *Heartbreak Park and Campground.* I've always known it was there; I've just avoided this route for the past few months in an effort to forget about the accident. Avoidance has always been my defense mechanism.

I make a sharp turn to the right, tires squealing loudly as everything in the car jerks to the left. My phone slides across the passenger seat and onto the floor beneath the pedals.

"Sorry, baby, I didn't mean to frighten you in there." Smoothing my hand over my bump, I look in the rear view mirror to see if I've left some tire tracks on the road. Sure enough, two black tire marks are tattooed on the cement behind me. They curve in the direction of the Heartbreak Park sign. The smell of burning tires envelops me as I drive slowly past the sign and into the park. Green pine trees line both sides of the road, as if they are urging me and cheering me on to get to my destination.

Without being told, I know exactly where Jason was rock climbing the night of his accident. There are several giant boulders in the park, but Jason, being the daredevil that he is, always went to the most treacherous of the boulders. I know this because once he took me here in an attempt to teach me how to rock climb, and instead of starting on the smaller boulders and working our way up, he brought me straight to "Big Wally." Another quirk of Jason's was his habit of nicknaming everything. Our Coleman cooler was named "Coley," his Black and Decker vacuum cleaner was named "Blackie," and his favorite rock to climb was named "Big Wally."

Since school is still in session, the park isn't flooded with 4-H groups of children. There's a small group of moms pushing running strollers. From a distance I can see the muscle definition in their arms. I watch the four of them as they park their strollers in a grassy open space, sanctioned off by picnic tables. They each place a hand on their stroller and start doing synchronized lunges. I'm overcome with envy as I think about the plush lifestyles they must live. They spend their days gossiping and burning off their pregnancy fat while their loving husbands work in corporate America. I'm sure they'll never have to worry about their baby not having the best of everything. I, on the other hand, am worried about how I will afford diapers, let alone a fancy jogging stroller. I'm sure they would look down on me as a mom. I've never been a bitter person, but I'm starting to feel bitterness creep all around and closing its walls in on me.

I pull over to an empty spot along the road. Of course Big Wally is off the beaten path, as Jason is always one to go outside the norm. He could have easily climbed any of the five other rocks in clear view, but he's always had to be different. I pull apart two branches that are arched over the tiny dirt path that leads to Big Wally. I'm certainly not dressed for this trek through the woods. My cotton maternity tank top keeps getting caught on branches along the path, and my arms are itchy from the little bugs that are clinging to my skin.

"Ouch!" My belly is just big enough that it keeps getting whipped by branches that extend into the pathway. "Sorry, baby. But your father always takes the path less traveled." After waddling down the path, I pull apart the last set of branches and step into the open plot of barren land below the massive rock. Jagged edges protrude from the gray rock, reaching out to me as if daring me to climb it. I walk over to the rock and place one hand on my belly and one hand on the rock, rubbing its hard, chunky surface. I think about what was going through Jason's mind as he gripped the rock before falling. I slide down to the ground and sit, my legs splayed out before me and my belly a small round mound in front of me. I rest my elbows on my somewhat bent knees and hold my head up with my hands as I drop my neck and watch tears drop onto the ground below. I sob for what seems like forever, apologizing to my baby. I fumble around in my jacket pocket for a tissue, making a mental note to pull out all my spring clothing and put the winter stuff away.

As I wipe the leftover wetness from my nose and dab below my eyes, ridding any mascara marks that may have trickled from my lashes, my eyes are drawn to a shiny splash of silver peeking out from a lonely leaf on the ground. Too lazy to get up, I crawl over to the silver speck, my belly hanging toward the ground as twigs dig into my palms. My body gets exhausted so quickly now that the four feet I crawl feels like twenty. A tiny silver key looks up at me, and I push the leaf aside to pick up the key and massage it between my thumb and index finger, jogging my memory at the same time. This is the key to Jason's bike lock. He kept it in the pouch underneath his bike seat. It must've somehow fallen out of the lock or his pocket. I continue rubbing the key as if it has the power to unlock my sadness. Months have gone by and winter weather has come and gone and the key remained as if it was meant for me to find. As I walk back to my car I continue rubbing the key, my index finger and thumb create tiny little circles as if to soothe my thoughts. I drop the key into my pocket and plop my body into the driver's side seat and shimmy my belly behind the steering wheel. On the drive home, I feel the key digging into my upper thigh, as if Jason is trying to tell me something.

I toss my satchel on the bed before I even close my apartment door. Digging into my deep maternity jean pockets, I pull out the key that I'm sure belongs to Jason's bike lock. Across the room, Jason's bike is leaning against the white wall with the accordion-like lock dangling from below the seat, right under the pouch where he used to keep his money, this key and his license during his biking adventures. I silently curse myself for all of the times I would nag him for having this stupid bike. I complained at least a dozen times that its rubber handlebars made a permanent black mark on our white wall, and that it took up valuable space that we needed. But now I would let him mark up all the walls and store five bikes in here if only I could have him back to his normal self. His bike is his prized possession. He's never spent a lot of money on himself, and he always gets things at the second-hand shop, but he had saved for months to purchase an expensive on/off road Trek mountain bike.

I remember him talking about it on our first date at the coffee shop. He kept looking out the window to make sure the bike was safely locked up at the bike rack on the corner. He told me how much more reliable and affordable a bike was than a car. *Just think,* he'd said, *I will never have to pay to get the oil changed on this baby—not to mention the positive effects on the environment.*

I always knew the truth behind his bike obsession though. I saw the uneasiness that overcame him when he got in a car. As soon as the engine would start, his hand would grip the passenger side door, and he'd gasp at every sudden stop and highway merge. I never wanted to ask him why he was so petrified—whether something had happened in the past or he was simply one of those people who felt fearful in vehicles.

He was so proud of that stupid bike, and I was such a witch about it, I think. *Who cares about the stupid walls in this apartment anyway?* I walk over to the bike, pulling the handlebars toward me, revealing a round black smudge on the wall. I lick my thumb and press it lightly against the smudge, circling against the grainy white surface. It only takes a minute and the smudge is gone. If only I could use the same technique on my broken heart. He worked so hard for this bike, and he may never get to ride it again.

The red frame is spattered with mud, but the word "Trek" still shines brightly on the bar in shimmery silver. I lean the bike up against my belly as I reach over to test the key in the lock. With one quick turn, the lock opens, as if springing the bike to life. I lean it back up against the now smudge-free wall and unzip the black pouch below the seat. As I pull apart the pouch to make sure the key sinks into place, a red-tipped pen stabs me.

"Ouch!"

When I start to pull the pen out of the pouch, I realize it's clipped to a piece of folded-up notebook paper. I dig my hand in deeper and wrap it around a bottle of pills. The paper is tightly folded but still a little wrinkled and torn on one edge. I walk backwards the short distance to the bed and plop down. Setting the pills down beside me, I unclip the pen and undo the perfectly folded paper.

Dear Abby Girl,

> *Before I even begin, I want to start out by saying that you are the best thing that has ever happened to me, and I will always love you with every bit of my heart. You made my life complete, and I will thank you for that forever. I want you to know that none of what I am about to say was any of your fault; it happened before I ever laid eyes*

on you. You enhanced the life that I did have, but there were things about me that nobody could change or fix. I am broken. The things that I saw in Iraq fill my memory every single day (that is pretty poetic for someone like me to say, huh?). I have tried so hard to ignore them, to pretend nothing happened, but that didn't work. Neither did my frequent trips to the doctor. There is nothing that anyone can do to erase my pain. I should have died over there and I can't rid myself of the guilt that I feel for surviving. It was my responsibility to get my platoon back to our tents, and I failed to do that. I am telling you what happened to me so that you feel peace knowing why I chose to leave this world and know that I will be in a better place.

As soon as I got to Iraq my platoon leader assigned me to be the driver of our designated Humvee. I was responsible for making sure all of my marines reported to the Humvee at 04:30 every morning as we departed for our mission. And I was responsible for accounting for all five of my marines as we completed those missions and headed back to our camp. I took my job as driver very seriously and I was known for my harsh safety rules. Soon, I was known as "Sgt. Safety" instead of Sgt. Barnes. I was fine with that, as it was my mission to protect my marines. On my seventy-fifth day in Iraq, I was starting to feel more comfortable in my role, and I was so tired from the thirty-six hours of searching for civilians in need of help. I was so tired. The lack of sleep started to get to me physically and mentally. I was growing more delirious the longer I went without sleep. At one point I even thought that I saw a ghost in the desert. The sand storms had whipped so much sand into my eyes that I felt like I had to literally pry them apart just to see. I told my youngest marine, LCPL Wilkins, that he had to drive this day. Being the young, innocent marine that he was, he obeyed my order. I could always count on that kid to obey an order. We ensured that all the safety checks were complete and all marines were accounted for. I told LCPL Wilkins to drive us back to the tents for the night. We had done this route every day since we arrived, so he knew the route well. By the time the Humvee's engine even started, I was sleeping soundly. I would occasionally jolt awake when the tires would dip down into the sandy ditches along the route, jerking the vehicle side to side. I remember my helmet knocking lightly on the side of the passenger door. But the last time that I was alerted to wakefulness was different. I woke to LCPL Wilkins shouting SERGEANT BARNES, SERGEANT. BARNES! WE ARE UNDER FIRE! I woke up immediately, as all of us were trained to do. I could feel the vibrations of the bullets ricocheting off of the Humvee, there were so many shots being fired at once. I started shouting orders at Wilkins, regurgitating what I had memorized in my mind, since I was the one who was supposed to be driving. "TURN LEFT! I WANT YOU TO PUT YOUR FOOT ON THAT PEDAL AS FAR AS IT WILL GO. DO YOU UNDERSTAND ME, LANCE CORPORAL WILKINS? I turned to him, shouting as he tried to stay calm and listen at the same time. He was only eighteen; he had gotten out of boot camp just two months before he received orders to go to Iraq. He took his eyes off the road for about five seconds and we made eye contact for what seemed like hours. He looked like a little boy. My other marines were all ready to fight, guns positioned for combat, but LCPL Wilkins was flustered. I could see the fear in his eyes. He was so scared; I could hear the cracking in his voice. I remember looking at his white knuckles gripping the steering wheel, his helmet bouncing up and down on his dirt-stained pale skin. He looked so young. He hadn't been trained to do this job. I put him there. We somehow managed to outrun the enemy fire before anyone got hurt, but our vehicle had picked up so much speed and one of the tires got punctured by a bullet, so when Wilkins turned left the Humvee spun out of control and flipped into a ditch. Time stood still as I watched LCPL Wilkins' hands get ripped off the steering wheel from the force of the flipping Humvee. The accident only lasted for about one minute, but it felt like forever as we were jerked from side to side and tossed inside the vehicle. At one point during the accident, I remember feeling completely safe and calm, as if someone were holding me in a comforting embrace. After flipping several times, we came to a perfect stop, landing on the driver's side. As much madness had just happened, it was miraculously quiet when the vehicle stopped rolling. They say I was unconscious for about a minute before I sprang up, gasping for air and picking shards of glass from my face. One of my arms was dangling out of the window, covered in broken glass, and my body was leaning over onto the driver's side. I woke to two of my other marines shouting in the background. SERGEANT BARNES! SERGEANT BARNES! I remember thinking, even in that moment, that this was serious, because they hadn't called me by my real name in weeks. I looked over to see the lower half of LCPL Wilkins' body lying limply on the driver's seat, one hand resting on top of the steering wheel, all full of blood. I couldn't see his top half because it was out the window and under the vehicle. The two conscious marines and I maneuvered our way out of the Humvee, jumping out of the passenger side and falling even deeper in the sandy ditch. Adrenaline took over our bodies as we counted to three and pushed the Humvee upright. LCPL Wilkins' body was still hanging out the window. He looked like all the life had been sucked out of him. He was just dangling there. That is the image that I see in my head every day, Abby. Every day. It is not something that time can erase. I pulled his body out of the vehicle and rested him on his back. I tried to save him; that is what we were trained to do. But it was too late; he didn't budge. I pulled his helmet off and rested his head gently on a pillow I made out of the sand. When I pulled his helmet close to my chest, something fell out onto my lap. It was a photo of LCPL Wilkins and his mom. He was standing tall and proud in his dress blues at boot camp graduation, his lanky arm wrapped around his mom, her smile beaming with pride and love as she looked up to him. That is another image that replays itself in my mind all the time. My other two marines did a decent job at reviving the three others, but none of us will ever be the

same. CPL Watson went home with no feeling below his
waist, and LCPL Ryan lost an arm and had a concussion.
CPL Ericson got so much glass in his left eye that he lost his
vision in that eye forever. I walked away from the accident.
Everyone says that I am the lucky one, but there is nothing
lucky about this. I have to live with these haunting images
forever. I can't do it anymore. I can't keep imagining the
look on LCPL Wilkins' mother's face when she was told the
news that her son was dead. All because I wanted to rest
my eyes for a few minutes. There is no medicine or therapy
that will be able to take this pain away. I know that some
will say it is selfish that I took my life, but I know this is
for the better. I hope you understand. I'm sorry, Abby. You
will be better off without me. I love you always and forever.

By the time I finish reading the letter for the third time, it's covered in splatters of teardrops. I wave the paper to dry the moisture and set it on the nightstand. *Jason was planning on committing suicide that day.*

I know he has issues from Iraq; I even sat in on one of his therapy sessions. One day, he asked me to go with him to see Dr. Cohen for his monthly visit. I sat in an uncomfortable chair beside him in front of Dr. Cohen's desk. It had been nothing like I had ever imagined a therapy session. There was no comfortable couch; Dr. Cohen didn't have a calming tone in her voice. Every question or statement from her mouth was abbreviated and impersonal. At the end of the session she said she was going to up his dose of anxiety medication. This was after he broke down crying in front of both of us. She just sat there with an icy stare as if she were looking right through him. A grown man crying is obviously a sign that something is wrong, but she just sat there looking at him almost as if she were seeing the exact same patient before and after him. As if she were sitting in a boring movie that she had seen a dozen times. He told her that he panicked when he was in a car, that large crowds frightened him and that he woke up every night to nightmares. She never asked him what happened. I had a bad feeling about that doctor ever since she refused to look me in the eye as she shook my hand limply. It was as if her hand had no muscle; it just hung in my firm grip like a dead fish. It just didn't feel right. No wonder Jason hated going to those appointments. He was better off reading self-help books on his own. I look over at the metal bookshelf in the corner of the room. There are at least a dozen books that should've served as an alert that Jason was in this much pain. *Power of the Mind. How to Move Beyond Your Past. Get Out of Your Own Way. The Time Cure.* I'd just assumed he read them because of his messed-up childhood. I never realized what was really lurking beyond his carefree, fun-loving spirit.

I rest my hand on my belly and feel the baby swimming and fluttering around inside. This is the only thing that has made me feel alive since Jason's accident. Somehow, I feel as though this baby has saved me. I still don't know how I'm going to raise this baby alone if I have to, on my waitressing salary. I've pushed these thoughts out of my mind for the past few months like a snow plow in a blizzard. My desire to see Jason at this very moment is so strong. I gather my things and this newfound letter and head to the hospital.

I race through the reception area and walk through a surprisingly empty waiting room, grateful that I can spend some time alone with Jason. I need to pray for a miracle, to somehow make a deal with God to save Jason.

I've never considered myself to be in shape, as I'm a sloth by nature, but pregnancy makes me even more out of breath when I pick up my walking pace even the slightest bit. When I finally get to his room I practically have to hover over my knees in a resting pose to catch my breath. To my disappointment and surprise, Dale is in Jason's room, sitting erect in one of the uncomfortable chairs alongside the bed. I swear I hear him talking to Jason, but I'm so consumed with trying to cover up my disappointment that I don't question it.

"Dale!" I say in a tone that comes out far too cheerful.

"Oh, Abby. Hi." He is startled and possibly embarrassed. I see him covertly drop Jason's hand, covering up the fact that he was holding it. I'm touched by this but act as if I didn't see. There is no need for him to be embarrassed. He gets up quickly.

"Here, sit," he says as he motions toward the chair closest to the bed. "I was just leaving."

"No, don't leave." My voice cracks as I unzip my giant black purse. "I made some banana bread." I dig through the purse, pawing at loose paintbrushes and containers of makeup, finally settling my hand on the loaf wrapped in shiny tinfoil. I look up as I set the loaf on the side of Jason's bed. Dale looks at me confused.

"Banana bread is Jason's favorite. I know he can't eat it, but I guess. . ." I trip over my words as I realize I sound like a complete lunatic. "I guess I just. . ."

"I understand." Dale slides the chair by the door close to the other side of the bed. We sit on opposite sides of Jason's bed talking about him as if he's a ghost in the room.

I slice the bread with the plastic fork I brought. I've been bringing Jason's favorite foods to him for the past two weeks, but I've been good about keeping it a secret. It allows me to feel some normalcy, and it gets me to actually eat. The baby has been slowly driving my appetite up, giving me cravings that I never had before.

"You like banana bread?" I ask Dale as the first few slices fall over onto the unfolded tinfoil like a row of dominoes.

"I do." Dale looks up, and I get the feeling he thinks I'm crazy and is waiting for me to snap.

"I hope you like walnuts." I pass a thick piece to him. "Jason just always HAS to have it with walnuts."

"I prefer it with walnuts actually." He takes a small, polite bite. "Wow. This is amazing. I see why he likes it." He takes a bony finger and brushes some crumbs off his upper lip.

"Baking is about the only thing that I do in the kitchen. I don't know, I guess it's a stress reliever for me. When I found out banana bread was Jason's favorite baked treat, I started experimenting with all different ingredients—chocolate chips, almonds, raisins. But walnuts always remained his favorite."

I find myself babbling to Dale like I'm in a therapy session. I barely even know him, yet I feel an odd comfort in his company. "Jason has always been the cook, and I've always been the baker. He always told me that he cannot stand the exact science behind baking. That cooking allows you to be creative."

I remember how he'd sprinkle different spices in our meals, always trying to take it up a notch and try to get me to like super spicy things.

"That sounds like Jason." Dale folds the napkin I gave him into a tiny square and sets it on the table by Jason's bed.

I feel myself suddenly fill with jealousy as I realize Jason had a life before me, that he shared his quirks and his personality with others. I grow hot with envy because Dale and Samantha might know Jason as well as I do, if not better. They had more time with him, more years to learn and discover him.

I look over at Jason for the first time since I've been in his room this morning. I take in his face, swallowing every feature and marking, trying to make up for lost time.

"It's funny because I'm the creative one—I'm the artist—but when it comes to some things in life, I like an equation that will end in a guaranteed result."

I think about the irony in this statement and how badly I just want to know that Jason will live and we'll go about our lives. I think about how much I'll appreciate our lives together if he wakes up. I'll never nag him for his friendship with Samantha; in fact I'll encourage it. I'll be the best girlfriend in the world. I'll participate in all of his silly antics and hobbies; I'll get him the help he needs, even if it puts me into debt. I'll make him banana bread every day for the rest of our lives and eat all of his spicy Southern concoctions. I find myself making a deal with God to keep him alive.

"I'm the same way," Dale says. "I love a guaranteed result. I've always been one to err on the side of caution. I think that's why Sam's mom and I didn't work out. She was wild, always pushing the limit."

He slides his fingers through his hair and looks around the room as if he's afraid someone else is in the room hearing his deep dark secrets. Every time I've been around Dale, he's been quiet, not opening up much, so I'm shocked when he mentions Sam's mom. "I think Samantha had a little bit of that wildness in her when she was in her early twenties, but she seems to be turning into her old man over the years."

When he says *early twenties*, I know he's referring to the years Samantha and Jason were married. Part of me has always been intrigued by the mystery of their years together, but the other part of me would rather not know. Now that I know Samantha, my desire to know about their past together has waned, kind of like if you actually see a celebrity in real life and you realize that they aren't as perfect as they appear on television and in the magazines.

"Did you like Jason when you first met him?" I taunt myself with the question.

"Oh boy." He laughs as his eyes drift toward Jason. "No, he was so high-strung and such a daredevil. I was always afraid he'd talk my Samantha into doing something dangerous and that she would get hurt." He pauses and lets out a sigh. "Nobody was good enough for my daughter though. It took a while to warm up to Jason's ways, but once I dug underneath his tough surface, I learned who Jason really was, and I think a part of me fell in love with him as a son."

He pauses and looks over at Jason as if he is part of the conversation. He seldom makes eye contact with me, and for the first time since I've known him, I can see another side of Dale—someone who has a fragile interior underneath that tough surface. I contemplate telling him about the baby, but I'm so afraid he'll judge me. For some reason I yearn for Dale's approval, as if he were my own father. I wonder if Sam has broken the news to Dale, if he can see the growing bump under my flowy maternity shirt. I discard that thought, as most men are oblivious to these things.

"Jason and I are nothing alike. He's so brave in his thinking and the way he views the world. I always play it so safe, and I guess that's what I always wanted for Samantha. Someone who plays it safe. Sounds pretty conceited that I always wanted my daughter to marry someone like me, huh?" He asks me the question sincerely, as if he really wants my opinion.

"No, not at all. I think that's pretty typical. Jason is actually a lot like my own dad in some ways, and maybe that is why I fell for him. I guess it's that whole fly-by-the-seat-of-your-pants attitude that somehow attracted me, maybe because that's opposite of who I really am." I think about how much Jason has loosened up my tightly wound personality since I first met him.

"'Opposites attract' is what they say, right?" Dale shoots up to a standing position and drives his hands into his jean pockets.

"Yep, that's what they say." I look over at Jason and grab his hand, using my thumb to smooth his thumb.

"Well, I better get going." He gives me a nod and heads toward the door.

"Dale?" His name does a back handspring out of my mouth.

"Yeah, Abby?" He turns on his heel, hands still buried deep in his pockets.

"I'm pregnant. I'm having Jason's baby." The words shoot out of my mouth before I can stop them and they are followed by a pause that feels like forever. I sit, searching Dale's eyes and trying to extract his thoughts. After what feels like the longest minute of my life, he looks into my eyes directly for the first time, as a grin rips across his face. "That is the best news I've heard in a long time." He nods and maintains a tight-lipped smile almost as if he's relieved. Then he turns away rigidly and walks out of the room.

After Dale leaves, I find myself excited about this baby for the first time. I slide my chair flush with Jason's bed and guide his slack hand to my belly.

"Jason, this is our baby," I say softly as I hold his hand on the small bump. It's not quite big enough to rest his hand on alone and falls to the side when I let it go. "Come on, Jason. Please wake up for us. If you don't do it for me, do it for our baby. Our baby needs a daddy." I start to cry as I think of the reality of losing Jason. "Please, please, please."

My cries turn into begging sobs, and I rest my head on the side of his bed while holding his hand tightly against my belly. Suddenly I feel a little flicker underneath the spot where Jason's hand is planted. I shoot my head up in alarm and look around the room as if I just saw a ghost. "Jason. Jason baby, did you feel that?" I pull his hand tighter to me as two more little flickers erupt from my belly. "That's our baby. That's our little boy or girl!" I announce breathlessly, as my tears come down harder and faster, a combination of happiness and sadness tangled into one. "This baby needs you. Please, Jason. Wake up."

Feeling the baby kick for the first time makes reality set in. I thought seeing the baby in the ultrasound images was real and amazing, but the baby's movement inside of me has pushed that aside.

The only other time I made a deal with God was when my mother was diagnosed with breast cancer. Before we knew the severity, I begged God to take her cancer away and to make her healthy. I promised God that I would be the best daughter a mother could ask for if he did this one favor for me. Two weeks later, we found out that the cancer could easily be removed with just a few treatments. My mother hasn't had another bout with cancer since, and over time I've lost the appreciation I once had for how easily she escaped what could've been a nightmare. Today was the second time in my life that I made a deal with God, except this time I promised two things in return: to be the best mother and best girlfriend that I could be. I thanked God for saving my mother so many years ago, and I asked him to save Jason.

CHAPTER EIGHTEEN

Samantha

THE ROCKY DIRT CRACKLES beneath my feet as I near the end of my five-mile run. My arms propel my body faster as I pick up speed, stretching my legs as far as they can go while reminding myself to breathe. Thinking of Jason makes me run faster. The combination of sadness and regret lengthen my stride, pushing me harder and faster. With each step that hits the ground I think about a memory that we shared, good and bad. If I had stuck out the marriage maybe Jason would be alive today, maybe I could have tried to control his bizarre spontaneity, maybe Abby wouldn't be stuck with a fatherless child. On the other hand, I was raised as basically a motherless child and I think I turned out fine.

Sunday mornings are my favorite time to run, to loosen the stress built up over the previous week. Just ahead of me, I see one of my favorite sights—Alex is on the front porch of our small ranch. Legs crossed, he is staring intently at the *Philly Tribune* with Chauncey curled in a ball by his feet. The sound of my feet hitting the pavement of our street alerts them to my presence. As if on cue, both of them look up at me. Chauncey stands, wagging his tail, anxiously anticipating my arrival.

"Hi, Handsome." I tousle the hair on Chauncey's head and lean in to kiss Alex on the forehead.

"Hello." Alex pulls me onto his lap, tossing the newspaper onto the floor.

"What makes you think I was talking to you?"

"That's true, I should've known better—always giving the dog more attention than me." Rolling my eyes, I lean in and begin pecking him all over his face, making loud obnoxious kissing sounds with my lips.

"You brat." He gets up, spilling me onto the wooden slats. "You got some mail. It's on the table."

I gather his already read newspaper pages and head into the kitchen, dumping them into the recycle bin on the way. I admire the centerpiece of dried flowers sitting on our round glass kitchen table. I helped Abby pick out the flowers to display in Jason's room. On one of the days that we were just downright frustrated with the boredom of the hospital, we ventured out to the nearest gardening store and purchased a display to brighten up Jason's room. We both agreed that Jason would've wanted something green and natural embracing his earthy side, so we chose green cymbidium orchids surrounded by eucalyptus. We had the florist sprinkle in some blue forget-me-nots throughout the arrangement to symbolize the blue in his eyes. At the end of my trip there, Abby and I broke up the arrangement and created a bunch of smaller ones that we placed all around Abby's apartment. She urged me to take one home.

"Sammie, you've played such a huge role in Jason's life, you deserve to take one home. Please." She had handed me the arrangement as if presenting an award. I wrapped the flowers in paper and created a space in my carry-on so that they wouldn't squish and roll around in my bag.

Weeks later and the flowers still miraculously looked beautiful; they were just starting to crumple and brown on the edges. A few pieces of dried flower were sprinkled on the table around the edge of the globe vase I had placed them in. I grab the envelope on the table and use the edge to sweep the dried pieces into my hand. I take a long look at the green orchid; its red center is staring back up at me. I drop the dried edges into the trash can as I look down at the piece of mail from Wells Fargo, addressed to "Samantha Barnes."

Every now and then I get mail with my old last name, but this time it stings and tugs at my heart. Maybe if I were still married to Jason, he wouldn't be in a coma. I trip over the word "coma." Just the pronunciation of the word sounds odd in my mind. It sounds like he's off on some vacation on a remote island. I catch myself idling on bad thoughts and settle myself into the "now." If I were still married to Jason I would've never settled down with the love of my life.

Tossing all delicacy aside, I tear open the envelope and drop the remaining shreds into the trash. A three-page document unfolds itself in my hands like an accordion. I feel my eyebrows scrunching in disbelief as I scroll down the pages of a life insurance policy. I flash to the bold print that reads **$42,102.52.**

While I had clung onto so many memories from my life with Jason, there was one I had forgotten: He and I had opened a savings account together and tried living on just one of our military paychecks for a while. It had been a lot easier than we had expected since almost everything in our young lives had been covered by the military for those few years. After we started a good-sized chunk, we started to get addicted to saving. For every weekend night we didn't go out, we'd add $100. It started to add up fast and we had loved to see it grow, but after all of these years I had completely forgotten about it. The bank must've had a tough time tracking me down at all my different addresses over the years. And with all of my name changes. I was Barnes, then I went back to my maiden name, and now I am forever Samantha Colton. I'm surprised they ended up finding me at all.

I remember the day I changed my name to Barnes like it was yesterday. A frail white-haired woman named Claire was our Justice of the Peace. The entire ceremony took twelve minutes. I stood facing him, his hands held by my sweaty grip as some stranger legally bound our lives. He was wearing cargo shorts, and a green military T-shirt peeked out of his button-down pale blue short-sleeved shirt. I was wearing jean shorts, wedge sandals and a tank top that bordered on being a belly shirt. I remember it being so hot and partially blamed the heat for making such a spontaneous decision that I knew in my gut was wrong. I was too young and too naïve, and I ignored all the signs that stood right in front of me along the way, all of my military friends who warned me to wait. We just had to be together; we couldn't spend another minute apart. *Young love.*

We got married the first time I had visited him at Camp Pendleton. We drove two hours off base to the Justice of the Peace in Fatefall, California. I chalked that up to be a sign, simply because the word "fate" was in the town name. The dry heat made Claire's hair frizz up as she recited some generic vows that I'm sure she used on all of her young military couples. Her two neighbors, both coincidentally having Mexican last names, signed our marriage certificate as witnesses. Instead of running off to honeymoon in a sunny remote location, we went straight back to base to the legal office and filled out all of our paperwork, including my name change. It was as if I couldn't get away from my past life fast enough.

One of the perks of being in the military was that every base was like a one-stop shop: We could process our life insurance policy, power of attorney and name change all in one office. We just signed our names and the young marine behind the desk did the rest. It's no wonder why there are so many young marriages in the military.

I'm not happy that I'm still entitled to half of this sum. Alex and I are well-off, Jason is only living on his disability money from the Marine Corps, and here I am holding the key to unlock probably all of the savings that Jason has while he is in a coma, hundreds of miles away. I made a vow and walked out of our difficult marriage and landed in the arms of my soul mate and a world of happiness, while he was left behind with no one.

I'm still haunted by how easy it was for me to leave on that December day. As fate would have it, our court date fell on December 7, Pearl Harbor Day. Maybe that was a sign that the combination of the two of us was a disaster from the start, one that would leave a mark on both of us forever. There were a few strangers in the courtroom while we made our statements, as if our poor decision had been placed on display for the world to see and critique. I remember seeing an older couple sitting in the back of the room, an antsy toddler tangled between the two of them. The mother kept squeezing the little girl's arm trying to get her to settle down while the father got up and went outside for cigarette breaks what seemed like every few minutes.

While the process of our agreed-upon divorce was simple and went as smoothly as it could have, it was the words that Jason added to his statement that nearly choked me, making it impossible not to start crying. After we both stated that we mutually wanted a divorce due to irreconcilable differences, at no prodding from the judge, Jason added, "Our hearts were in the right place, but the timing was wrong." It was as if he saved up those words for this moment. While divorces are usually filled with hate and anger, he emptied himself of pride and brought a level of humanity and truth to the courtroom that I think made everyone in the room think for a moment. Even the judge's rigid face seemed to soften for a moment as if he had never heard someone present such heartfelt honesty during a time that is usually coated in a batter of hate. I paused, startled by the words that came out of his mouth. When I had looked over at him, as if to question our decision, I saw one lonely tear trickling down his cheek. A barrage of memories from our early days strangled me until my own tears couldn't help but surface. I still wonder if that judge ever thinks about how peculiar we were as both a married couple and a divorced couple.

Walking out of the courtroom that day was bittersweet. I was tangled between the fear of a new beginning and the relief of no longer living with someone I could no longer help. It felt good to give up trying to recreate a love that had died when part of Jason died, but it was also scary as hell to leave the only adult life that I knew.

While most newly divorced couples walk out of the courtroom with battle scars and looks of disgust penetrating one another, Jason and I linked arms as we walked out of the tall columned doors and into the crisp December air. The cold air had felt symbolic of a new beginning for both of us. And that new beginning was celebrated by a few drinks at our favorite local pub. As one last hurrah, the two of us threw back pints of beer and reminisced about the journey we had endured together as a couple and the friendship we would promise to maintain.

"So what was that mushy stuff you fed the judge?" I asked him in between bites of pretzel sticks at the dark wooden bar.

"Oh, well I guess it's just how I feel." His eyes set like stone as he craned his neck to look at me. It was the first time in months that he said alluded to any emotion still inside there. Even behind the deadpan stare, it was hope that he was still capable of feelings. "Oh, and about our savings account. You can have it. I don't need it." He had looked down at his worn jeans and faded sweatshirt. "I don't exactly need a lot of money to live on,." he said with a wink.

"But Jason, that account was your idea, and you did most of the work saving. If it had been up to me, I would've used that money to buy stuff or go on a vacation. You were always so good about saving."

"Don't worry about it," he said as he snapped his front teeth into a pretzel stick. I didn't want to push it, so I changed the subject. Several beers later and a couple of games of competitive pool, we stumbled to our separate places, never to discuss those emotions again. We had agreed that I would stay in our apartment and he with a new friend. Compared to most, it was a clean split, but we both knew there was unfinished business between us. While we never discussed it again, I had a strong sense that he wasn't telling me something.

Chapter Nineteen

Abby

MY EMOTIONS ARE LIKE a creaky roller coaster ride, dipping and accelerating, jolting side to side. I've always been temperamental, but the pregnancy is making everything double. When I'm sad, I'm twice as sad; when I'm angry I feel as if I'm going to bust out of my skin. The other day, I left the grocery store before I was done shopping because I was so angry with a sweet little old lady who accidentally hit my heels with her cart in the canned vegetable aisle. I fully admit that I'm a monster as a pregnant woman. The restaurant has been my saving grace. Now that we're in the busy months, I don't have a chance to think about anything other than the present moment on my six-hour shifts, as I dance from table to table serving and trying to please the high-end customers.

"Hey, girl. How are you holding up these days?" Elliott gently sets down a tray of empty martini glasses on the stainless steel counter in the service kitchen. After he tosses out the remaining liquid at the bottom of the glasses, he leans against the brick wall looking at me as I impatiently wait for table three's plates.

"I'm okay." I smile with tight lips and look away to hide my pain. Knowing Elliott's determined persona, he will pry my feelings out of me.

"Abs, I know you better than that. Do you realize who's sitting at table four?"

"What, who?" I respond, confused.

"Adam Sandler. Adam Sandler is sitting at one of your tables, you just served him a filet mignon, and you didn't even notice. So Abs, please don't tell me that everything is okay, because I can see it all over your pretty little face that you have a ton on your mind, and that is completely understandable. You can put on your fake happiness for the yuppies that you serve, but you don't need to do it for me. It's okay to be sad, you know." He extends his index finger, circling it in front of my face before pivoting on a heel and sauntering through the two-way doors and into the dining room.

I let out a sigh, my lips fluttering dramatically. I've taken enough Art Psychology courses in community college to know that eventually I'm going to explode. I can only hold so many conflicting emotions in my head about Jason's death before they get the best of me. Elliott is right.

After my shift, I decide to walk around Main Street and browse the local shops. The air is still a little cool as the first signs of spring shine through. I dodge random puddles on the sidewalk while absorbing rays of sunlight to make up for the loss of warmth during the long winter months. Up ahead I see a moving truck and people going in and out of one of the store fronts with boxes and equipment. It would be great if a new boutique or art store moved in to add some variety to the street. As I get closer, I realize that all of the activity is coming from Sebastian's. I pick up my pace slightly to see what's going on. The store front awning has been taken down and the movers are loading the truck up with appliances. One of the movers hefts a dishwasher onto a dolly and moves it up the truck ramp with fluid efficiency. All of the tables and chairs are cleared from Sebastian's, and there are only a few empty coffee mugs left on the counter where the register used to be. The chalkboards remain on the wall, but the word CLOSED is scribbled in place of the daily menu.

"Excuse me. Sir?" I stop in front of the store and peer in at a mover, like a hopeless puppy.

"Yes?" The guy looks up from sealing a box with packing tape.

"Do you know what happened to the café?"

"I don't have any details. I'm just paid to move their stuff. But I will tell you that I heard a rumor that they couldn't manage the rent." He swipes the back of his hand across his forehead to wipe away a few beads of sweat.

"That's terrible!" I shout louder than I intend to. "This was one of my favorite places."

"It happens. I see a lot of these businesses go under because of the high cost of rent. I'm sure another one will move in shortly so you can get your coffee fix." He says with a touch of sarcasm as a shy smile peels across his face. He has dark brown eyes that squint in the sunlight and a few wrinkles that reach toward his temples as he smiles. I catch myself looking at his muscular build and fill with guilt instantly. For the first time in months, I'm looking at another man who is not Jason.

"But this was my and my boyfriend's favorite place." I emphasize the word "boyfriend" in an attempt to make myself feel better for checking out the moving guy. I realize too late that I sound like I'm whining.

"Well, I'm sure you and your boyfriend will find plenty of other places to frequent. There are always new restaurants popping up on this street." He tosses a box onto the back of the truck with the slightest bit of effort and heads back in for the rest. I take a few deep breaths and watch as Sebastian's Café closes. I walk away somber, as if I'm leaving another part of my life behind.

"Hey!"

I turn around to the voice shouting behind me.

"You want this?" The moving guy hands me a coffee mug that says *Sebastian's Café* in cursive across the front of it. "You know, as a souvenir or something."

"Yeah, that would be great. Thanks." I take the mug in my hand and outline the rim with my thumb.

"I would've given you another for your boyfriend, but it looks like there was only one with the name on it left behind." He holds my stare for a little while as if he knows exactly what's going on in my life. As if he can sense my pain.

"That's okay," I say as I turn on my heel and lift the cup into a "cheers" gesture.

CHAPTER TWENTY

Samantha

I CONSIDER MYSELF LUCKY when I compare myself to other travelers who commute into Philly for work. Our home is just far enough away from the city: Not too daunting of a commute, just long enough to daydream without having to sit in overwhelming traffic. We refuse to conform to the suburban culture, but we also refuse to live right smack dab in the city, so we recently purchased a small ranch that was built in the '80s in Reading, Pennsylvania. It doesn't have the large yard that we always dreamed of, but not having to spend my summer weekends doing yard work certainly makes up for that loss.

I've become so used to my commute that I seem to make it home without even thinking about the route. My obsession with audio self-help books also helps to pass the time. I'm ridiculously obsessed with self-help books, magazines and websites. Alex goes along with my obsession and orders me a subscription to *Psychology Today* for my birthday every year. He mocks the magazine covers' headings every month when they arrive in the mail, but I continually find them moved on the bathroom magazine rack and pages dog-eared.

Approaching my street, I interrupt the author's words on *Teaching your Mind to Think Happy Thoughts* and press "stop" on the CD player. Since we are the last house on the right, I usually spend the last stretch of my commute waving to the neighbors and dogs that inhabit our quaint little neighborhood; however, now that we are in the midst of winter, my street is sullen and quiet. My eyes dart to the bright green Camaro parked at an angle in my driveway.

"What the hell?" I say under my breath, right before it all clicks into place. I pull up in front of the house, park in front of a "No Parking" sign, push open the car door and march up the pathway leading to the front porch. Emma Jane is sitting on my front steps, a cigarette dangling out the side of her bright red lips, leaning back on the heels of her hands. Her legs are outstretched and crossed as if she's completely at home on my front porch. One pink leopard print peep-toe pump dangles over the other, revealing bright red toenails with tiny silver specks. The temperature is in the teens, yet she's dressed like she's going to a summer party.

Leaned up against the Camaro is her latest fling. He spits into a Coke can and looks me up and down with two beady brown eyes. He wears a torn jean jacket with several patches sewn on in a poor attempt at covering the holes up.

"Emma Jane? What on earth are you doing here?"

"Oh, Samantha, I think we both know the answer to that."

"Actually, Emma Jane, I don't know why you're here. Please enlighten me."

I can't help but hear the sound of spit hitting the bottom of a can and peer over at her boyfriend, his dirty Timberland boot grinding into the grass at the edge of the driveway. He grips a beer can in one hand, faded tattoos winding up the saggy skin on his forearm. I can't fully make out the colored images of the tattoos, but I can clearly see the spider web in black ink, enveloping his pointy elbow. I vaguely remember a Security Police friend of mine in the Air Force saying that the spider web tattoo symbolizes time in prison. He looks up and smiles, chewing tobacco seeping out from between his gritty yellow teeth.

"You have something that belongs to me, Samantha." Emma Jane stands up adjusting her high-waisted jeans.

"How did you even find me, and why are you here? Did you drive down here from New Hampshire while your son is in the hospital?" While Philadelphia isn't across the country from New Hampshire, it's certainly not just a town away.

"I have my ways. I want the money that I deserve, Samantha. Jason is my son; you were nothing but an ex-wife to him." She steps forward in one long stride, crossing her arms over her chest. She gets so close to my face that I can smell her sunless tanner wafting off her skin. Even though it is Emma Jane being her ignorant self, her words sting all the same.

"I'm guessing you are referring to my and Jason's money." I focus on the smudged mascara that is crammed into her deeply etched under-eye wrinkles as I attempt a deep breath.

"Damn right I am. That money belongs to me." Her voice rises at the end, emphasizing the word 'me.' "And with all of Jason's new medical expenses, I need that money."

"You're not fooling me, Emma Jane. I know for a fact that all of those expenses are covered through the VA." I don't back down from her, even though her size alone could probably knock me over with one small move. Once my anger starts bubbling to the surface, I am unstoppable. I can see "Mr. Right Now" lurking closer to us. He stands slightly behind Emma Jane, shoulders slouched, exuding his lack of confidence, his baseball cap so low I can barely see his eyes.

"But, but there are other expenses that go with his hospitalization." She stumbles over her words as her eyes dart side to side so rapidly that she looks like a lizard.

"Do yourself a favor, Emma Jane, and get off of my property. NOW!"

"I will not leave you alone until you cough up the money. You can kick me off your property, but you can't kick me off the public street. And you can't stop me from getting what is rightfully mine!"

As if her image isn't loud enough, her booming voice echoes through the neighborhood. I silently thank God that it's winter and all of the neighbors are tucked into their warm homes. If it were summer, this would be a scene, and I would be the talk of the street.

Mr. Right Now wakes up from his meager stance and grabs onto Emma Jane's elbow, leading her to the car as she continues her babbling. Pushing all crudeness aside, for a brief moment I'm thankful for his assertiveness. I can just imagine what this exchange looks like from an outsider's perspective. I'm guessing it is similar to the *Jerry Springer* shows that I used to get sucked into while working the long shifts in the Air Force.

"Let's go, Emma Jane. This ain't over." Mr. Right Now leads her to the passenger side of the Camaro and pushes her in the door, cutting off her words.

"We'll be back." He points one bony wrinkled finger, spit spewing out of his mouth as he speaks. He folds himself into the car, leaning too far back from the steering wheel, and backs out of the driveway without looking. I watch as he rolls over the corner of my yard, nearly hitting the birdhouse mailbox along the way. A loud squeal rings out as they peel out down the road. I watch the bumper, covered in stickers as the car drives off. A band of bumper stickers of various colors clings to the entire back end of his Camaro. One that says *I stop for Hookers* peers back at me.

When Jason and I were in the process of filing for a divorce, I was looking forward to saying goodbye to his mother for good. Although I had still maintained my friendship with Jason, I happily cut my ties with Emma Jane. The woman makes my blood boil. It doesn't even feel right to call her a "woman," as she is more monster than human.

It suddenly dawns on me how she even knows about this money in the first place. There must've been a statement lying around somewhere. I think back to how the hospital gave Emma Jane all of Jason's belongings right after his accident, before they realized his mother was a wacko. I am going to do everything in my power to keep her away from his money. Alex and I are well off and we don't have the financial strain of having children, but this money will never be allowed in the hands of that monster.

Since I had my very first bank account, I'd put little chunks of cash aside with the hopes of having a nice little nest egg for my future children. That nest egg continued to grow like a snowball rolling down a hill, accumulating size over time. I wanted my children to be able to choose their colleges and excel; I had planned for their college to be a hefty expense, but one worth saving for early on.

I had known from the time I was a little girl that I wanted to have babies. It was as if I had this inner need to be a better mother than my own. As young as five, I would sneak out of bed at night to cradle my Cabbage Patch Kids and rock them to sleep. Of course, I never really had to sneak around, as my mother was usually passed out by the early afternoon on weekends. I'd drape an afghan over her limp body on the couch and tend to my dolls for hours. I'd push a chair up to the countertop and climb up to reach the cereal so I could feed my dolls their afternoon snack. I'd fill their bottles with the skim milk in the fridge and rock them in my arms.

I treated those plastic dolls like they were real babies, as if I had this God-given instinct to be a mom. After a while of raising my dolls in the comfort of my lonely little world, my mother began to notice that we were going through milk awfully fast. From then on, I'd have to fake that I loved milk so she wouldn't find out I was dumping it out after it got too warm to feed my dolls. She was usually too drunk to realize that I actually hated milk—I never allowed it to make its way past my throat, spitting it back into the cup during the few meals we shared together.

It was either laziness or something hidden in my subconscious that prevented me from changing that savings account when I found out I physically could not have children. The day I had been diagnosed with endometriosis was one of the most devastating days of my life. Being told I would never be able to conceive was like an athlete learning he couldn't play his sport. Two years ago, after trying to conceive for a year, I was diagnosed with severe endometriosis blocking my fallopian tubes, making it very unlikely that I'll ever be able to have children. After some time, I have accepted the fact that I'll never be able to express my maternal instinct to my own little creation, but the pain still stings every time I see a mom pushing a stroller or a pregnant woman glowing. What hurts even more is when I see unwanted pregnancies terminated or unfit mothers waddling down the hallways of the hospital that I work at every day. I've pondered why God gives and takes things from each and every one of us, and my spirituality has me believing that certain things are "meant to be." But it hurts all the same. Having Emma Jane back in my life resurfaces all of the anger about not being able to have a baby. Emma Jane is so incapable of being a mother, yet she has been given the gift of being able to conceive at least two times that I know of.

She has been harassing me every day since she showed up on my doorstep with her scrawny boyfriend with the prison tattoo. I made the mistake of giving her my phone number when Jason was first in the hospital, in case she found out any news before I did. Most mornings, I wake up to at least two nasty drunken voicemail messages demanding Jason's money. A few nights ago, I'm pretty sure that she actually passed out on the phone, as the message ended with a few snorts and heavy breathing.

Although I want nothing more than to delete anything that has a trace of her voice on it, I have kept every single one of these messages for evidence. It frightens me that they know where we live, which is why I have notified the police. Considering Philadelphia PD has its fair share of crime, they took the complaint seriously, even though there isn't much they can do about it. I made sure to give a very detailed description of both Emma Jane and her boyfriend.

"Sounds very similar to about fifty percent of Philly's criminals, but I'll put this on file in the event that this incident escalates." The police officer let out a humorous grunt when I didn't hold back on my details. I found his response shocking, as I figured Emma Jane and her boyfriend would stand out around here, being the Southern white trash that they are.

Keeping every bit of the Emma Jane saga hidden from Alex makes me feel like I'm living a double life. I just don't want to drag him into this drama that I myself shouldn't even be involved in. I'm pretty sure he is onto me though, as he has caught my angry expressions and eye rolls while I hold the phone up to my ear in the mornings, listening to Emma Jane's angry banter.

"Crazy witch!" I shout too loudly as the dial tone penetrates my ears. Alex is in the next room watching some sports show.

"I hope you're not talking to me in that tone," he snickers as he saunters into the living room, setting his glass down on the coffee table.

"No, it's nothing. Just this new girl at work keeps calling me." I make a poor attempt to hide from the real conversation I was having with Emma Jane.

"Well, is there anything I can do to help? I know I deal with floor plans more than people, but I've been known to be a great judge of character," he says as he wraps his arms around my waist.

"Nah, it's not a big deal." I brush it off. He's clearly on to me, but I'm not ready to fill him in on the saga. I prefer to keep the life I have with Alex and Chauncey simple and quiet, free from all the past drama. I sink into his embrace.

* * *

Courtney strides toward me with a coffee cup in each hand. She presses one of the hot Styrofoam cups into my hand as she slides into the seat across from me in the hospital lounge. I'm a creature of habit, and I demand that we meet at exactly 9:30 every morning at the exact same table. She tries to persuade me to use security to sneak us into the doctor lounge to change things up a bit, but my need to follow the rules stops her in her tracks.

"Good morning, sunshine." Courtney's mouth peels open into a smile, perfectly applied makeup leaving her skin glowing. She is all girl, and I am more tomboy than anything else. She's been trying to get me to wear her fancy makeup products for months now, but I've never felt comfortable in makeup, as if it doesn't sit on my skin right. Maybe it's lack of experience.

"Hey, Court." I lean in to sniff my coffee. "Ahhh, dark magic with two pumps of hazelnut?"

"You got it. I figured we would need the dark roast with our lineup of back-to-back patients today. Did you read the file on the kid who got his foot ground in a bike spoke?"

"Eeek." My face crumples in repulsion. "Haven't had the pleasure of reading that one yet. "What the hell?" A stream of coffee dribbles out of my mouth and onto my shirt as I look up to see Emma Jane and her sidekick at the info desk. I can tell from the other side of the room that the nurse looks stressed; her hands are held up in front of her, palms facing Emma Jane. Before I can organize my thoughts and propel myself into action, Emma Jane slams her hands on the desk and hovers over the small middle-aged woman, clearly threatening her. I've never seen this nurse before, so she must have been hired recently with the new batch that just came on board. They're required to work shifts at the info desk when they first start, to familiarize themselves with the hospital.

"Are you kidding me? Who would give that poor little nurse a hard time?" Courtney says, her neck turned toward the action.

"Emma Jane would! That is Jason's mother!" I stand up, slamming my cup on the table, sending coffee splashing over the edge. I start to march over to the desk, but five steps in I turn around, grab my coffee cup and slam the rest of it. "I'm going to need this!" I spin around and dart toward Emma Jane.

"What are you doing here, Emma Jane?" I grab her by the wrist and pry her away from the nurse, who is clearly frightened by this Amazon of a woman.

"Samantha, I have decided to take things into my own hands. If you don't give me that money, you're going to have some big problems in your life." She pokes a long red fingernail at my face, nearly touching my nose. Nothing bothers me more than when someone gets up in my face, but I try to remain cool.

"The money is not yours. What don't you understand about that?" I stand taller even though I'm still inches shorter than her. I see her lowlife boyfriend hovering in the background, eyeing the young nurses as they walk by. I lower my voice so I don't make a scene. In my peripheral vision I can see Courtney standing to the left, arms crossed in a defensive stance. "I refuse to talk to you about this at my place of work, Emma Jane."

"Well maybe if you would answer my phone calls, I wouldn't have to come here!" she belts out as if I'm not standing directly in front of her. I start walking toward the exit, hoping she'll follow me out of the building. The only person in this hospital that knows anything at all about my private life is Courtney. I take pride in maintaining a private outside life, and I only keep my work relationships professional, always being careful not to cross the line when it comes to gossip.

"Where the hell do you think you are going?" Emma Jane grabs my right shoulder with her hand.

I spin around so fast that I nearly knock her over with one of my arms. "Don't you EVER put a hand on me!" I discreetly look past Emma Jane to the security guard post. Luckily my favorite guard, Officer Walton, is on duty and he catches my eye, sensing that something is wrong. I silently applaud myself for bringing in cupcakes for his birthday last month and for always taking the time to make small talk. I've always felt bad for the guards; they sit there for twelve-hour shifts all alone and bored out of their minds, I'm sure.

"Is something wrong, Samantha?" Officer Walton approaches, walking in perfect military step. He stops in front of us, thumbs dangling from his belt loops.

Before I can answer, Emma Jane steps forward with a fake smile plastered across her face. "Sir, I was just visiting Miss Samantha here on her break." She points a red fingernail seductively at his chest.

"Ma'am, I'm going to have to ask you to leave. This section of the hospital is for staff only." Officer Walton takes a step back, blushing slightly.

I turn on my heel and start walking toward Courtney.

"This isn't over, Samantha!" Emma Jane bellows as Officer Walton moves closer to her in an attempt to block her. She gathers her squirrely boyfriend and is led out the exit.

"What the hell was that?" Courtney takes my arm and leads me back to our table, even though we have gone way beyond our allotted break time.

"It's Jason's mother being herself. She wants his some money that he and I saved up a long time ago."

"Wait, he's technically alive and in a coma and she's already snooping around for his money?" Courtney's eyebrows crinkle up and meet each other.

"Yeah, claiming she needs it for hospital fees for Jason. I think we both know she doesn't plan on using that money on anything other than drugs."

"Wow, that is some crazy stuff. I mean, I knew you guys were close, I just didn't know that you were that close. What are you going to do with the money? Does Alex know?" Courtney's eyes widen into two big blue circles.

"No, I haven't told him yet."

As the weeks have gone by, my worry over Jason hasn't lessened; instead it's become a habit. I consume myself with work and running, and sometimes I end the day with a call from Abby updating me on any changes or progress. Five days have gone by and I haven't heard from her, which I'm sure means she's extremely frustrated. I have argued with myself about whether or not I should fly back out to New Hampshire but have settled on waiting for more information on Jason's progress or lack thereof.

I've researched everything I possibly can on comas and head trauma. I come across one story about a little boy who fell off of a twenty-five-foot cliff and had severe trauma to his head. He was in a coma for two months before the swelling went down and he woke up. That little boy is now twenty-three years old, and he gives talks about helmet safety all over the country. I need any hope I can find to hold on to. I get lost in my laptop screen as the little boy stares back at me. The picture had been taken post-surgery. He has a bright smile plastered on his face as his family and friends stand around him. His mom must've looked at him right as the camera flashed because her head is tilted down toward him; her hand is delicately resting on his shoulder as if she is afraid of breaking him but also afraid of losing him at the same time. I zoom in and notice a tear trickling down her cheek. She was probably so thankful that her little boy survived. I imagine that's the way Abby will feel when Jason wakes up.

The vibration of my phone pulls me away from the computer screen and my heart does a dance as I see Abby's name appear on my cell phone screen. An update. She must have an update.

I stand up and answer the phone at the same time; my body can't sit still and take the anticipation.

"Abby!" I yell into the phone as if I was predicting her call. But all I hear on the other end is sobs and sniffles. "Abby? What's going on? Is everything okay?"

"No. Oh my God, Sam. No, it's not okay. Dr. Bennington has scheduled a meeting for all of us to talk about Jason. He won't tell me anything." She pauses to catch her breath between sentences. "He said he has to meet with the whole family. I don't know what to do, Sam. What if he's telling us bad news?"

"Hold on, Abby. Just take a deep breath, okay?"

"Okay." She obeys me like a toddler being consoled by her mother.

"Now, when is this meeting?"

"It's on Monday. Two days from now. How am I going to wait two whole days?" Her words plead as I'm simultaneously thinking about how I'm going to fly there in just two days. My right hand instinctively rests on my mouse and clicks on my bookmarked airline pages.

"Let's not jump to conclusions, Abby. Jason has made it this far. I'm sure Dr. Bennington has good news for us. Before I get off the phone with her I have my flight booked for the following morning. I've been flying so often I can do this in my sleep.

Based on my experience watching Lifetime movies, it's never good when a doctor has to schedule a meeting with the family of the patient. Abby, Emma Jane, my dad and I all sit around the tiny conference room next door to the waiting room. We dance around our fear by making small talk. Abby's curvy figure is doing a good job at hiding her pregnancy, and I thank God that Emma Jane doesn't seem to have noticed the bump underneath Abby's baggy art shirts.

I slide into the seat next to Abby as something sets off an alarm in my head. "Don't let Emma Jane know about the baby. She'll haunt you forever if she finds out." I lean toward Abby conspicuously as Emma Jane blabs away about something from one of her gossip magazines.

"So how is that good lookin' husband of yours, Sammie?" Emma Jane rests her pointy chin on her palms as bangle bracelets slide down her forearms, creating a clanking sound.

"He's good. Been busy with work."

"What about you, Emma Jane? Any new boyfriends?" I pry, trying to find out where she has been sneaking off to in between her visits with Jason. Abby mentioned that she's barely been here and only comes by for a few minutes at a time.

"Oh you know, it's the same ole thing. Going on dates here and there."

What Emma Jane calls a date is in actuality a one-night stand. She always meets her victims at bars, then after a few shots of whiskey and a couple rounds of pool, she stumbles out the door, clinging to the most desperate man in the bar while slurring promises to them.

"Glad you're staying busy," I say with just a touch of sarcasm. Thankfully our conversation is interrupted as Dr. Bennington quietly opens the door after one soft knock.

"Good morning. I see everyone has their coffee." He peers around the room as we all watch him slide into his chair, eager to hear what he has to say.

"I invited you to this meeting because I want to update you on Jason's physical condition."

I can feel Abby's tension as she adjusts her position nervously.

"It is clear that the four of you are his closest family and friends."

"Jason doesn't have many friends." Abby speaks up, almost as if to defend him.

"Yes, well sometimes less is more." Rubbing his scruffy chin with his index finger and thumb, he gets right to the point. "Jason has severe brain damage due to the accident. The right side of his brain has had a massive amount of bleeding, which has led to damage that is irreversible."

I grab Abby's hand under the table. I can feel her shaking next to me. Accepting my hand, she sniffles and takes a deep breath. "Are you saying there is no good outcome, Dr. Bennington?"

"I'm saying there is nothing more that we can do to help Jason. The breathing machine is what is keeping him alive physically. Jason will not be able to function on his own. I'm sorry. We've done all we can. The most critical point with a brain injury like this is getting the patient care right away. Unfortunately, because it was dark out when Jason fell, too much time had passed before he was found and could get care." Recently we have had other patients that have experienced the same type of trauma and we were able to save them. I had hopes that we would have the same success with Jason. I'm sorry. We did all we could."

"Oh God, no!" Abby rockets herself from the chair. Her legs give out as she melts to the floor. "No. No. No. This can't be happening."

I squat down in front of her, trying to be strong, as tears escape my eyes. I pull her into my embrace, smoothing down her soft black hair. "I'm here for you, Abby. I'm right here." I feel my dad anchored behind us, Emma Jane crying lightly at the table.

"So, what are our options, Dr. Bennington?" My dad's strength takes over, as always.

"In my professional opinion, I would advise you to let Jason go. Based on what you've told me, Jason was a very active young man, and his happiness relied on his ability to be mobile and coherent."

I think back to all the times Jason made me mad because of the stunts he'd attempt. But the truth is, all he was doing was living. He was a free spirit. Far from the typical person who unhappily sat in a cubicle day after day trying to fit in with the "norm," Jason marched to the beat of his own drum. Time didn't just pass through his life; he carved his own way through it, breaking down any of the barriers that make a person conform, like a little boy discovering the marvels of the world for the very first time.

For this reason, I always thought he would be good working with children. He could relate. Like a child, he would focus so intently on the activity he was doing, waving away all of the naysayers and civilized adults, leaping away from the norm. One year we volunteered at a muscular dystrophy camp. It was clear that these kids looked forward to this two-week-long getaway all year long. It was their one time to feel like they fit in, because they were all different, which made them essentially the same.

There was one little girl who was quieter than the rest. Every day she would sit in her wheelchair in the back corner of the auditorium by herself while all the other kids would sing and dance and act out productions on the stage. Every day I would see Jason approach her, inching his way into her mind, hoping she would feel more comfortable with the other kids. I could tell he wanted nothing more than for her to meet friends and gain that sense of belonging. She was deathly shy at first, but over time, I would see a smile slowly illuminate her face when Jason would walk in the room. By the end of the first week, Jason had managed to introduce her to a dozen other kids, and by the next week she was even performing on stage with the others. He took her under his wing and took it upon himself to make sure that she felt right at home.

The two of them were inseparable for the entire two weeks. Jason would push her wheelchair, bustling her between the various activities and taking her wherever she wanted to go. Against the camp rules, he even took her "off-roading" on the nature trails that the wheelchairs were warned against. He didn't think it was fair that the kids who already had the misfortune of having to live in a wheelchair couldn't enjoy the same things as the others. So he formed a group of wheelchair campers. Each day they would spend some time in the arts and crafts room, decorating their chairs with glitter, ribbon and signs, embracing their uniqueness. At the end of each day, Jason would take the parade of colorful chairs out to the trails with the help of some of the other rebellious camp counselors, including me. He made those kids feel normal if only for a span of two weeks, before they had to go back to living their lives as outsiders. That little girl probably still thinks about Jason today.

Chapter Twenty-one

Abby

MY REACTION TO DR. BENNINGTON'S news is like a movie scene. I fall to the floor, the legs I've always relied on to keep me standing give out completely, and I sink, dropping in one gut-wrenching thump. I've never been a victim of hardship; I've always sailed through life dodging the death of family members and managing to get from one phase of life to the next safely. Until now. It's as if all hardship and sadness in my life has been saved up for this one moment, for the loss of my soul mate, my best friend. The man I knew I was meant to be with from the moment I met him. The thought of losing Jason hurts so bad that it can't be real. I must be having a nightmare. I look up as Samantha envelops me in a tight hug. She has become my rock through all of this.

"Why? Why is this happening?" Tears race down my face and drip into Samantha's hair. I'm somehow not embarrassed by this as I'm completely caught up in a sobering sadness.

"I'm here for you, Abby." She smoothes the hair away from my face as if she's consoling a toddler.

"Dr. Bennington. How much time do we have?" Samantha's strength balances out my weakness.

"That depends. The breathing machine is the only thing keeping him physically alive, so the sooner we take him off, the easier this may be. For all of you. I'll let you discuss this in private. Again, I'm so sorry." His eyes make their way around the room before settling on the floor. He walks out of the room, closing the door quietly behind him.

"My baby! If I were here this never would've happened. I wouldn't have let him out of my sight! You girls these days have no idea how to treat a man!" Emma Jane shouts as if she's reciting lines in a play, arms flailing dramatically. As soon as she mentions her baby I instinctively place my hand on my belly, and it's in this moment that I realize I'm going to be a single mother. My baby won't have a father.

"How dare you, Emma Jane! Where were you all those nights when Jason was home alone taking care of his little sister?" Samantha bursts from the floor; the anger in her voice is piercing. Her long legs allow her to make it across the room in two strides so she is face to face with Emma Jane. A protracted index finger pointing in Emma Jane's face, Samantha is making up for never having had a chance to let Emma Jane know how she really feels. Her usually calm demeanor is instantly washed away, as if an aggressive wave has taken it out to sea.

"You didn't even have the decency to write to your son when he was in Iraq. Do you even know when his birthday is? Because as far as I know, you never even sent him a card the entire time I was married to him!"

Emma Jane backs up toward the wall, a mixture of tears and mascara roll down her face.

"You have no idea what it's like, Samantha!"

"What it's like? Your lack of parenting skills? Your obsession with money and men? No, I don't know what that's like…"

"Enough!" Dale loses his patience and jumps up, separating the two of them. "The last thing Jason would want is for you two to be fighting right now." A bright red Samantha, shaking with sobs, clings to Dale..

"Let's go get some air. Abby, you should come with us." Dale extends a hand, helping me up from my spot on the floor.

CHAPTER TWENTY-TWO

Samantha

I WAKE UP THE NEXT DAY to the sound of my dad clinking dishes in the kitchen of his small Cape Cod style house. My room still has remnants of my adolescence. A New Kids on the Block poster clings to the wall over my twin bed. The edges of the poster are starting to peel so I make a mental note to take it down and replace it with something more up-to-date. Another reminder of Jason. The first time that I took him home to meet my dad he made it a point to make fun of my teen New Kids on the Block obsession.

I toss the pale blue comforter off my achy body and make my way toward the full-length mirror hung on the back of the door. I couldn't forget yesterday's news if I tried, as my red-rimmed swollen eyes are proof of the tears I've shed. My throat is dry and scratchy from the showdown I had with Emma Jane. I don't regret a word I said though. That woman is a self-consumed witch. *Thank God for Visine*, I think as I tilt my head back and dispense two droplets into my bloodshot eyes.

"Good morning, Sammie. I hope you were able to get more sleep than I was." My dad hands me a mug of coffee as I plop down at his two-person table.

"You know me, Dad. Nothing keeps me from sleeping." I cup the mug, warming both of my hands. "Once a Marine, Always a Marine" is splayed in red lettering across the mug. I'm sure this was an oversight on my dad's part, but it hits me all the same.

I remember the day that Jason gave this mug to my dad. It was Christmas of 2001. Jason hadn't met my dad yet, and he was so nervous about what to give him as a gift. We had been out shopping all day, hopping from one California mall to the next. At first he had wanted to get my dad some little gadget from Brookstone, but I steered him away from that, knowing that my dad is not the least bit technologically savvy. We had zigzagged in and out of stores as he searched for the perfect gift. Right when I thought he had settled on a golf shirt, he changed his mind again, afraid that clothing was not a good gift for a man to give another man. I had never seen Jason so consumed with what someone thought about him. It was as if he knew that my dad would end up being his life raft through all of the storms he would suffer through. Oddly enough, he settled with this mug at the store on base. I look down at the mug and outline the words with my thumb. Today is the day we say our goodbyes to Jason. As much pain as I am in, I'm guessing Abby's is doubled.

My dad sets down a plate of chocolate chip pancakes in front of me.

"I figured you'd like your favorite today."

"Thanks, Dad." I force myself to eat his special creation for me. Each bite brings me closer to the reality of the day. In less than six hours Jason will be gone. I trip over my emotions as I stare at my plate and think of the day when I envisioned a long future for the two of us. One specific day stands out in my mind like fluorescent colors against a collage of black and white.

The year was 2003. It was my last day in the Air Force. Sitting in traffic on the California freeway, I couldn't have been happier, as it was the last time I would have to creep through the exhaust-filled air while watching my gas light drop and the minutes go by. I promised myself to never work a job where I had to spend so much time as a prisoner in my car. On my way to LA Air Force Base the traffic never bothered me as much, as it gave me time to sip on Starbucks and zone out into my private world of dreams—dreams of a life when Jason and I were out of the confines of the military, when we could choose who to be and what to do without having the stamp of the military tattooed on our lives. The drives home from my boring twelve-hour shifts were always the hardest, as I reflected on the day and realized I had accomplished nothing.

Radio blasting Avril Lavigne, I pulled into the apartment complex where Jason and I had spent the last two years. I peeled off my hat and unbuttoned my top before I had even approached the top step to our third-floor apartment; I was ready to hang up this uniform forever.

"Hi, Sam. How is Jason doing? Have you heard from him?" asked Mr. Baker, looking up from his potted plants in the community garden, eager to talk to someone.

"Just a couple of letters. I hear they don't have much time to write home. You'll be the first I tell when I hear something Mr. Baker." I adjusted the military-issued sack on my shoulder, deciding to stop and spend a few minutes with the retired police officer.

"I remember when I was in the service. I didn't have much time to write either. My wife wasn't too happy when I returned with a pile of letters that I never had a chance to send."

Always moving, Mr. Baker had to keep his hands busy or he would start to go crazy. Most mornings, he could be found in his garage as early as 2:30 a.m., tinkering in his tool box or fixing a bike or toy that belonged to one of the neighborhood kids. He was known as' 'Mr. Fixit Fast' throughout the complex. Kids could be guaranteed that their broken bikes would be fixed by the next morning if they dropped them off before he went to bed at 10 p.m. I was always amazed by how little sleep someone could function on.

"But being in the service yourself, I'm sure you're used to the lack of time they have over there."

"Yeah, that's true." I gave a polite smile as I approached the flight of stairs leading to the mailboxes, thinking about the vast difference between the Air Force and the Marine Corps. I could never get used to living the lifestyle of a marine. Country first, family second.

Even though I hadn't received any letters from Jason in the two months he'd been gone, I still got anxious before turning the key to the tiny metal mailbox that belonged to unit 3B. I tore through the usual junk mail as I walked back up the stairs to our apartment. By the time I reached our front door, I was down to the last piece of mail. It was a lonely piece of cardboard from a ready-to-eat meal package, covered in messy writing that was exposed, too big to fit inside an envelope. I could hear Jason's voice as I read the letter:

Hey Sammie,

Things are really starting to feel like combat around here.
But I guess this is what I signed up to do, right? All I seem
to hear these days is shots being fired. My ears are ringing
now — I hope this doesn't affect my long term hearing. ☺
Last night, all of a sudden the sky went completely black. It
was so dark that you could close your eyes and then open
them and you still couldn't tell the difference. We froze for
about a good seven hours last night. The only thing that
kept me from falling asleep was my uncontrollable shaking,
or shivering, and of course thinking of coming home to you.
I'll tell you more when I get home.

Love you always.
Jason

I lifted the letter to my nose, hoping to smell Jason and somehow
feel closer to him. I was filled with mixed emotions: happy that I
finally had a letter from him but sad to think of him cold, shivering
and in harm's way.

When we'd first gotten the news that Jason would be deployed
to Iraq, I tried my hardest to look on the bright side of things. One
of those things that kept me going was knowing we'd get to write
letters back and forth, just like in the old war movies. The dreamer
in me fantasized about our relationship flourishing through words
and imagination, even though we would be wrapped in two
different worlds. I stood by the old saying *Absence makes the heart*
grow fonder as I spent every day dreaming about our post-Iraq
future together. I never took into account that the world he was
in would change him forever, while the world that I was in left me
feeling swaddled in safety like a newborn. Guilt surged through
me whenever I enjoyed a nice meal in the comfort of our home. It
made an appearance whenever I went shopping and purchased a
non-essential item that would bring me pleasure, knowing he was
making the best of what little he had: a uniform, a weapon and the
camaraderie of his fellow marines. He left with his head up and
turned toward the sky, confidence bubbling out of him like a freshly

opened bottle of champagne. He returned with his head down and eyes darting all over, never being able to focus on an object or a person for more than a minute.

Each day that passed put me one day closer to Jason, but my bittersweet thoughts led me to wonder how he would be when he finally made it back. I had heard stories. Witnessing Mr. Baker's antics alone was enough to scare anyone. Trembling hands, fear of crowds and loud noises. That empty stare? *Once a Marine, always a Marine*—the famous quote that Jason and his fellow jarheads had been told since the day they joined.

"Sammie?"

"Yeah?" I'm jerked back to the present day by the sound of my dad's voice. "Sorry, I was daydreaming."

"Are you ready to head to the hospital soon?" He gives my shoulders a little squeeze and plants a gentle kiss on my head.

"Yeah, I just gotta get changed." I look up and feel the warmth of a teardrop gently rolling down my cheek. It must have made an escape as I was thinking about the past.

"Okay, take your time, honey."

I make my calls to Alex and Courtney to fill them in on everything. Tears make their way into every word that manages to escape my mouth. I scroll through my phone and punch "send" when Alex's picture dances across my screen.

"How is everything going?" He picks up the phone after two rings.

"Well, it certainly could be better." I decide to jump right into it. "The doctor has advised us to let Jason go."

"Oh, Sam, I'm so sorry." I don't know if it's the sound of Alex's calming voice or the feeling of finally saying the words out loud that makes me suddenly lose control of my emotions.

"Just like that, someone is gone. Just like that, Alex. How can someone be here one minute and just gone the next? I—I just don't understand." The words manage to escape between sobs. "When my mom died, at least I knew she had been sabotaging her health her entire life. Jason doesn't deserve this."

"I know, honey. It just doesn't make sense." I can tell that Alex feels uncomfortable and doesn't really know what to say, which doesn't surprise me. He's great at a lot of things, but sorting out someone else's emotions is not one of them.

I try to change the subject. "How 's Chauncey doing? Does he miss me?"

"Of course he does. He's been sitting by the door every night, just waiting for you to come home. Every time he hears a car door shut, he perks right up. I actually feel really bad for him; he keeps getting his hopes up."

"Well, give him some kisses for me and tell him I'll be home soon."

"Speaking of, when will you be home? No rush, stay as long as you need to, but we do miss you."

"I'm going to search flights today; hopefully there's something affordable the day after the funeral. I miss you. And I miss our bed."

"Well, regardless of how much Chauncey misses you, he doesn't seem to mind sprawling out on your side of the bed every night."

I laugh for the first time in what feels like forever as I picture Chauncey with all fours in the air on my side of the bed. "Tell him to move over 'cause his mama will be home soon."

"Will do. Love you, Sam."

"Love you too. Goodbye."

I call Courtney next, and repeat all of the details about Jason's condition. I feel a little bit more free to go into detail with her than I did with Alex. While Courtney rarely has a difficult time with words, I can sense the loss of them when she responds with the polite "I'm so sorry" over and over again. Her perky tone is taken down a notch as she tries to console me. The absence of her usual firecracker remarks feels odd, but she knows when to listen and stay quiet, and she knows when to change the subject to elevate my mood. She fills me in on everything at the hospital and assures me that my work is covered for as long as I need time off. It will actually be somewhat of a relief to go to a hospital and only have to deal with broken bones instead of broken hearts.

Chapter Twenty-three

Abby

I WOKE UP FEELING SICK to my stomach. I even dry heaved a couple of times as I was getting ready to go to the hospital. I refuse to accept the fact that I'm losing the love of my life today. I always wondered how people coped with death. I don't know if this is anything I'll ever know how to do. Do you ever get over losing someone?

Since the day Jason and I met in the coffee shop, I've been in awe of him. They say you date the person whose qualities you most admire or whom you most aspire to be like. I've always wanted to be a free spirit, living every day as if it were my last, but until I met Jason, I had such a tight grip on life that I never could.

I can't believe I'm already thinking about him in the past tense, and I feel guilty for it. He always laughed at the strict rules I placed on myself. He always told me artists weren't supposed to be so disciplined. He said I was the most contradicting artist on the planet, but that's what made me so special. I had my daily lists and goals, as if I were in a rush to get such unimportant things done. Why couldn't I just give up a day of cleaning our apartment to go out bike riding with him or participate in one of his million hobbies? Apparently cleaning was far more important to me. As if life won't go on if there's a dust ball in the corner of a room.

By the time I get out of my own way and make it to the hospital, the waiting room is filled with the usual suspects: Emma Jane, Dale and Samantha. I bypass Emma Jane and walk up to Samantha, who has clearly already been crying, which of course makes me lose it immediately.

"Hey. So, this is it." I embrace Samantha in a hug. If I didn't feel close to her before, I certainly do now. It's as if we are long-lost sisters. I completely regret my pestering Jason about their friendship. Regret is something I seem to be having a lot of lately: It wraps around me like a rope, pulling me into the past and filling me with a sense of urgency of what could've been. Now I can see that she only had good intentions in their friendship. She's been the only one who's been able to get me through this.

We take a seat in silence, not making eye contact with Emma Jane or even acknowledging her presence. Samantha's eyes dart toward my baggy button-down shirt that balloons out at my waist as she winks at another attempt to hide the baby from Emma Jane. Luckily baggy clothes are in these days, and my artistic sense of style doesn't make this outfit appear out of the ordinary for me.

One by one we go into the room to say our goodbyes. I volunteer to go last. Emma Jane waltzes back into the waiting room after her goodbye, tears silently rolling down her cheeks. For a moment, I feel bad for her. Losing a child must feel like losing a piece of yourself. When I would tumble or fall as a child, my mother would always come running over to me to scoop me up as if she had the sole power to heal me, like I was one of her very own limbs. I remember the look on her face when I came home from school crying because the mean girls at school picked on me. Her brow furrowed in such sadness it was as if she was more hurt than I was, as if the sight of me in pain was far worse a pain than she could ever imagine for herself. My mother always told me that a mom is only as happy as her saddest child. I wonder if a woman who seems as insensitive as Emma Jane would feel the same way, or if, like a wild animal, she can simply disconnect herself from her child.

"I'll schedule a friend to come pick up Jason's stuff from your apartment. I already have the things he had with him when he got into his accident." She looks at me in disgust before walking out of the room. Without giving me a chance to respond or argue about Jason's belongings, she throws her tacky purse over her shoulder and walks out of the room, her jean pockets encrusted with fluorescent jewels, her behind wagging side to side. And just like that, my sympathy for her disappears. I no longer feel bad for her.

"Don't let her get to you. She won't get Jason's belongings either. She has no business here. The woman doesn't acknowledge her own son's existence his entire life, then she has the audacity to come here sniffing out his belongings like a bloodhound. I guarantee you she would just sell them off anyway." Samantha pulls me in to a seated side hug.

"Will you go in there with me to say goodbye?" I look up at her like I'm a child leaving her mother on the first day of school. "I can't do this on my own."

"Of course." She pulls me up from the chair and we head toward Jason's room for the last time. My steps are slow; my head is down. I can't bear to look up, can't stand to see the pity in the doctors' and nurses' eyes. I'm suddenly taken down by a wave of nausea.

"I'll be right back." I race into the nearest restroom. I make it just in time, as vomit shoots into the toilet, spraying the seat and splashing back in my face.

"Abby, are you okay?"

"Yeah, I think the stress is getting to me." I flush the toilet and head toward the mirrors to touch up my swollen pink face, which is now spattered with tiny particles of the cinnamon toast I had for breakfast.

"Understandable." Samantha pulls out a wet nap and dabs at my face. "You are one of the only people I've ever seen who actually still looks pretty after she vomits. It's not fair."

"I don't know about that, but thanks for the compliment."

The lights are dim in Jason's room. Maybe they do this so family members can weep in darkness. Samantha stands back as I placed myself front and center, pulling the chair as close to his bed as possible. He looks exactly the same as I saw him last, except his head is turned toward me as if to acknowledge my presence.

"Jason, I love you. I love you so much. I will always love you." A tiny little laugh sneaks out between my sobs. "You should see me now; I'm best buddies with your ex." I grab his hand and squeeze as more sobs escape me. "She's actually quite nice. I see why you stayed friends with her." I look back to see Samantha, her face now drenched in tears. "I'm sorry. I'm sorry for fighting with you. I hate myself for it. I can't do this." I look up at Samantha with pleading eyes.

"Abby, this is not your fault. Please, please do not blame yourself. Jason was—is—a daredevil. This was bound to happen. He always threw precaution to the wind; you know that. If he had to die, this is how he would want to go, doing something he loved." She stands on the other side of the bed gripping his other hand, her blue eyes glistening behind tears.

"Damn it, Jason. You've never given us a dull moment. You are one in a million." Samantha smoothes the small section of his short hair that is exposed and leans in, gently kissing his forehead. "Have a blast jumping and climbing things in heaven. I'm sure you'll be looking down laughing at us."

Samantha's words make me cry harder as I think of Jason's silly antics, always risking his life and living so fully, a child in an adult's body. It reminds me of the time he was determined to get me to go sledding in Coughlin Park. He had one of those saucer sleds that spin out of control.

"Come on Abs, sled with me." He had grabbed my hand, pulling my resistant body up the hill.

"I hate these things. They spin out of control."

"You have too tight a grip on life, Abs. You don't always have to be in control," he said as he plopped down on the saucer, making room for me in between his legs. "Just let go of life for two minutes. I promise it will be fun."

"Fine." I had shimmied into the spot he made for me and gripped his thighs. He wrapped his arms around me; his puffy winter coat was like a giant body pillow. For once in my life, I felt safe and free. Digging the heel of his boot into the snow in front of us for leverage, he sent us spinning down the hill. The saucer swirled smoothly and soon we were facing backward, then forward again. Jason's giggles blended with my screams as we spiraled our way down the slick snow and slid across the flat bottom of the hill. When we finally came to a slow halt, the saucer rocking side to side, I was so filled with adrenaline I could no longer feel the frigid air.

"Let's do it again!" I had jumped up, bouncing up and down like a child, my cheeks like icicles from the whipping wind of the ride. "That was so much fun!"

"I told you. Sometimes you just have to let go, Abby Girl." He draped an arm across my shoulder as we trudged back up the hill for another round.

I catch myself smiling as I think about the memory, forgetting that I'm here to mourn, to say goodbye. I get up from the chair, gripping his hand tighter as I embrace his body, shielding him and not wanting to ever let go. I no longer care about being cautious around the delicate machines. I kiss his head one last time, memorizing his face and taking in the smell of his skin. Just when I think I can't get up and leave his side, I'm filled with strength.

"Goodbye, Jason. I will always love you. And I swear I will follow through with all of the promises I made you." I walk out of the room, motioning for Samantha to stay; I just want to be alone.

Chapter Twenty-four

Samantha

AFTER ABBY STEPS OUT OF THE ROOM, I say goodbye to Jason and leave the room for the very last time. This is the second time in my life that I have said goodbye to someone in the confines of a hospital room.

After I had been in the Air Force for only a few months, I received an urgent call from my base commander. My mom's sister was requesting my presence in New Hampshire. Just months after I realized my mom would never change and would continue to break every promise to sober up, she had gotten into a car accident that took her life. My aunt told me the roads had been slick with rain that night, but I knew that it had less to do with the roads and more to do with my mother's shaky hands on the wheel and drunken eyes on the road. She spun out on the road and slammed into a telephone pole head on, luckily not hurting anyone else in the process.

When I lived at home, my biggest fear had always been that she would hurt some innocent stranger when she got behind the wheel. Before I was old enough to realize how unorthodox this all was, I would hop in the passenger seat during my mother's drunken joy rides. At the time, the scent of alcohol and my mother's unsteadiness were all completely normal because they were all I knew. It wasn't until my seventh grade drug and alcohol class that I learned her symptoms were odd and that she had a problem. I was too embarrassed to tell anyone and too scared to deal with the aftermath of her anger, so I just lived day to day as if all was normal and thought of creative ways to keep both of us out of trouble along the way.

Once she got to a certain point of drunkenness, I would hide her keys somewhere she would never be able to find them. Instead of monitoring how many drinks she would have, I instead learned to monitor certain things she would say or do that would reflect just how drunk she was. When she started reminiscing about her younger years when she wanted to be a Hollywood starlet, I knew she had a good buzz on. It was when she started talking about my dad that I had to hide the keys. She would shout, angrily jab her arms in the air, or weep hunched over on the couch telling me how much he damaged us. If she could stay awake long enough during either of these drunken states, she would stumble out the front door and drive around aimlessly. The booze kept her slow and turned her mind to mush so she didn't have the energy to search too long for the keys after I started hiding them. I didn't have to try too hard because sooner or later she would just pass out and forget what she was looking for in the first place. I sometimes hid them in odd places like the freezer or the cookie jar, but sometimes it was so easy that I could simply walk them up to my room, the keys noisily jangling from my hand. The counselor at school had taught us never to try to reason with a drunk, but I had learned from experience that if you wait long enough a true drunk will pass out and fall into a coma-like state so you can get almost anything past them.

Years and years of doing this drove me to flee her presence and join the Air Force. We spoke twice on the phone since I'd left: once when I was allowed to make one of my weekly calls in boot camp and once when I had called to tell her I had received my duty assignment in Texas and would be graduating from training soon. Both times she had sounded hurt and seemed to take on the role of victim, like I had abandoned her. My mother never took the blame for anything, whether it is her drinking or something as simple as burning a slice of toast. It was always the toaster's fault, or whatever other inanimate object she was tooling around with while slurring obscenities.

After her accident, she had hung on for three days in the hospital, just long enough for me to fly home and say goodbye. I like to think she hung on those last days for me, but I can't say I fully believe that. Her hospital room wasn't filled with balloons and flowers, and there was no line of people in the waiting room prepping to say goodbye. It was simply me and my Aunt Kathleen. Aunt Kathleen was mom's older sister, who had basically raised her when their own mother disappeared in her own states of drunkenness. I think Aunt Kathleen felt so bad for my mother since she was so young at the time that she continued to make up excuses for her until the very moment she died. Aunt Kathleen gave up any type of life of her own to raise my mom, sacrificing nearly everything, so when my mom died she was devastated. The room that she passed in wasn't much different from Jason's, which made my mind revert back to that day nearly ten years ago. At the time I was still in training, so I had to travel in my dress blues. When I showed up at the hospital, she was hanging on by a thread. Aunt Kathleen had taken up residence in the room; her cot and belongings were huddled in the corner.

"Hi, Aunt Kathleen." I raced over to her before even looking at my mom's bed, because I knew that once I looked it would be hard to hold a normal conversation.

"Hi, Sweetie. I'll give you some time to be on your own with your mom." She gripped my hands before leaving the room. The sound of the machines served as background noise as I approached Mom's bed. She had so much white dressing on her head that it looked like a pillow was extending from her hairline. Although her head injuries were severe, it was the internal bleeding that ultimately caused her death. I sat in the chair alongside the bed that Aunt Kathleen had been using and reached for her hand. The deeply etched wrinkles on her face and hands were one of the many marks left behind from her years of binge drinking. I turned her tiny, dry hand over in mine so that her palm was facing up. I gently began to trace the line that carved its way from her index finger down to her wrist.

"I predict you will be a Hollywood starlet in your next life." A tear trickled down my cheek as I said the words. "Remember when I was little and we used to pretend that you were the magic palm reader, Mama?" She blinked so long that I thought I lost her, but when she opened her eyes I could see she was just trying to hide her tears. The tears glazed over her eyes, making it look like she was looking at me from the bottom of a blue-green ocean. With her other hand, she reached for my basic training ribbon that was pinned to top of my left breast pocket and squeezed her index finger and thumb over the colorful bar. Her hand went slack and she dropped it on her lap before coiling her fingers into a fist and raising her thumb. I didn't need to hear her words; that was enough to tell me she was proud. It was all it took to send me over the edge into a fit of tears. I had to look away if only so that her last memory of me wasn't one where I was sobbing uncontrollably. If basic training taught me anything, it taught me to keep my emotions under control and fill the mind with a happy place. I thought about running somewhere exotic, somewhere beautiful. I thought about the future and what it held for me. When I finally gained my composure, I stood up and kissed my mother on her pale, cold cheek, her skin already growing cold, and I knew it wouldn't be long before I lost her forever.

"Bye, Mom. I love you. I hope Hollywood is good to you in heaven." I squeezed her hand one last time and watched her close her eyes, as if she had seen all she had wanted in this life and was saying goodnight one last time. I'm glad I had those last few sober moments with my mother, and for once in my life I felt like I had done right by her and made her proud. For once she saw me through sober eyes without her anger and resentment attached.

I grab Jason's hand one last time as emptiness hovers over me like a black cloud. "Goodbye, Jason. I promise to take care of Abby and the baby for you. I'll look out for them the way you've looked out for everyone your whole life. Love ya, kid." I turn on my heels and walk out of the room.

The next few days go by slowly as I stick around to help with Jason's funeral arrangements. A tiny guilty portion of me is happy that I will never have to deal with Emma Jane again after this. She has been playing the "poor, sad mother" role since the doctor gave us the bad news. She never cared about him when he was alive; I don't know why she feels the need to act like she is so devastated to lose him. I don't use the word "hate" often, but I can, without any restraints, say that I hate this woman. I'm growing homesick and I long for my normal life again. I miss my husband and my bed, and I miss occupying my mind with the mundane tasks of everyday life.

The morning of the funeral, I wake up to the clearest blue skies. Sunlight peeks in between my bedroom blinds, leaving a bright yellow line on my blue comforter. The smell of coffee brewing lures me downstairs in a zombie-like state. I've come to terms with the fact that I'm not a morning person. I love my late nights, reading books and watching *Nick at Nite* in bed. I love the silence and calmness associated with a late night. After most of the world is sound asleep, my deepest thoughts surface, allowing me to analyze and question in the silence and darkness of the night. My dad once told me that the only way my mom could get me to take a nap when I was a baby was to put dark blankets over the windows, turning my nursery into a cave. If any light snuck through the cracks of the room, I would wake up instantly crying and beet red, punching my fists in all different directions.

My dad knows me all too well and hands me my mug of hot coffee as soon as I approach the landing at the bottom of the stairs. He lets me get three good sips in before he allows a word to come out of his mouth.

"Are you doing okay, honey?"

"Okay, yeah. Good, not so much." I rest my chin on one cold hand, the other hand cupping my mug as I sit at the breakfast bar. "I just feel so bad for Abby. She really loved him."

"You know what I've always said: Things happen for a reason." My dad stands at the stove, flipping an egg with delicate perfection. "I'm making your favorite eggs if that helps any." He looks back, winking effortlessly.

"Thanks, Dad. Thanks for everything." He strides across the small kitchen in two long steps and scoops two eggs onto a plate in front of me. Two over medium eggs stare up at me like two eyeballs. I cut into the yolks and watch them ooze out like teardrops.

As expected, the funeral is unbelievably sad. The sound of bagpipes alone sends me into a state of sobs that leave me blinded and breathless. It doesn't feel final until they lay the flag over Jason's casket, the red, white, and blue so bright against the somber surroundings. The flag is folded to perfection and handed to a weepy Emma Jane, who is dressed completely inappropriately: A short black skirt sits on her oversized hips, while a zebra print shirt peeks out from behind her bright pink suit jacket. It's clear she has rehearsed her act of "grieving mother" thoroughly, as she falls to the ground in sobs after receiving the flag. Her current boyfriend interjects himself into the scene and lifts her up, walking her back to the crowd of onlookers. She walks in a daze as if she's drunk, hovering over her short, scrawny boyfriend. I wouldn't put it past her to be under the influence of something.

My dad graciously offers to host a post-funeral gathering at his home for the small group that attended the funeral. It was pretty somber as we sat around remembering Jason's silly antics. Emma Jane decided to show up drunk, swaying side to side and slurring the few inappropriate memories she had of Jason.

"I remember when I caught Jason in bed with his high school girlfriend." Hanging onto her boyfriend to steady herself, she retold the story, taking frequent pauses to get her drunken thoughts back on track.

"Emma Jane, maybe you should lie down; it's been a long day." I let her finish the story before pulling her aside.

"Get your dirty hands off of me! You're nothing but a tramp, you and your little friend over here!" She points an unsteady finger at Abby while falling backwards into the tiny wooden table that's serving as a bar. An open wine bottle falls off the table, red liquid splattering all over my father's pale blue walls. Abby grabs my arm and walks me out of the room, trying to prevent any more damage.

"That woman is a monster!"

"She is, but just think—we will never have to deal with her again after today." Abby looks away, tucking her hair behind an ear. "Hopefully."

CHAPTER TWENTY-FIVE
Abby

I LOCK MYSELF IN my tiny apartment for three weeks following Jason's funeral. I am unbelievably tired, which works to my benefit as sleep offers a nice escape from the world. The hardest part is waking up and having to reconnect myself with my sad world. My sleep is interrupted every few hours by a friend or a family member calling to check in on me. I haven't picked up my paintbrush in weeks. Since meeting Jason, I had painted every day because he filled me with so much life and passion. Now I feel as if everything inside me is missing, as if I'm a balloon that has just been deflated of all air.

I toss the covers off as though I'm mad at them. Even though I've washed the sheets over the months, I swear Jason's scent lingers. It haunts me every night when I burrow my face in our shared pillows and blankets. Getting out of bed is one of my harder tasks these days, as my belly wants to keep me weighted down.

I stumble across the apartment and catch myself in the mirror. I'm a mess. My hair is sitting in one big lump on top of my head, making me look like Elvira. I haven't washed my face for days. It would be amazing if I still had any lashes under the clumps of mascara that have been caked on my eyes for so long.

I trip over a box as I make my way to the sink. "Damn it!" I reach down to grab my toe but am stopped by my belly. Dozens of photos of Jason spill from the box and splay out before me. I had put them away after he died, not having the drive to paint his face anymore.

One of the photos stands out against the rest: Jason is standing with his bike in front of Sebastian's Café. He looks proud as he always did in photos, as if he were trying to convey his winning personality to the world. I pick the picture up and stare at it. I'm pulled out of my depression for a few minutes until I realize I'm looking at two of my favorite things that are no longer here: Jason and Sebastian's Café. I lift the lid to one of my paintbrush boxes and lift out one of the vintage brushes Jason got me. Before I know it, I'm lost in my colors and this photo. I spend hours recreating the picture of Jason in front of the café. I feel alive for the first time in weeks.

* * *

Abby

One Month Later

I'm three weeks away from my due date and I feel like a beached whale. The only difference is that beached whales don't have to work and move around, and I'm sad to say that I envy them right now. Every movement takes all of my effort, and I get out of breath just taking one of several trips to the bathroom.

Eliott has tried to get me to stop working and go on bed rest, but I need all the money I can get right now. Early on, I figured I'd have a good nine months to save up, but my rent got raised, my car needed new brakes, and of course there's all of the baby stuff I've been accumulating. It's amazing how many little things a baby requires. If Jason were here, he would laugh at the ridiculousness of it all and insist people back in the day didn't need all this junk to raise a baby. Aside from his stockpile of sporting goods from his various hobbies, he was a minimalist at heart, but I confess I kind of like all of the cute little baby toys and miniature clothing.

If baby decides to stay in there past my due date, I can't blame him or her. I'm not sure if I would want to come into a world where all you have is a single waitress-slash-starving artist for a mom and no father. My parents have been as helpful as they can, but their money troubles make it hard enough on them. I fear that I'm passing down our family's money trouble to the next generation. But I just keep pushing on, trying to move in the right direction. Samantha lives by that motto and has taught me to do the same.

I take a few moments to talk to baby as I lie in bed before starting my day. As I use all my effort to flop onto my side I feel baby tumbling and kicking in my tummy. "It's okay, baby. We'll get through this together." I take a deep breath and hurl myself up to a seated position, swollen ankles dangling from the bed like two raw sausages.

As soon as I saw the baby in the first ultrasound, I decided to not find out the gender. I'm not big on surprises, but I know Jason would've wanted to be surprised, and I feel like I owe him this. He always thought it was cheating when people found out the gender of their babies before they were born—there are so few surprises in life once you're a grown-up, and generations before us managed to survive before technology could tell us. I found my pregnancy to be enough of a surprise, but I have honored his wish, and that makes some room in my conscience. I go about my daily routine of sleeping in until 11 a.m., showering, eating and heading back into work for a double shift. I have begged Eliott to give me all of the extra hours that he would normally give students home from college on summer break. He isn't too happy about how uncomfortable I look and his nurturing nature has compelled him to take care of me between peak hours, but I need the money badly. I haven't even allowed thoughts of day care bills to infiltrate my head, because I cannot handle the worry that will add to my already stressful condition. I have no choice but to live one day at a time.

"Hey, mama." Eliott pops his head into the break room. When he sees that I'm alone, he prances over to me, sits in the chair I've propped my feet on and begins massaging my sausages. One of the bonuses of having a gay man as your best friend is they are great at massages and you never have to worry about them trying to make it around the bases.

"Hey, E." I succumb to the magic that his fingers are creating in my water-filled calves.

"Your doctors better not scold me for allowing you to work when you're about to pop, literally any minute."

"My doctors won't know and I promise I will be fine. Think of the manual labor women did while they were knocked up back in the day."

"Yeah, but those women weren't nearly as cute as you." He winks and springs to his feet, gently setting my feet back on the chair. "I got an interview with a college boy who wants to be the weekend bartender. He's lucky he's cute. I just might give him the job."

"How do you even know what he looks like?"

"I Google all of my candidates, silly." Eliott gives me a wink and twirls on his heel, exiting the break room.

Before I was pregnant I never sat down between peak times because it was always so hard to get back up and in the groove of serving tables. Now, I don't have a choice, as my whole body aches. Breaks have become my saving grace. I plop by feet off of the chair and on to the floor as I slide the *People* magazine that I was reading onto my footrest chair. Taking a deep breath, I get into a squatting position and hoist myself up. In the middle of standing upright, I feel a grueling cramp in my lower belly. I try to stand but another cramp follows and keeps me hunched over, grabbing my belly. This is what I read about in the dozens of pregnancy books that I have sitting on my nightstand at home. I'm in labor.

Chapter Twenty-six

Samantha

I'VE MADE IT A HABIT to take my phone on long runs with me ever since there was a local news story about three women who were separately attacked while running near my usual route. Alex instantly bought me a top-of-the-line treadmill and demanded that I run in the safety of our home, but the boredom of the treadmill began to suck the life out of my runs. I love the sounds of my sneakers hitting the cement, and I live on the high I get from running in nature. After several weeks of convincing Alex of this, he armed me with runner's mace and insisted that I bring my phone with me every time.

I'm startled when I feel my phone vibrating in my back pocket. I use a sweaty palm to slide it out of my fitted running pants. A strange number with a New Hampshire area code dances on the screen.

"Hello?" I question the caller.

"Hi, is this Samantha?" A dramatic male voice asks hurriedly.

"Um, yes. This is Samantha." My voice is out of breath.

"Hi, Samantha. This is Eliott. I work with Abby. She's in labor as we speak. You were on the list of people she wanted me to call. Breathe, honey, breathe." His voice calms as I can hear her panic elevating in the background. "I'm driving her to Brookside Hospital now."

"Thanks, Eliott."

I hear some fumbling in the background as Eliott yells. "Gotta go before she rips my arm off."

Before I can say anything, the dial tone cuts me off and rings in my ear like an alarm clock. As I finish my run and head back to the house, my mind is filled with images. I imagine what the baby will look like, if it will have any of Jason's traits. He always had this old-fashioned desire to have a boy to carry on his name, and for this reason I secretly hope it is a boy. A mini version of him to carry on his legacy. On the other hand, my feminist side urges me to hope for a girl, as she could carry on that legacy just the same. Jason was a good-looking guy and Abby is one of the most striking women I have ever seen, so I'm pretty sure they will have a good chance of having an attractive baby.

I haven't been home to see my dad since Jason's accident, so I plot ways to get up there without interfering with work. Ever since I've been on a Monday-through-Friday schedule, I try to make most of my trips on weekends, and I've built up quite a few frequent flyer miles because of it. I even think of surprising Abby. Another vibration on my phone stops me in mid-thought. Unknown number. Must be Eliott or Abby at the hospital again.

"Hello."

"Hello, Samantha," my least favorite voice in the world whines on the other end.

"Emma Jane. I told you to leave me alone. What don't you understand about that?"

"I'm not leaving you alone until you give me what is rightfully mine."

"Well, I guess you'll have to talk to an attorney about that because I'm not giving you a dime of Jason's money so you can blow it on drugs and God-knows-what-else. Goodbye, Emma Jane."

The second I hang up, I regret not finding out where she is. The gypsy could be anywhere right now: standing outside my house, parked on my street in her dumpy car, or even in the house.

"Shit!" I think about the hidden key. Without anticipating something like this, we'd put the spare house key under the front doormat, one of the most obvious spots. I launch myself into a full sprint until I'm standing at our front porch. When I see that she's not here, I hover over and rest my hands on my knees, catching my breath. "Phew."

I leap up to the front door, skipping steps in between. I tear open the door and peel up the corner of the welcome mat, revealing the spare key. As I lean down to pick up the key and let myself in, a piece of paper flutters down from the door. I catch it with a sweaty hand.

Samantha,

I came by to get my money. I want it by next Monday before I go back to Louisiana. If you know what's good for you, you will hand it over.

Emma Jane

The note is scribbled in the penmanship of a five-year-old. "Please go back down south, where you belong," I say to myself as I unlock the door and let myself in. Chauncey must have heard Emma Jane drop off the note because he's sitting alert at the front door instead of sleeping in his usual spot at the top of the stairs.

"Hey, buddy. Did you see a crazy lady around our house?" He looks up with adoring eyes and lets out a little cry as if to acknowledge my comment. He circles me as I try to walk further into the house. "What's the matter, buddy?" I walk through the house, Chauncey dancing beside my every step. He stops in front of the back door that leads out to the deck, standing at attention. He releases two more loud cries, his lips rippling like a flag blowing in the wind. He raises a paw, directing it toward the door, and looks back at me with sad brown eyes.

"What's the matter, Chauncey Bear?" I pet the top of his head and catch a glimpse of our backyard. Complete disarray seeps into my peripheral vision. "What the hell?"

Before I can stop myself, I fling open the door and step out onto the deck. I leap down the deck stairs, my hands quivering in anger. Chauncey sidles up to the fence, sniffing along the edges. My eyes are led to three big sloppy red words spray-painted like spatters of blood on our brand new white fence: IT'S MY MONEY. A chill sprints down my spine. I used to brush Emma Jane's antics aside, assuming she was just selfish and ignorant, but this time is different.

Before I can get far, the color red stops me in my tracks. All along our wooden deck, red spray paint winds messily along the railing and drips down to the deck floor, like arms reaching for something.

At the bottom of the deck stairs, trash is strewn everywhere, our two cans dumped over and rolled on their sides.

Chauncey continues to trail behind me, sniffing the shredded papers and old soup cans. Some of Alex's old boxer shorts are even on display, torn at the edges and tattered at the waistband. (I had been on a spring-cleaning mission last weekend and demanded that he get rid of all of his old stuff with a promise that he could get a new toy from Best Buy.) Old bills cover the ground, cut in half and laid out like dead soldiers on a battlefield. Chauncey makes it to our old wooden shed before I see him stop dead in his tracks. His body freezes; his shoulders and head lift in one fluid motion while his ears perk up like two bunny ears. His head tilts to the side as if he's pausing to make a decision.

"What is it, Chauncey?" I walk toward him, my anger quickly transformed into fear. I feel like my life has been invaded. Emma Jane and her clan are crazy; there is no telling what they are capable of.

Suddenly a burst of energy jerks through Chauncey's body as he bounds for the shed door. He starts barking like rapid fire, so fast and furious that his bark becomes hoarse and aggressive. His front paws lift, launching his body from side to side. I slowly tiptoe toward him, trusting his instinct. "What's the matter, buddy? What's the matter?" Whispers escape me. I slide my hand across his smooth coat and try to lure him away from the door, but before I can pry him away, a loud crash erupts from the shed, sending Chauncey leaping up onto his hind legs with his front paws pressed against the shed window. I grab him from behind, looking into the window to see a mound of blond hair peeking out from behind the lawn mower. I pull open the deteriorated door, pieces of wood flying off the frame. Chauncey squiggles his way past me, preventing me from going in first.

Emma Jane's two bloodshot eyes peer up at me, days-old makeup smudged all around them. She tries to pull herself up using the metal utility shelf but stumbles backward, falling into a pile of ceramic garden pots, soil spilling out from the cracks in the pots and onto the dirty wood floor.

"You!" She points at me with one long, shaky finger. She leans forward on all fours and pushes herself up to her feet. Blood drips from her forearm from where she landed on one of the cracked pot pieces.

"Where is Jason's money? I want it now." The slurred words pour out of her mouth like a train emptying a crowd of passengers all at once.

"First of all, Emma Jane, you are trespassing on my property. Second of all, I don't have Jason's money, and even if I did, YOU are not entitled to it!" I lie about not having access to it, hoping she's dumb enough to believe it.

"Like hell, I'm not entitled to it. He was my son!" She starts to walk toward me but stumbles on the edge of an old doormat and grasps onto the lawnmower handle for balance. She manages to keep her oversized purse on her shoulder at all times, but it's challenging her balance as she leans to one side.

"Emma Jane. You are drunk. Why don't you go home and get some rest?" *You can never rationalize with a drunk,* I repeat to myself as I recall all the times my drunken mother argued with me over petty things.

"I don't HAVE a HOME! Give me that money and I'll leave!" A far-off look glazes over her eyes and she reaches into her bag. Chauncey stands in front of me, blocking me from moving any closer to Emma Jane. Her hands trembling, she unsteadily pulls out a handgun and aims it directly at me. Before I can register what's happening, I freeze, shock running through my veins. Chauncey leans down into a bow; slow growls erupt in between his barks.

"Emma Jane. Put the gun down. This isn't necessary," I plead, raising my hands like I've seen them do in the movies. Memories flash in and out of my mind like waves reaching for the shore. She's so close that I can see down the barrel of the gun as it moves from left to right in her shaky grip. I lose my breath, but I'm afraid that if I try to gasp for air, the movement will set her off and make her pull the trigger. A stoic expression is planted on her face as if she's somewhere else; her eyes open and look in my direction but appear to be looking through me. Her lips slightly parted, her breathing echoes in my ears like background noise. For the first time, I realize she's actually crazy enough to kill me for money.

"Shut your damn dog UP!" She kicks a piece of ceramic pot toward Chauncey. It bounces across the dirt-covered floor and hits him in the snout, just as he lets out a cry.

"Okay, I'm just going to lean down and pet him so he quiets down." I crouch down, one arm still raised in surrender. "It's okay,

Chauncey, Emma Jane is a friend," I lie, trying to soothe him as sobs erupt from my gut. Besides the brief M-16 training I had in the Air Force, I've never been within two feet of a gun, let alone had one aimed at me. But having grown up with an addict, I know they'll do anything to get their hands on their drug or drink, so I know Emma Jane will pull that trigger if it will get her closer to Jason's money. Chauncey stops barking, but he is still on edge; I can feel it in his rigid, upright position.

"Now where are you hiding the money? Do we need to make a trip to the bank?" She keeps the gun raised, the flab on her arm jiggling back and forth.

"Emma Jane, I promise you that I don't have his money. I never processed it. I haven't filled out the paperwork." I look up as the words come out from between sobs.

"You lying little bitch!" She shouts so loudly that Chauncey jumps.

"I'm not lying, I promise!"

"Well, if you're not lying, why don't we go together and process that paperwork?" She looks at me through crossed eyes.

Suddenly a loud crash explodes from behind me as rotten wood pieces fly in different directions, some landing in my hair.

"What the hell is going on in here?" Alex steps over the door frame and into the shed.

"Alex, leave, just leave. I'll handle this." As relieved as I am to see him, I don't want him to get hurt in all of this. His face goes pale as he realizes Emma Jane is holding a gun.

Clearly feeling outnumbered, Emma Jane takes a step backward, pulling back the trigger on the gun and preparing to shoot.

"Put the gun down NOW." Alex reaches for his side, raising a silver handgun in one fluid motion as if he is a sharp shooter. My jaw drops. I've never seen Alex raise his voice, let alone hold a gun. I can feel the nervous energy wafting off Emma Jane as she starts shaking uncontrollably. She walks backward, dropping the gun to her side.

"Hand it over." Alex steps toward her, his hand extended, as calm as a trained police officer. She obediently places it in his hand. He steps back, directing me to take Chauncey and leave the shed while maintaining his perfect shooting posture, keeping his eye on Emma Jane the entire time. "Call the police, Samantha."

Moments later the police arrive, ready for action. I go over what happened as they document my statement and hear the background story leading up to it. They make the face that everyone makes when they hear the part that she is my ex-husband's mother: "Wow, I thought *I* had some crazy in-laws." The older cop's words sneak out from behind a cough.

Emma Jane is charged with breaking and entering, vandalism and carrying an unauthorized weapon. It turns out that just days ago, she was caught shoplifting but released after she sweet-talked the mall security guard.

"Have you ever seen anyone with her since she's been in Philly?" the younger cop asks as the older one assesses the area.

"Well, the few times I've seen her she was with some guy. I guess he was her boyfriend."

"Sergeant Reilly, can you come here for a second?" His face acquires a look of recognition as he motions for the gray-haired officer to join us.

Sergeant Reilly steps into our circle, his hands on his hips. "What's up?"

"Do you have the images of the Webster Homicide on your phone?"

"Yes." A look of confusion wipes over Sergeant Reilly's face as he scrolls through his images.

"Can you show Mrs. Colton one of the photos of the victim?"

When Sergeant Reilly is satisfied with the proper picture to show me, he turns his phone around so it's facing me, while keeping one eye on Emma Jane, who is now cuffed to our deck.

"Mrs. Colton, do you recognize this guy? Is this the man that you saw with Emma Jane?" The young officer grabs the phone from Sergeant Reilly and turns it so I get the horizontal view.

The squirrelly man is sprawled out on his back in the image. A protruding elbow bends and his slack hand reaches up to his face. His lanky body is wearing the same torn jeans he wore when he was standing by his car, dirty and tattered. The image on his face stitches a mark on my memory, his eyes open and his expression one of shock. In the photo, blood is dripping from the single bullet hole in his chest. If Emma Jane was the one who shot him, she must have been sober at the time, because I cannot imagine the shaky hands that I saw today having such impeccable aim.

"Yep, that's the guy she was with the last time I saw her," I say with confidence.

"Sergeant Reilly, I think we have our suspect."

I turn around to see Emma Jane pouting like a two-year-old in time out, and I can't help but laugh at the sight before me: my ex-mother-in-law handcuffed to my property, her makeup-stained eyes peering at me like a raccoon hiding from a predator.

"You're lucky your husband came to the rescue when he did, Mrs. Colton. There is no telling what she would've done. We see crazies like this all the time. Addicts will do absolutely anything to get their fix."

I peer over the officer's broad shoulders and see Alex reorganizing the disarray in the shed. "Excuse me for a second, Sergeant Wallace." I walk over to him; the gun that he handled so professionally sits on his left hip in a case. "Sooo, what is the deal with the gun?"

"Listen, I know you're not a fan of gun ownership." Alex flattens out the upturned doormat with his foot. "I got it when I was working on the projects that we were redesigning in the Sully neighborhood." Sully is the section of Philly where the junkies hung out. I wouldn't be surprised if Emma Jane had made herself at home there. "Some of the others guys at work had one, so I figured I should protect myself too." He picks up an overturned chair, setting it just right, resting his hands on the back and leaning forward. "I know that I should've told you but—"

"I'm not here to scold you, babe; I'm here to thank you for saving my life." I step over the broken ceramic pots and embrace him in a long hug. "And when on earth did you get so good at handling that thing?" I point to the holster on his hip.

"Well, I've been kinda sneaking out on weekends to take target practice." He leans back on his heels, looking down at me as the truth slides from his lips.

"Ohhhh, so you haven't really been going to the gym on Saturday mornings?"

"Nope. Haven't you noticed this growing?" He rests his hand on his belly and rubs in a circular motion.

"I think I could get used to you being my superhero." I wink and lean in, reaching for his hands.

"Mrs. Colton, could I ask you to make a statement in court?" Sergeant Wallace walks over, interrupting our moment.

"Yes, absolutely."

"I don't think it'll take much persuasion, but as long as you can describe this guy to the judge, the process should be pretty smooth." He holds up his phone, waving the image of Emma Jane's victim in front of me.

After exchanging contact info with Sergeant Wallace, I watch as each officer grabs one of Emma Jane's elbows and hauls her into the cruiser, pushing her giant head down and guiding her into the backseat. As the car is pulling out of our driveway, I can see her flailing around in the backseat like a fish out of water. I can hear her muffled shouts as they drive away, but the only words that I make out are "money" and "mine." I feel sympathy for those officers; I'm sure Emma Jane is going to be a handful in jail. I turn to Alex, who is standing behind me watching in awe, Chauncey at his side, chest protruding and beaming with pride.

"Yep, now do you see why I've kept in touch with Jason all of these years? Because, besides a sister that he hardly sees, THAT is his only family."

Alex dangles an arm around my shoulders and guides me into the safety of our home as Chauncey trails behind.

CHAPTER TWENTY-SEVEN

Abby

I'M NOT ONE OF THOSE WOMEN who has a master birth plan. Until now, I've actually thought very little about the day I'd go into labor and tried to focus on everything else leading up to it instead. I don't feel the need to be in control at all times, so I put all of my faith and trust into the doctors.

As soon as I get to the hospital, I'm wheeled into the maternity ward. During pregnancy, I avoided all books and the Internet, in hopes of staying away from other women's horrible experiences. I simply didn't want to be tainted by someone else's story. Although I don't consider myself a religious person, I wanted my own story, written the way God intended.

The tightening clenches my stomach from all angles, as if the skin on my belly is being stretched to encompass my entire body. The cramping isn't as bad as I thought it would be or as bad as the numerous strangers had told me it would be. I think back to the woman who went into great detail about her labor while scanning my weekly items at the grocery store. *Back in my day, we didn't have those fancy medications so the pain was all natural. When I gave birth to my daughter I thought I was going to die, just die right there, the pain was so bad.* A smile peels at the corners of my mouth as I think about how wonderful it will be not have to listen to these stories anymore. To drink as much coffee and wine as I please and not be continually monitored by strangers, as if a pregnant woman's body is up for public discussion. My smile continues through the pain as I fanta-size about not having to hear *You're carrying low; it must be a girl. You are SUCH a cute pregnant lady.* Looking back, I think being called "lady" may have been my most insulting remark. It makes me sound like a little old frail lady waddling around with a gut.

A cluster of nurses swarms around me. One starts taking my blood pressure while the other demands that I change into the gown that she is holding. They roll me into the birthing room as I try to breathe through the contractions. Eliott's fingertips are starting to turn white because my grip is so tight around his knuckles.

"You got this, girl. Just breathe." He hovers over me and helps the nurse prop me on the bed. I start to take my shirt off, but I'm immediately stopped by a growing contraction that is clenching into a ball in my gut. It feels as if the baby is being strangled by my muscles. "Is the baby okay? Is the baby okay?"

The older nurse waddles over. "The baby is fine. That's just your body getting ready to push your little angel out." She gently pushes me back on the bed so my upper back rests on a mound of pillows, my body angled in a birthing position.

"I'm Jane and I will be here the entire time. Is this your designated labor partner?" She waves her hand toward Eliott, who is standing in the corner of the room, eyes wide and hands nervously tucked in his pockets. I give him a pleading smile. The one thing I didn't want was to have my mother in the room with me. I knew her anxiety and nerves would just put me on edge and make me even more stressed out.

"Yes, I'm her labor partner." Eliott practically leaps toward the nurse, one hand raised as if he's an eager student in a classroom.

"Okay. Your name?"

"Eliott. Eliott Payton." The words erupt from his voice in a nervous slur.

"Okay, Eliott. I'm going to need you to put this on over your clothes, and you must wear this mask at all times while in the delivery room." She looks at him, scanning his restaurant attire: black skinny jeans with a button-down black shirt and a black tie loosely dangling from his neck. "It looks like you two were headed to a funeral, not a birthday." The nurse giggles as I silently push through another contraction, trying hard not to make a scene.

Once Eliott is donned in his scrubs, he stands by my head, awaiting instructions from Jane. "I owe you my life, Eliott. Thank you." I look up at him; tears erupt from my eyes, half pain and half emotion.

"Abs, this is nothing. I grew up with three sisters. Don't worry about a thing. The only thing I'm worried about is—oh, shit! The restaurant. No one is running the restaurant. I gotta call George and see if he can take over!"

Eliott gets permission from Jane to leave the room for a quick phone call. The younger nurse layers me with blankets and starts prepping what appears to be birthing tools.

"I know this is none of my business, but sometimes it helps the delivery process to know the details. Is Eliott your boyfriend?" Jane adjusts my bed so I'm sitting slightly more upright.

"No, Eliott is a friend. A good friend." I hesitate as my face scrunches into another contraction-bearing grimace. "My boyfriend," I catch myself and retrace my words, "the father, died two months ago." Before I can stop myself, I start spilling everything to the nurse in between groans and cries, and surprisingly I find it somewhat therapeutic. "Jason, the father, was in a rock-climbing accident. Over at Heartbreak Park. We fought. I fought with him right before he left and did a risky climb. He died. And I feel like it's all my fault. And now, this poor baby is going to be without a father."

Jane grabs my hand and smoothes the hair that is now melted to my head from sweat. "Don't you think you're taking on an awful lot of responsibility to say that his accident was your fault?" I can tell she's conversing with me to keep me distracted from the pain.

"But it is. If I hadn't nagged him about his ex-wife, then he would've never left in anger."

"Listen, Abby, if I've learned anything from being a nurse for thirty-five years, I've learned that we don't have control over accidents and death. So, do me a favor, at least for the sake of your baby. Just let go."

CHAPTER TWENTY-EIGHT

Samantha

THANK GOD FOR FREQUENT FLYER MILES, because I would be broke flying to New Hampshire so often. This time, Alex has decided to accompany me, even though I insisted he stay home. Since all of the drama with Emma Jane, I've spilled all the details about the past few months.

After gathering our baggage, I spot my dad amid the crowd of people picking up passengers. I could pick him out of any lineup. His spindly arms are anchored to his side while his hands are pressed so deep into his jean pockets that he has probably worn a hole in the material over time. His shoulders naturally shrug upward from the position of his tight limbs. His face is rigid and serious, rooted with a deeply carved map of wrinkles. When he spots me, his face softens and a warm smile carves out of his face as if on command.

"Dad!" I pick up the speed of my steps, my stride propelling me ahead of Alex.

"Hi, hon." He pulls me into a rigid embrace before darting his hand out to shake Alex's. After all of these years, he still relies on the formality of a firm handshake with his son-in-law. Some things never change.

"Good to see you, Dale." Alex leans in, returning the handshake just as firmly and strongly.

"I guess we can both agree that this trip home is under better circumstances than the last one, huh honey?"

"Yeah, that's for sure." I sink into his embrace as he dangles one lanky arm around my shoulders.

"Hey Alex, how do you feel about hitting some balls after? While your wife does her girl stuff?" Dad cranes his neck back toward Alex, who is trailing behind us.

"That sounds like a great idea. I can only take so much obsessing over babies." Alex winks while I lean back and pinch his arm. He straightens his right arm and rotates it backward while grabbing his shoulder. "It's been awhile, though; not sure how good I'll be, Dale."

"Oh, you'll be warmed up in no time, son."

"Says you, the baseball legend."

Back in the day my dad coached little league baseball and had quite the reputation in our hometown. Alex was one of his little leaguers, so from a very young age Alex learned how to handle his impetuous nature on the ball field.

Dad offers to take me directly to the hospital to see Abby and her new baby, but I'd rather take a little while to get settled in and drop my stuff off at his house first. As we file into my dad's front door, the faint, familiar smell of pine cradles me as it always does, as though the Christmas season is continually upon us. I take our shared travel bag into my bedroom and place my clothes and toiletries on the stenciled, pale blue dresser. While Alex can live out of a bag for weeks, I can't stand the unsettling feeling of digging through a bag to get my belongings while on vacation, even for just four days. I like committing fully to my destination.

In the midst of refolding my clothes and setting them delicately on the dresser, I'm startled to see in the corner of my eye Alex, who is standing in the doorway leaning on one sturdy arm, crossing one foot over the other as if he's posing for a cologne ad.

"Geez. You scared me! Are you spying on me?" I joke as I smooth my hands over a freshly folded hooded sweatshirt.

"I'm always spying on you." He saunters into the room, sliding his hands suspiciously into his jean pockets.

"Stalker," I joke, pushing past him to set my water bottle on the nightstand. "Want me to fix you a sandwich or something? My dad always has that good bakery bread that you like," I tease in a singsong tone.

"No thanks. I think I'm going to catch up on some plans for next month's hotel renovation." He pulls his laptop out of his messenger bag. I give him my best pouty face, attempting to lure him away from his work. "I'll only work for an hour. I promise. Then I'll let your dad beat me up on the baseball field while you go do baby stuff."

"Fine, I guess I'll just hang out with my dad and eat a sandwich by myself." I kiss him on the forehead before pseudo-sulking my way out of the room and into the kitchen.

My dad stands with his back to me, one hand gripping the yellow refrigerator door, the other reaching for deli meats. I think my dad lives on sandwiches. As a creature of habit, he never seems to get sick of eating a sandwich for lunch and dinner every day. Sometimes he varies the bread, the meat and the condiments, but it's always some form of a sandwich. It makes me sad that he doesn't sit down with a nice woman for dinner at night. Instead, he most likely eats alone standing at the kitchen sink and leaving a sprinkling of crumbs behind as he looks out the window into the neighbor's yard.

Mrs. Austin, a widow of thirteen years, has lived in the house next door as long as my dad has lived in this house. She's a firecracker of a woman with three grown sons of her own. I know my dad secretly has a crush on her. She's managed to age gracefully, and her preppy designer clothes make her look ten years younger: Even when she's gardening, she sparkles in button-down crisp shirts and perfectly pressed khakis. I always know when she's around because I can hear the clanking of her gold bangle bracelets. Her shoulder-length hair has streaks of gray that somehow make her look young and hip instead of old and gray, and I can only imagine what high-end skin products she uses to give her a perpetual dewy glow on her olive-toned cheeks. The subtle scent of her Ralph Lauren perfume is just strong enough to leave a trace behind. Minus the widowed part, she's exactly the type of woman I want to be in thirty years. I know she's a phenomenal baker, too, because the last time I was home, I discovered a loaf of chocolate chip banana bread tucked in the corner of my dad's counter, wrapped in foil and a delicate red ribbon. As I peeled open the foil I had asked my dad where this secret loaf arrived from, knowing full well he's not capable of baking and wrapping to such perfection.

"Oh, Mrs. Austin came by and dropped that off yesterday," he'd replied.

"Mrs. Austin?" You mean to tell me that the two of you aren't on a first-name basis yet?" "Jane," he'd said coyly. "Is that better?"

"That is better. Now what are you waiting for? Ask her out already." I have pushed this topic for years, and I've made it my mission to continue pushing it.

"She's my friend, and she's not interested. How many times do we have to go over this, Sammie?"

"Dad, you sound like a junior high kid. She's hand-delivering you baked goods wrapped in RED ribbon. Red is the color of love, Dad. Don't you get it? She's obviously waiting for an invitation to dinner," I had scolded.

This time, I survey a half-eaten blueberry pie tucked in the corner. A fork rests on the edge of the cobalt blue pie plate.

"I see that Mrs. Austin has been by with her special baked goods again?" I tease, trying to pry out some details of his life and hoping he has something to spill.

"Yes, it's very good. Try a piece." He brushes me off as if he has no idea what I'm trying to get at. "You've always been a dreamer, Sammie." He shakes the mustard bottle and shakes his head in disbelief.

"Seriously, Dad, it's time for you to meet a nice lady friend, and Mrs. Austin—Jane—is perfect for you. I see the way you two look at each other. I'm not a child, Dad."

He continues to focus on his sandwich as if the task requires his undivided attention. He slides a small plate toward me without looking up and continues his attempt at changing the subject. "I need to tell you something, Sammie." When he finally looks up to make eye contact with me, I see serious eyes peering back at me.

"What's wrong? Is there something wrong with you, Dad?" The words rush out of my mouth in a panic as I jump to the conclusion that he's about to tell me he only has six months to live. My worst fear is losing my dad—besides Alex, he's my only family.

"It's not me, I'm fine—it's just something that happened. Something that I feel like you should know."

I put my sandwich down, suddenly no longer hungry, preparing myself. I unintentionally grip the laminate countertops to steady myself, afraid his words will make me lose my balance. "What—what happened?"

"The day that Jason fell. The morning right before his accident, he came here." He massages some gray stubble on his chin with his thumb and forefinger.

"Yeah, for what, your weekly visit?"

"No, he came over to talk to me. I should have seen the signs, Sammie. I just didn't think he would do something like this."

"Dad, what do you mean? What are you talking about?" His words are sending me into a confusion that I can't control, and it's making me aggravated and heated.

He pulls one of the kitchen drawers out and reaches in for something. I see him wrap his hands around small box, gripping it tightly.

"His behavior was erratic that day. He told me he didn't deserve to live—that it should've been him dying in Iraq. He was all over the place. His hands were shaky, he was jumpy, he just couldn't sit still. I finally calmed him down. I thought he was okay. I thought he was just having a moment, Sammie. I have friends who went through what he went through in Vietnam, and they'd all go in and out of depression and bouts of anger, but they all seemed to recover. I feel like I could've stopped him."

"Dad, what are you saying?" A lump starts to form in my throat, barricading any more words from coming out.

"I don't think Jason fell that day. I think he jumped." His eyes penetrate mine. I can see the various shades of blue that are identical to my own.

"But he always did stuff like this, Dad. He was always doing stunts. You don't think he just fell during one of his stunts?"

"No, Sammie. I don't." The words come out stiff and firm, softened on the ends and in between with a compassionate pause. His long fingers unwrap themselves from around the item he pulled out of the drawer. His palm reveals a suede gray jewelry box. "He gave this to me to give to you. He said to tell you he'll always love you and that you've been a better family to him than his own. I thought maybe you two had just stopped talking because of Abby or something, so I didn't think it was strange that he was giving this to me instead of you."

Before I can say anything, I pluck the box from his hand with my index finger and thumb. As I bend back the top, the hinge springs to life, revealing a thick men's gold band. "His wedding band." I look up at my dad; his eyes turn down in a sympathetic frown. "There's something else too." He pulls a crinkled envelope out of the drawer. "I didn't open it." He hands me a letter opener from a pencil jar on the counter. Only my father still uses a letter opener. I slice through the tightly sealed envelope and unfold a piece of pink-lined notebook paper, tattooed with small writing in black ink.

Dear Sammie,

If I have learned anything over the years it is that there really are different types of love in this world. You were my rock. I was incapable of making decisions without your thoughts, guiding me and leading me. Thank you for being my family and for loving me when no one else could. By now, I am sure that you have met Abby. Isn't she an angel? I always knew you would approve of her. She can be feisty at times, but she is a teddy bear at the core. Please look after her. It may take her a while to warm up to you, but it will be worth it once she does. Once she accepts you as a friend, she will never let you go and that is why I love her so much. She is loyal and faithful. I guess that trait of hers is what kind of reminds me of you.

I told your dad to give you my wedding band. I never told you this, but after we got divorced, I had it engraved on the inside. It is now yours to keep. We'll always have California. I love you, my best friend.

Love,
Jason

The words leave a mark on my heart, like a scar that was caused by a good memory. My dad turns to face the window that looks into Mrs. Austin's yard. I can tell he's trying to give me my space while I take this all in. A fat teardrop spreads onto the letter, morphing some of the words so that they blend together. I pluck the ring from the box and angle it to read the writing on the inside. *Sammie, my rock forever* dances delicately along the inside of the ring. I smooth the ring with my fingertips, wishing it could bring him back to life. I start to wonder how long he had this all planned, but I stop myself knowing that turning the details over in my head will just torture me.

"You were right, Dad." I take two long strides and melt into my father's arms.

"I'm sorry, Sammie. I feel like I could've stopped him," he whispers in my ear, smoothing my hair like I'm a little girl again.

I can't help but let out a giggle. "Dad, you know there was nothing you could've done to stop him. When Jason had his mind made up, no one could stop him." I swipe an index finger under each eye and push the tears out of the way so my vision is no longer clouded. "I guess he's in a happier place now." I curse myself for saying such a cliché. "Isn't that the truth? Remember the time he climbed up the tree in your front yard to get the neighbor's cat down? He had no support, nothing except for a short ladder. I remember telling him he was going to fall."

My dad tucks a strand of my hair behind my ear, trying to soothe the new batch of tears flooding down my face like an angry river. It's the memories that are always the hardest part of grief. The mind allows us to sink back into the memories as if we're watching the trailer to a new movie we'll never have the chance to see.

"But just like a monkey, he managed to make it to the top of that tree. I don't know how he did it. He just kept climbing and clinging to the bark like an animal. He saw in his head that he could do it, so he wasn't letting anything or anyone stop him."

I keep rambling as I stare off over my dad's shoulder and into Mrs. Austin's yard. I stare blankly as Mrs. Austin kneels down on a garden pad to water a coppery pot filled with pink impatiens. Her wide-brimmed sunhat tilts forward as she leans, angling the green stem of the watering can into the flowers.

"The cat was so frightened that it clawed him when he picked it up, but even that cat's sharp claws weren't going to stop Jason from getting it and bringing it down. His arms were all bloody with cuts from that mean old cat."

My dad hands me a tissue. I wipe away the blend of moisture that's now flowing steadily out of my eyes and nose. Somehow talking about the memory is making me feel better about it all. None of us stood a chance in stopping Jason from killing himself just like none of us ever stood a chance of stopping him from his crazy stunts. His determination far outweighed what anyone else thought of him or what he had in mind for his own agenda.

"If he had just used that determination elsewhere, maybe to find the right help, maybe we wouldn't be standing here today crying." My tears come to a halt as I finally take a breath and look into my dad's eyes.

"Jason wouldn't have wanted you to cry over him. He probably would've wanted you to celebrate him and honor him." My dad pulls me in to his chest. I graze my hand along his back gently, his bony structure protruding through his thin, lanky body.

"You're right. He probably would've made fun of all of us for being babies." I take a few deep breaths and lean back against the countertop.

We both turn toward the stairs when we hear a creak on the old hardwood floor and see Alex quietly hop off of the last step and into the kitchen. Although I've never been one to wear makeup, my skin tone and eye color never allow me to cover up the fact that I've been crying. I'm sure Alex senses the somber tone in the kitchen, but I can't hide behind my red-rimmed blue eyes.

"Hi, honey!" I look up with false excitement in my tone. He can see right through it.

"Hello. Is everything okay?" Alex stands behind me and rests his hands firmly on my shoulders as if he's about to shepherd me around the room.

"Yeah, now it is." I look up and embrace his face with my sweaty palms before planting a kiss on his lips.

Alex sits quietly on the living room couch as I reiterate everything I just learned about Jason. He holds my hand and lets me get everything out as if I'm his patient in a therapy session.

"Does Abby know?"

"I don't know yet." I was so consumed with the news that I didn't even think to wonder if Abby knew. "Do you think I should tell her?"

"I don't know. But if you do, I'm not sure you should tell her right after she delivered a baby. You should probably give her a little time to bask in what happiness she has in all of this."

"Good point." I can always count on Alex for a candid answer.

"What do you say, Alex, you want to go hit some balls while this one goes and does her girly stuff?" My dad steps into the entryway of the living room, confidently tossing an old tattered baseball into the air with one hand.

"You bet!" Alex hesitantly gets up from the couch as if he's being forced into a party he doesn't want to attend. I bounce up from the worn cushions and pull him into a hug. "He's going to kick my butt, Sammie," he whispers into my ear, sinking into the hug.

"Just remember, he's a lefty—always aim for his right side," I giggle back a little too loudly.

"Hey, no telling him my secrets, Samantha!"

"You boys have fun and stay out of trouble." I watch my dad lead Alex out the door. Alex clumsily trails behind, trying to balance a bag of equipment on his shoulder. I dig my hand into my deep sweatshirt pocket and pull out the gray box that holds the ring.

Chapter Twenty-nine

Abby

I'VE READ THAT YOUR PERSONALITY sometimes correlates with how you came into the world. If there's any truth to that, this baby is going to always walk to the beat of her own drum. She was positioned feet first and decided to make her appearance three weeks early. Maybe that was her way of telling me she wasn't ready to be thrown into this world.

After the nurses prepped me for the C-section, I didn't really feel much of anything, and since I was shielded from the surgery, I blocked out what was going on below the curtain. I had read about C-section procedures; however, I used mind power to avoid thinking about how they take out my insides and set them on the table in order to get the baby out. Unfortunately, poor Eliott saw enough for the both of us. During the procedure he thought he was going to be brave and take a peek behind the sheet, and the sight set him over the edge. Luckily a burly nurse caught him in time and set him on the reclining chair by my head.

When the nurse rests my brand new baby girl on my chest for the first time, everything in the world clicks into place and makes sense. All the fear I had ever had about not being a "baby person" subsides, and I can't imagine how I ever lived without this pink little bundle. I may never be a baby person, but I will always love this little creation that is a piece of Jason and me. She looks up at me, her eyes squinty and smooshed from the past nine months of being in tight confines. But she is perfect. Her tiny hands are clenched into fists as if she's cheering me on as her new mommy.

We can do this, Mom. All my fears about money and raising this baby on my own escape the very instant she opens her eyes and looks into mine.

"Hello, baby girl. I'm your mommy." I feel free to talk to her during these few moments when we're all alone. The nurses gave me some alone time with her, and Eliott went to the café to get a soda and to try to recover from what he witnessed earlier. I gently smooth out the dark hair that is plastered to her head.

"You're going to have your mommy's hair and your daddy's personality, aren't you, little girl?"

Her petite heart-shaped lips are stained a shade of red, just dark enough to reveal themselves from behind her little round pink face. "You are perfect."

She nestles into my chest. I'm hot and sweaty from the lights in the delivery room, but I don't care. I could stay like this for hours as we melt into one another. "I gotta be honest with you, little girl. I don't know what I'm doing, I don't have any money, and I'm frightened as all hell. But you know what? We're going to make it together. That's one thing I do know." I look her directly in the eyes as if I'm interviewing for a job and she's my potential boss.

"Is it safe to come in yet?" Eliott's head pokes around the corner of the doorframe.

"I think all the blood is cleaned up." I smirk and motion for him to come in with a tilt of my head.

He unwinds his long fingers, revealing a can of Diet Mountain Dew as a look of mischievousness cuts across his face. "I'm not sure if I'm supposed to have this in here, but I know it's your favorite so I couldn't resist."

"Thanks, E. What the heck would I do without you?"

"Well, for one thing you'd probably have fewer chairs in this room." We both look around the operating room and see a reclining hospital chair parallel to another chair that was used for Eliott's collection of ice packs and sugar tablets after he passed out.

"You did great, E."

"*You* did great! Look at this perfect little angel." He leans in, kissing her forehead and caressing her cheek. "Be honest though, now that you know it's a girl, are you a little scared of the teenage years?"

"Well, if she's anything like me, then yeah, I'm scared. I was a monster as a teenager. Then again, if she's like Jason, she's going to be one stubborn little girl."

I think back to the time when Jason simply refused to get dressed up to go out to dinner one night. I had worked diligently for months planning a surprise party for him at Oliver's, our favorite restaurant. The restaurant was more upscale then we were used to, but we loved it so much that we treated ourselves to it on rare occasion. It was his thirtieth birthday, and by that point we had established a solid group of New Hampshire friends together. Out of the thirty I had invited, twenty-five RSVP'd yes. It was the biggest and only party I had ever planned, and I was nervous. I had worked hard to get every little intricate detail right, even incorporating mini skateboards into the centerpieces. The restaurant had a strict dress code, so no jeans were allowed, and since we only went there on special occasions, I couldn't simply tell him to dress up for that reason. I wanted to pull off the best surprise ever. I begged and pleaded for him to wear something other than jeans, but he insisted that if the place we were going to couldn't accept him in what he was comfortable in, then he didn't want to give his money to them.

Knowing full well that everyone attending his party would be wearing their best, I was so nervous they'd think he looked like a fool dressed in jeans and a tattered Pacific Sunwear T-shirt—and even worse, that he wouldn't be allowed into his own party. But there was no navigating his decision toward mine. He was set on what he was wearing, and there was absolutely nothing that I could do to change that.

We managed to sneak by the hostess before she had the chance to give us a disapproving once-over. The surprise went off successfully. All of our friends really expected nothing less on his birthday than stubbornness. Even though Jason never let anyone in far enough to get to know him well, all of our acquaintances could detect his stubbornness from the start. It was one of his strongest personality traits.

After everyone had left and the party was over, the two of us leaned into one another at the dark bar for last call. He asked me, "Why didn't you just tell me we were going to Oliver's so I would dress up?" The words slurred from his mouth from too many birthday Jack and Cokes.

"Ha! Do you honestly think that would've changed your mind and you would've magically put on your Sunday best?" I had laughed, feeling the first signs of my buzz wearing off.

"I just don't understand why we have to dress up in expensive fancy clothes to spend more money at a place to eat. That's society's way of making us spend more money on useless things."

"I know you don't get it, but it's just the way it is, and I don't think us trying to fight it is going to change anything. Some people like to dress up, you know." I pushed his overgrown hair out of his eyes.

"Well, I am me. What you see is what you get." He motions to his now-stained and even more tattered outfit. "If these places can't accept me for who I am, then I don't want to spend my money here."

"Well, they seemed to accept you for who you are tonight, honey. They even let you dance on the bar." I slid the empty glass away from me so I didn't have to smell the green apple vodka anymore. "Now, let's get you home so you can make it to your thirty-first birthday."

Jason's stubbornness was so strong, I sometimes thought it got in the way of him accomplishing big things. If only he could've just gone with the flow sometimes. While he was simply trying to express himself and his rights, that stubbornness blocked him in like he was in a cold jail cell.

"I think you're going to be a natural, Abs." Eliott leans in and kisses me on the forehead and kisses the swirl of dark hair on my baby's head. "So, I know you've been avoiding this for months, but have you thought about a name yet? We gotta call her something."

"Yes, I have, actually." With more confidence than I've had in months, I look up at Eliott, who is anxiously waiting the unveiling of her name. "I'm going to call her Bridget. It means strength."

"I like it. A bit more Irish than I ever imagined for you, but I like it. And I think her mommy is the strongest gal I know, so it's fitting." He looks at me intently for what feels like forever. I see a little emotion start to pass through his steely gray eyes.

"Are you getting sappy on me, E?" I grasp his hand in mine. "You know that you're a guy and you can't blame it on the hormones right?"

"Yeah, yeah. I'm not getting sappy. I'm just so proud of you. Of everything that you've gone through this past year, and how you're somehow still smiling with this sweet little bundle of joy. Your life is just beginning, Abs. And I want you to know that I'm here to help you one hundred percent. It's not like I'm going to have a kid of my own anytime soon."

Sadness washes over Eliott's face. I know he's always wanted a child, but his lifestyle has made that difficult. I think about how unfair it is that some teenage moms don't want their babies and end up raising them in terrible environments, while someone like Eliott, who would make an amazing father, doesn't have the option.

"Well, I couldn't have done this without you, E." I squeeze his hand in mine.

"I gotta get back to the restaurant to check in. Without me or you there, the place has probably already gone to shambles." He winks as he saunters toward the door. He stops and grabs the doorframe with one hand and turns, remembering to say something before he leaves. "Oh, and Abs?"

"Yeah?"

"Love you, mean it."

"Love you, mean it, E." I return the sweet banter that we've shared for years. Eliott is so ridiculously good-looking and so perfect of a man, that sometimes I find myself extremely frustrated that he's gay. His body is smack-dab in the middle of thin and muscular, not swaying too much to either side. He has the type of hair you rarely see on a man: It's black and silky and sweeps across his forehead, accenting his mysterious gray eyes. For years, he's claimed he never goes to a salon, that he trims it on his own when it reaches a certain point on his forehead. His chiseled jaw line and facial structure serve as a perfect home for his full set of lips. Making sure he never looks "too gay," he has a rule that he always leaves just a sampling of stubble on his chin. He looks just masculine enough to fall into my category type without looking like a pretty boy. But if he wasn't gay, I'm sure he'd be tossing the ladies around as if he were playing hot potato.

My C-section has landed me in the hospital for a four-day visit instead of only two. By the time I'm settled into my recovery room, I'm exhausted but filled with adrenaline, introducing Bridget to everyone.

My parents have been a bit worried about me over the past few months, and I'm sure they are still scared about how I'm going to raise this baby on my own, but you wouldn't know it by looking at them. They are both over the moon with joy as they meet their new granddaughter. My mom cries, which is no surprise. My dad shows his love by saying, "Good job, Abs. I'm proud of you." I know they both wish they could help us more financially, but they're stuck in a rut trying to catch up to their past decisions that have left them in a bind. Usually in a marriage, one spouse is better with money, but not in this case. They've both lived one day at a time, bouncing from one big purchase to the next, instead of saving for the future. Still, I know the love they will give Bridget as grandparents will far outweigh any money. My mom has already scheduled weekly dates with her granddaughter, and while she may not be able to buy her a boatload of presents, she'll certainly shower her with kisses and cuddles and teach her things that I cannot.

"Oh Abby, she is just beautiful." My mom plucks her from my arms as my dad hovers over her shoulder. She paces back and forth in the hospital room, stopping to sway side to side every now and then to soothe Bridget's little whimpers. She seems to have the magic grandmother touch already.

I've made myself comfortable in my hospital room, and to be honest, I'm quite scared for the day I have to go home. I'm sure most couples are thrilled to take their new little bundle home and get into a routine, but this is frightening for me. I know I'll have a lot of help from Eliott and my parents, but for the most part it will just be Bridget and me. I'm daunted by all of the little things I have to worry about, but I try to balance that out by simply being thankful that Bridget is healthy and forcing me to approach this enormous project of raising a child one step at a time.

CHAPTER THIRTY

Samantha

I SWING BY THE HOSPITAL gift store on my way to Abby's room. I'm lost in a sea of pink and blue as I thumb through the baby clothes. I still don't know what the gender is, and although I'll find out in minutes, I don't want to show up empty-handed. I settle on a brown teddy bear wearing a Boston Red Sox shirt. If she doesn't like baseball, she can always unstitch the shirt and take it off, maybe throw something pink and sparkly on it.

I lightly tap on the door before poking my head around the entryway to Abby's room.

"Samantha!" Abby's face lights up.

Even after giving birth, she looks beautiful. Her pale skin is touched by a dash of pink on her cheeks, and her eyes are wide and bright as ever.

"Abs!" I take a speedy stride across the room and hug her gently, afraid of hurting her.

"This is my mom and dad. I think you may have met them at the funeral." Abby looks down somberly. I can tell all this recent joy has helped lessen the pain she's suffered with the loss of Jason.

"Yes, it's good to see you, Mr. and Mrs. Jacobson. Congratulations!" I give them a wave as they shoot me back big smiles. If they think Abby's and my friendship is awkward, they don't show it.

The baby is a perfect combination of Abby and Jason. She seems to have all of their best features: her mother's dark hair and perfectly heart-shaped lips and her dad's wide-set eyes.

"Thank you, Samantha." Mrs. Jacobson strides toward me and greets me with a hug. The baby is set in her arms effortlessly, wrapped in a pale pink blanket. "Would you like to hold her?"

"It's a girl!" I look over at Abby, who is glowing and nodding her head excitedly. I stare at the baby's tiny features as Mrs. Jacobson guides her into my arms. "Oh Abs, she is perfect."

I don't admit it, but I'm nervous holding her. She's so delicate and angelic, I'm afraid any move I make could damage her. This is perfect proof that life is so fragile, that it can change in an instant and pull us down a completely different path than the one we originally set out on. I can't take my eyes off her. Jason was meant to pass on his legacy and share it with the world. I know he's watching over us now, with a proud smile planted on his face. He will guide this little girl through life and keep her protected.

"Her name is Bridget." Abby interrupts my thoughts. "Bridget Jason Jacobson."

"I love it. I absolutely love it, Abs." I walk closer to her bedside, scared that any sudden move is going to scare Bridget. She lets out a whimper. I lean down and set her on Abby's chest. "I think she wants her mommy." Bridget nuzzles her face into Abby's blue scrubs and stares back up at her as if she's in the comfort of her home.

"Thank you for making the trip to see me, us," Abby corrects herself, settling into her role as mother.

"I've been looking forward to this day for a long time, Abs. I'm sure you have too."

"Pull up a chair and stay for a while." She gestures toward the black guest chairs lined up along the wall. I slide one of the chairs up to her bed so I'm eye level with her.

As if picking up on a silent cue, Abby's mom walks over and kisses Abby on the head. "Honey, we're going to go down to the cafeteria and get some lunch. Give you girls some time to catch up. Do you want us to bring anything back for you to munch on?"

"No thanks, Mom. I think my appetite is still shot."

"No thank you, Mrs. Jacobson."

I immediately interrogate Abby about what labor feels like. She recaps the delivery room chaos as I listen intently. It turns out that my image of what a woman in labor looks like is very off. Unlike what the movies portray of a screaming, sweaty labor, Abby assured me that while the contractions were extremely painful, they weren't as bad as what I pictured. Although Abby is five years younger than me, I feel as if overnight she has surpassed me in experience now that she has given birth. Now that she has gone through pregnancy, she's been welcomed into a club that I'll never have the chance to be a part of. My sadness is lifted when I see how content and happy she looks with Bridget in her arms. She's holding her so naturally, as if this is exactly what she was put on this earth to do.

"I know you're scared, Abs, but you're going to be such a great mother." I lean over and grab one of Bridget's pink hands that has made an escape from the swaddled blanket.

"Thanks, Samantha. That means a lot to me. I am scared. I'm terrified, actually. It's not just that I don't know what to do; it's that I don't know how I'm going to provide for her. I mean, I have enough hand-me-downs and stuff to get by now, but what about when she starts crawling and walking and needs more living space? My parents had trouble raising me, and there were two of them." I can see the stress building with each word that comes out of her mouth. "I'm trying so hard to try to get in the mindset of living one day at a time, but the reality is this—"

"Abs, stop. I need to tell you something." I pull her free hand toward me, putting a stop to her escalating hand gestures.

"What's wrong?" She stops suddenly, her eyes settling directly on mine.

"Nothing is wrong. That's just it." I release her hand and nervously intertwine my own two hands. "When Jason and I were married..." My throat is suddenly dry and the words come out fast, as if they are racing against one another. "When we were first married, we had started this savings account. You know how frugal Jason was and how little money he needed to live. With the exception of his hobbies, he hardly spent money on anything, and he practically lived off of canned goods."

She nods, confused, her eyes darting left to right as if searching for answers. A voice in my head is urging me to just say it.

"Well, when we split, he told me to keep the savings account. We were both still listed as account holders. I had honestly forgotten about the account, so it was quite a surprise. The bank sent me a statement. I swallow, trying to clear my mouth of the excess saliva that has built up. "What I'm trying to say Abs, is that we have $42,102.52 in this savings account. I spoke with the bank, and while I don't have the power to switch it over to your name, I can open a separate account where I can have monthly sums deposited. I want you to have this money. It's for you and Bridget."

Abby's mouth opens slightly in disbelief, her eyes wide and fixed on my words.

"I know he would've wanted you to have it. I don't need it, and I certainly don't think Alex would be comfortable taking money that was opened up by me and my dead ex-husband." I catch the bluntness in my tone after the words slink out of my mouth. "I'm sorry, I didn't mean to say it like that

"I, I don't understand." Her eyebrows furrow together, joining as if they are one. "You mean, just like that, you're giving me that money."

"It's not just my money, Abs. It's Jason's money too. And I know what you meant to Jason. And I know that Jason would've wanted his little girl to be happy and content. I made a promise to Jason that I would take care of you. He may have been sleeping when I made it, but all the same, I made a promise and I'm going to keep it."

"I don't know what to say. I've never had anything just given to me like this before. I feel like I need to earn it."

"Jason earned it, Abs. And Jason loved you and held you closest to his heart. He never paid attention to finances, so I'm sure he forgot about it. Now, will you accept what I'm proposing so we can move on and watch this little baby girl grow up happy and healthy?"

"Yes, yeah. Oh my God. I just can't believe this

"So, onto business. We need to get you listed on the bank account that I set up. So whenever you get released, we can go down to the bank together." I look down at Bridget, her face nestled into Abby's chest, her hand pressed up against her little cheek as she caves in and closes her eyes and falls into a peaceful sleep.

CHAPTER THIRTY-ONE

Samantha

Four Years Later

I ROLL OVER TO CHAUNCEY lying beside me, his head resting on Alex's pillow. A red and green Christmas scarf is tied loosely around his neck. I scratch his chin as he looks at me with tired eyes, almost as if he can read what I'm thinking. His snout is tinted with white specks of fur and whiskers, making him look wise. It saddens me to see him slowing down; his once agile puppy pace is now a slow swagger.

"Merry Christmas, Chauncey Bear." I kiss him on the top of his head and hop out of bed, eager to peak out the window to see what kind of Christmas day New England has brought us this year. The creaky stairs whine beneath my feet as I make my way down to the second floor landing. I peel open the sheer sage green curtains and look to the ground below. Not a speckle of snow on the ground but I can feel it in the air. The sky is an eerie shade of gray; the holiday leaves behind placidity in our neighborhood streets. The little boy across the street is dragging a new sled down his front steps, eager for a coating of snow on the ground so he can use his new toy. I can understand his excitement for the snow. There's nothing more calming than a white Christmas.

I'm especially excited this year because it's our first Christmas in our newly renovated home. With some urging on my part, Alex gave up working for his firm and dove head first into his dream of starting his own private architecture firm. It's kept him out of the dangerous neighborhoods and let him get creative with helping couples build their dream homes, our own being his first major project. Since the market for home renovations was already saturated in Philadelphia, we decided to move up to New Hampshire, where the trend was just starting to take off. I'm still working as an X-ray tech, but I'm taking night classes and pursuing my dream of becoming a pediatrician. It hasn't been easy with all the costs that go into starting a new business, but Alex has already found a few firm clients. I take pride in being his very first client, and I made certain he had a chance to practice his renovation skills on our house first.

We took several trips back to New Hampshire to shop for houses before we settled on a large gray Victorian in Brookside that was originally built in 1952. The house is in the perfect location, close enough to the small city shops and hospitals, yet nestled on the end of a street in a lot with plenty of trees for privacy. While the process of renovating our own home has been somewhat frustrating, the end result has been well worth it. We knocked down walls, pulled up carpet and updated just about every nook and cranny of the house. The only sign of its age is the creaky hardwood floors. I love the sound of the wood cracking beneath my bare feet as I pad around our dream home.

While Alex spends most of his time in the kitchen or living room, I have made the upstairs front room my little cave of solitude. The room sits at the top of the stairs and while it is small, it serves its purpose for me. A giant window juts out from the front of the house, creating a little reading nook for me. I've placed a navy blue chair angled toward the window, where I read and occasionally get interrupted by the children playing in the street below. On the days that I don't want to be interrupted, I unhook the curtain from its holdback and let it fall delicately in front of the window, blocking out the world. My school books and favorite mystery novels cover the walls on smooth mahogany shelving that Alex built just for me. Some of the books are angled upright, others are on their sides stacked with their titles facing outward, luring me in. I seldom use the small wooden desk that is catty-corner against the back walls. Instead, I prefer the comfort of my chair with my oversized school books perched up on my bent knees.

While I prefer to bury myself in complete silence while I work and read, Alex prefers background noise while he tinkers around the house, which is why I can hear Paula Deen's voice echoing up the staircase from the kitchen. She is confessing her love for butter, as if we didn't already know.

"Ugh, too much, Paula, too much darn fat!" His voice erupts in a loud whisper, blending with the sound of a whisk hitting the sides of a mixing bowl. I tiptoe down the stairs, Chauncey giving away my surprise with the tap dancing of his paws behind me.

"Merry Christmas, handsome." I hop off the bottom steps and hug him from behind. The kitchen looks like it was hit by a food tornado. Flour is speckled in random spots on the floor, and eggshells are shattered on the counters, some of the yolks still oozing out onto the granite surface.

"Did you have an itch?" I point out the flour handprint on the back of Alex's navy blue T-shirt. He cranes his neck to his lower back, twisting his body while still vigorously stirring his concoction in the bowl. A goofy grin slides across his face as he leans down to kiss me.

"Merry Christmas." He drops the whisk and pulls me toward him, nearly spilling out the contents of the mixing bowl. "Merry Christmas, Chauncey."

"Having another argument with Paula Deen I see?" I dart toward the coffee maker.

"Yes! Doesn't she know there are healthier ways to make the same tasty treats?"

"Are there really though?" I pull out a tub of margarine from the side door in the fridge. "While I'm all for being healthy and cutting calories where you can, that melted butter looks a hell of a lot tastier than this processed junk." I point to the TV screen while setting the margarine down by the toaster.

"Yeah, yeah." He rolls his eyes and pours the homemade batter into a rectangular glass pan. I watch as some spills over the edge of the pan and drips down the side of the breakfast bar. I bite my tongue, trying hard not to lecture him on tidiness. He's heard it from me enough, and it is Christmas day after all. "Speaking of butter, what are our lovely guests bringing for side dishes today?"

"Dad is bringing the usual." I generously spread the margarine on my whole-wheat bagel, handing Alex the other half of the bagel dry. While he loves food and flavors, he doesn't use sauces, spreads or dressings on anything. He claims he doesn't like to take away from the natural flavors, but I think the truth is that he doesn't want the additional calories compromising his figure.

"Ahhh, his famous canned cranberry sauce," he says with a chuckle. After a couple of attempts at making a simple green bean casserole, my dad gave up and succumbed to only bringing canned cranberry as his contribution to our holiday dinners. His patience has dwindled over the years, but I think we're all better off for it.

"Yes, but Mrs. Austin is joining him this year, and she's bringing not only green bean casserole but also her famous mashed potatoes." I take a swig of my cinnamon flavored coffee, cupping my New Hampshire College mug with both hands.

"Okay, I guess he's off the hook then. But he better bring me a Cuban cigar."

"Oh I'm sure he will."

Since we moved here, my dad and Alex have been getting together for weekly cigar-smoking sessions while I'm at my Wednesday night class. Whenever I ask what they talk about in their sessions, they both look at me as if I'm asking for the secret password to a club.

I shower and slide on a pair of fitted jeans, boots and my usual red cowl-neck sweater that I wear for Christmas every year. I break up Alex's cooking trance and demand he shower before the guests arrive while I clean up the mess he's left behind.

I look around the kitchen, feeling defeated. It looks as if two toddlers had a food fight. Melted butter dribbles off the side of a plate and onto a cutting board filled with leftover bits of stuffing. Alex clearly made no effort to conserve our flour supply; the white powder is sprinkled on nearly every surface. There's even a smattering on the wall above the stove. While I don't like to complain, since he's a magnificent cook, sometimes I think he intentionally leaves even more of a mess to challenge my cleaning skills. He claims the mess is a sign of his "artistic process," but I think I can only let him cling to that excuse for a little longer before I lose it.

Chauncey licks what appears to be egg yolk off of the pantry door. I trail behind him, armed with the bottle of Fantastik and roll of paper towels.

"Thanks, Chauncey. I'm sure you're just helping me clean, right?" I say as I hip check him out of the way. The smell of freshly baked rolls escapes from the oven, blending with the apple cinnamon candle on the breakfast bar. The smell of Christmas alone is enough to make me love the holiday.

Just as I'm sweeping the last evidence of leftover ingredients into the trash can, the doorbell rings. I give one last glance at our kitchen and family room, making sure everything looks presentable. I straighten some frames on the mantel and give my reflection approval in the mirror above the fireplace before I glide toward the door.

The cool air bombards me as I pull open the front door.

"Merry Christmas!" Mrs. Austin cries as my dad leans in for a hug, nearly dropping the stack of wrapped boxes cradled in his arms. Some of the gifts slide off the top of his pile and into my arms as I lean in for a hug.

"Merry Christmas!" I squeal back, leading them down the hallway and toward our open concept family room and kitchen. Dad delicately places each of the gifts under the tree as if each gift has a designated location. Mrs. Austin follows me into the kitchen as we sort out the side dishes she's brought.

"Where are the boys today, Mrs. Austin?"

"Please, Samantha, call me Jane." She places a gentle hand on my arm. "You know, when you have boys, they always end up going to their wives' families for the holidays. I lost them the day they proposed. Don't get me wrong, I'm blessed with three wonderful daughters-in-law. I just wish I could see my boys more." A glum expression settles on her face for a moment. "But they always invite me over to join, so that is nice."

"Well, you are always welcome here, Jane." I give her a warm smile. I like Jane a lot. She treats my dad well and keeps him on his toes, so that's an added bonus. "I'm sure Alex's family feels the same way. We tend to spend more time with my dad than with his family. Luckily he has a sister who keeps them busy."

I giggle thinking about Alex's high-maintenance sister. Kaylie means no harm and is one of the sweetest girls I know, but drama seems to follow her everywhere. One time it was an odd boyfriend. Another time it was when she invited a group of homeless people over to dinner when she was going through a hippy phase. Her parents always seem to be dishing out money when she hops from job to job, changing careers like the rest of us change underwear.

The doorbell interrupts my thoughts. "Speaking of, that's probably his family now." I swing open the door and am immediately swept into a political conversation that Kaylie is leading. "Tell them, Samantha. Tell them that corporate America is killing us all."

"Whoa, I'm going to sit this one out, Kaylie." I dole out hugs to Kaylie and Alex's parents and usher them to the living room. Before I can finish the introductions between Alex's family and Jane, the doorbell rings again.

By the time I get to the door, I hear fists pounding to the harmony of a little girl's voice shouting "Kissmas, Kissmas!" I open the door and scoop Bridget up into my arms.

"Sorry, she's a little wound up. I think she officially knows who Santa Claus is now too." Abby holds one of Bridget's stuffed animals in one arm and a pitcher of cider in the other arm. "I think I'm going to need some of this today." She raises the pitcher and walks toward the kitchen, followed by her parents, who are holding a sack full of toys.

"Sorry to clutter your house, but Bridget refused to leave our house without her new toys from Santa Claus." Abby's mom motions to the sack that her husband is clearly struggling with.

"She's a demanding little one, isn't she?" I take their coats and lead them to the rest of the guests.

"That's an understatement." Abby's dad drops his shoulder and the sack of gifts spills to the floor, relieving his arm.

"Did Santa Claus come to your house last night Bridget?" I nuzzle her nose and tuck a loose brown ringlet behind her ear. She nods back and looks down at the floor, suddenly shy.

"Well, I think Santa Claus left some gifts for you here, too." I motion toward the Christmas tree. There are so many gifts that they spill beyond the tree skirt and nearly reach the coffee table. I put her down and watch her dig through the sack of pink and purple toys. She takes them out one by one and looks up to make sure I'm paying attention.

By the time I reach the kitchen, Abby has poured us each a glass of spiked cider.

"Gosh, it smells amazing in here!" She opens the oven, making herself at home, inhaling Alex's signature holiday turkey.

"Hey, hey! No cheating!" Alex jokes as he hops off the bottom step, darting toward his creations in the kitchen.

"Yeah, yeah," Abby sputters in a teasing tone before leaning in to give Alex a greeting hug. Since we moved back here, Abby is here quite a bit, and she and Alex have formed a sibling-type bond.

"What, no drink for the chef?" Alex teases as he flicks his hand toward the pitcher of cider. Kaylie joins us, preaching to us about her latest platform.

Abby pours two extra-large glasses and hands them each one. The four of us clink glasses as the parents all make small talk and ogle over Bridget in the living room.

After dinner we all sink into our oversized living room furniture and watch Bridget open up more gifts. She sits at the center of the room tearing through the wrapping paper and intricately setting up her new toys to surround herself with stuffed animals, dolls and books. Bridget is a spitting image of Jason. It's almost eerie when she looks at me with those silvery blue eyes. She has his pudgy little nose and goofy grin too. The only feature she seems to have of Abby's is the dark hair. I can already tell she's going to be a beauty when she's older, and I'm sure Jason will be looking down on her and protecting her from all of those who dare to take her out on a date.

After Bridget is done opening her gifts, she looks around the room questioningly as if we should have some more gifts hidden for her somewhere.

"Oh, I almost forgot. The stockings!" It takes all my effort to pull myself up from the deep cushions. I make a mental note to have everyone dress in Christmas pajamas next year. An elastic waistband would be much more forgiving after a meal like that. I totter toward the fireplace. Stockings cover the mantel and rest alongside the brick. I positioned them yesterday, carefully so that none of the insides fell out. Stockings are my favorite part of Christmas. I get more joy out of the little gifts than the big ones. I hand out a stocking to each guest, one by one, setting the heavy decorated tapestry on their laps.

"You shouldn't have, Samantha," Jane says, admiring the personalized stocking on her lap.

"Trust me; she gets more joy out of this than anyone," Alex says, massaging his stocking and feeling the individually wrapped gifts.

"Over the years I've tried to make her stockings just as good, but they don't compare."

"And you know I don't want a stocking. I just like to give them." I plop down on the couch next to Alex and cuddle up to his side as everyone starts to pull out their items one by one. Pez dispensers, gum, ChapStick, toothbrushes and candy cover the coffee table and floor. Even Chauncey has a stocking filled with treats. After he gives up on trying to get his treat packages out of the stocking, he walks over to everyone else's little piles and sniffs around, looking for something edible.

"What about that stocking? Who is that for?" Abby points to the one lonely green stocking that is centered on the mantel.

"That's Jason's stocking. I figured that every year you and Bridget could add something to it so he's always in our memory." Abby pauses from unwrapping her mini gifts and pulls Bridget in closer. She looks at me sincerely, tilts her head and mouths "Thank you."

"Do you hear that, Bridget? That's Daddy's stocking."

"Daddy!" Bridget squeals and points to the stocking. She turns herself onto her tummy to get leverage, then slides off the couch. She darts toward the mantel and raises both arms, reaching for the stocking. "Daddy, Daddy!" She jumps up and down trying to get the stocking free from the mantel.

"Hold on, Bridget. Mommy will help you." Abby looks at me as if to ask if it's okay to take the stocking down. I nod.

Everyone continues to go through their tightly packed stockings, announcing each item. I always give them one meaningful, pricier item at the bottom. This year I got Dad an engraved keychain with his baseball number on it. Alex got a watch engraved with our anniversary date. I gave Mrs. Austin a gardening charm for her charm bracelet, and Abby's parent's got grandparent gifts: Her mom got a silver pendant engraved with "Grandma," and her dad got a keychain engraved with "Grandpa." I got Alex's mom an intricately carved silver bookmark and his dad a monogrammed set of golf balls.

Abby sits down on the floor with Bridget and reaches deep inside Jason's stocking. "Looks like there are already some things in Daddy's stocking, Bridget." Abby pulls out a small 3" x 5" photo frame of Jason in his dress blues, fresh out of boot camp. She stares down at the photo as a tear gently trickles down her cheek. Bridget leans in, reaching for the frame with two chubby hands. "Bridget, that's Daddy."

Bridget looks down, curiosity filling her eyes. "Daddy! Daddy!" Excitement stirs her into an upright position as she parades around the room with Jason's photo clenched to her chest. She bounces from guest to guest showing everyone the photo. Everyone looks on with emotion as they watch Bridget, so proudly showing off the photo of her daddy.

"Hey, Bridget." Abby pats the floor beside her, motioning for her to sit next to her. "Maybe you could draw a picture to put in Daddy's stocking."

"Okay!" Bridget gets excited and bounds toward the oversized bag sitting on the floor next to the couch. One by one, Bridget pulls out crayons and pieces of pink and yellow construction paper.

"She refuses to color and draw on anything other than pink or yellow paper," Abby adds with an eye roll.

We all sip on our after-dinner drinks and chat while Bridget sits at the coffee table, intently focused on her drawing.

"Mommy!" She comes bounding over clutching the pink paper in one hand and crayons in the other.

I hover over Abby's shoulder as we look at the picture. Three stick figures are scribbled in purple and green. One of the heads is topped with long, messy black hair and the other head has short spiky brown lines sharply scribbled in different directions. In between those two figures is a shorter stick figure with outstretched arms and black coils shooting out from a smiley face. Bridget looks up at Abby with wide blue eyes and points down to the figures one by one. "Mommy." She pauses before pointing to the little figure. "That's me!" She pauses again and darts her eyes between Abby and me. "Daddy." Then she points to a red, white and blue square darting out of the ground by their feet on the paper.

"What is that, honey?" Abby asks.

Bridget holds up the 3" x 5" photo of Jason in his dress blues and points to the flag that is perched behind him as he stands at attention.

"Oh, that's a flag. That's right, honey. That is daddy with a flag."

Bridget shakes her head proudly, her dark ringlets bouncing like little corkscrews. She focuses keenly as she folds the pink construction paper up into a messy square and stuffs the creation into Jason's stocking.

CHAPTER THIRTY-TWO

Abby

THE PAST TWO YEARS have been the hardest of my life. I have never worked so hard and so persistently at anything. I finally finished up all of my art classes and have painted every day, if only for twenty minutes. I had promised myself that I would put some effort every single day toward my goal of opening up my own art studio. Bridget has helped me stay focused on my goals, as I want to be the best role model for her. Bridget tugs on my hand as I lead her down Main Street.

"Keys please." I bend down and put out my right hand as Bridget drops the ring of keys onto my palm. I sweep the snow out of the way with my foot before I jiggle the lock and let us in. The bell over the door rings and welcomes us through the threshold. Bridget goes bounding ahead of me, bouncing on her tiptoes toward the little playroom I made for her in the back of the studio. I drop the keys on my desk, which sits against the main wall. The wall holds all of my best paintings, mostly action shots of Jason doing his different hobbies. As I've done every day since I opened my studio, I stand in front of the picture I painted of Jason with his bike in front of Sebastian's and whisper "I love you" before I start my day.

"Mommy, Charlie is here!" Bridget emerges from her playroom to the sound of the bell ringing on the door. She runs up to my first student of the day, Charlie Edinger. Charlie has autism, and he comes to my studio once a week to do art projects. His mother has seen a positive change in his mood since he started coming here the first week that I opened, two months ago.

I stand at the entryway cupping my Sebastian's mug as I watch Bridget greet Charlie with the energetic personality of her father. She takes her job as my little helper very seriously, and I reward her with weekly trips to the ice cream shop next door. I've kept the chalkboards on the walls. They used to hold Sebastian's daily menus; now I let the children draw freely with the various chalk colors.

"Welcome to Promises Art Studio!" Bridget shouts as she waves her arms around the room in greeting. She squeals in delight, proud of her first greeting of the day, and then bounces back to the playroom.

"Thank you, Bridget," I say as I lead Charlie back to the easels that line the back wall.

* * *

Jason

I run away from the waves, the damp sand molding around each foot, leaving a trail of prints behind. I keep running away from the never-ending waves as they grow larger with each step I thrust forward. The shadow of the expanding waves grows in the reflection of the sun on the sand in front of me. I try to run faster, but now my feet are trudging through dry sand, making it harder to pick up speed. The sand hits the back of my calves and pinches like tiny crab claws clenching my skin. The sun is hot, and sweat starts to trickle down my forehead, the salty water piercing my eyes. Suddenly I hear a tiny voice bleed through the crashing waves.

"Daddy. Daddy!"

I turn to the voice and see a little girl with fearful blue eyes running behind me. A small hand covered in splatters of sand reaches up toward me. There is something familiar in this little girl's eyes, in the way she looks at me as if she has known me forever. She keeps calling me Daddy.

Her little body is framed by a fast-approaching wave that looks like it could gulp her up in a matter of seconds. My body twists and runs toward her in one fluid motion as I scoop her up and keep running toward the shore. I feel the spray of water from the wave hitting the ground and being pulled back to the ocean. The dry air mixed with the salty water has scattered her dark ringlets in different directions around her face, as if she is a mythical creature with snakes sprouting from her head. Silvery blue eyes peek from behind a strand that is swiped across her forehead.

The waves have slowed to a calming flow, gently caressing the sand and reverting back to the sea, getting softer and slower with each cleansing repetition. The lyrics of the song *I'm Going to California* suddenly overpower the sounds. I stare into the little girl's familiar eyes before I set her gently on the sand. Her skin is pale with little blotches of red from where she was touched by the sun. Her pale green bathing suit hangs loosely on her little body as if she hasn't quite grown into it. Patches of sand coat her arms and legs and are sprinkled throughout her hair.

All the fear has lifted from her face, and her red lips expand into a wide smile, displaying a full set of baby teeth. She leans into me, wrapping her arms around my legs with a sweet tender touch. I crouch down so that my shoulders are level with her embrace. She releases the hug and frames my face with her little pink hands; a serious look transforms her childish features into one of an adult.

"Thank you, Daddy. I love you."

We form seats in the sand with our bottoms and look out into the water, watching the waves come and go. They glide over and over two sets of footprints, one set belonging to me, and the other set a clear imprint of her tiny little feet running behind me. The footprints remain as the waves wash over them, again and again.

ACKNOWLEDGMENTS

There are so many people to thank in the creation of this book and I feel like each person has equally contributed to *Saving Jason*.

First and foremost, I think the majority of my thanks should go to my husband for putting up with me and treating my stories like a true craft and not just a hobby. I think he believed in me before I believed in myself and he even bought me a fancy computer to bribe me to write. Thank you for not only allowing me to write, but encouraging me to write while you took care of everything else.

Saving Jason would've never been completed if it weren't for my daughter, Emily June. I'm dedicating this book to you my little girl, because from the second I found out you entered our lives, I made it a rule to sit down and write every day and finish what I started. Your kicks in my belly were encouragement along the way and one day I will get to be your cheerleader when you decide to conquer a dream.

There is one person who knew about *Saving Jason* from the very start-my mom. When I was only a few pages in and still so timid to share my writing with the world, you read my words and encouraged me every single step of the way. You believed in me and gave me honest input and advice. You always answered the phone eager to hear about my next chapter. Thank you for being my number one cheerleader. Thank you for seeing my gift and nurturing it. I wouldn't have continued beyond the first chapter if it weren't for you.

My dad deserves thanks from very early on in my life. From the time I was a little girl, you listened to my silly stories and played along with them like my true partner in crime. You have always put the fuel in my fire to write. It all started with The Great Turtle Catch of 1987. From ski trip sagas to lakeside dramas, you have always been by my side, eager to hear my next story. I believe once you even said, "You are working on the next Great American Novel." ;) LUMTYWELM.

Heather Huffman, my book manager—it always makes me believe in miracles when I think about how you came into my life. You are my true angel. You treated me like a "real author" and gave me the strength and encouragement to share *Saving Jason* with the world. You are a true professional. I will be thanking you for the rest of my life. Shari Ryan, you have the amazing ability to create the exact picture that I see in my head. I guess that is what makes a team! From the start Jesse James Freeman and Adam Bodendieck have been a huge part of this team. You both clearly love your jobs and everyone at Booktrope is so grateful to have you. Working with you is like seeing passion erupt every day.

Thank you Erica Cote and Kristina Caverly for reading those very first words. Erica, thank you for your honesty in how Abby and Samantha needed to be more "bitchy" to each other. I can always count on you to be honest. And Kristina – I love you and I love your reaction to the first words that were regurgitated onto *Saving Jason's* very first pages.

I owe a special thank you to Kristen Gilzean, my photographer, for making me look pretty and for supporting my book. Thank you Leahanna Neas for being my sidekick in life.

Thank you Rooch, for your military expertise and passion about the topic-you are a true war hero and I think I am your biggest fan.

And finally, I owe a huge thank you to my two dogs-Baxter and Brody. Thank you snuggling at my feet in the cold weather and sprawling on the floor beside me on hot days, as I created my plot and characters. And giving me your unconditional love along the way.

I have a list of veterans who go about every day making a difference and never ask for anything in return: Robert Baker, Brandon Clark Hymel, George "GEO" Allaire.

Thank you Chaplain Youstra for leading me in the right direction in my early Air Force days, or at least "trying to." ;) And thank you for dedicating so much of your life to our service members.

I'd also like to thank Peter Heald, Betty Hanagan and Jay Hanagan for being such a great support system and for being the audience to all of my silly stories since I was a kid. Thanks to all of my early readers who pushed aside their "current reads" and put *Saving Jason* at the top of their list. Thanks to Marysa Allaire—you are like a sister to me.

MORE GREAT READS
FROM BOOKTROPE

Fiery Hearts Collection by **Heather Huffman** (Romantic Suspense - ebook) Heather Huffman bundles three heartwarming and exciting romantic suspense novels about strong and diverse women whose lives intersect as each discovers her unique ability to leave her mark on the world; includes *Jailbird, Suddenly a Spy,* and *Devil in Disguise.*

Swimming Upstream by **Ruth Mancini** (Fiction) A life-affirming and often humorous story about a young woman's pursuit of happiness.

The River Valley Trilogy by **Tess Thompson** (Romance Collection) A surprising mix of romance, humor, friendship, intrigue and gourmet food - the River Valley trilogy entertains while reminding you of life's greatest gifts.

Seasons' End by **Will North** (Contemporary Romance) Every summer, three families spend "the season" on an island in Puget Sound. But when local vet Colin Ryan finds Martha "Pete" Petersen's body in the road on the last day of the season, he uncovers a series of betrayals that will alter their histories forever.

Discover more books and learn about our
new approach to publishing at **www.booktrope.com**.

CPSIA information can be obtained
at www.ICGtesting.com
Printed in the USA
FFOW02n1934260515
13597FF